GETTING STARTED IN MUSIC

Lois N. Harrison
University of the Pacific

PRENTICE HALL, Englewood Cliffs, New Jersey 07632

Library of Congress Cataloging-in-Publication Data

HARRISON, LOIS N.
  Getting started in music.

  Includes indexes.
    1. Music—Theory, Elementary. 2. Music—Handbooks,
manuals, etc. I. Title.
MT7.H266 1989   781   87–32687
ISBN 0–13–354911–9

Editorial/production supervision
  and interior design: F. Hubert
Cover design: George Cornell
Manufacturing buyer: Ray Keating

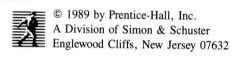 © 1989 by Prentice-Hall, Inc.
A Division of Simon & Schuster
Englewood Cliffs, New Jersey 07632

Printed in the United States of America

10 9 8 7 6 5 4 3 2 1

ISBN 0-13-354911-9

PRENTICE-HALL INTERNATIONAL (UK) LIMITED, *London*
PRENTICE-HALL OF AUSTRALIA PTY. LIMITED, *Sydney*
PRENTICE-HALL CANADA INC., *Toronto*
PRENTICE-HALL HISPANOAMERICANA, S.A., *Mexico*
PRENTICE-HALL OF INDIA PRIVATE LIMITED, *New Delhi*
PRENTICE-HALL OF JAPAN, INC., *Tokyo*
SIMON & SCHUSTER ASIA PTE. LTD., *Singapore*
EDITORA PRENTICE-HALL DO BRASIL, LTDA., *Rio de Janeiro*

THIS BOOK IS DEDICATED, WITH LOVE,
TO MY MOTHER AND FATHER,

THERESA MARTHA HUNGER
AND
JOHN DENIS NEUWIESINGER,

FOR GETTING <u>ME</u> STARTED IN MUSIC.

CONTENTS

CHAPTER 12 LISTENING 169

Continuation of emphasis on listening with concentration on two aspects: ear-training related to the elements of music and aural analysis with emphasis on variety in music literature.

MUSIC 185

Selections alphabetically arranged.

APPENDIX 234

MUSIC INDEX 347

GENERAL INDEX 351

PREFACE

Getting Started in Music is a resource for adults with little or no background in music. It provides materials to support different modes of learning, depending upon the teacher's style, facilities, equipment available, the size of the class, and the motivations of the students. When instruments are available, students in small classes can play the musical examples. Larger classes and those having limited access to instruments may depend upon the teacher to play examples, especially of pieces provided for illustration that the students cannot sing or otherwise perform. Even in the large classes, some highly motivated students may wish to pursue performance opportunities outside of class; independent instruction materials are included for them in the instrument section of the Appendix.

Different tracks are indicated in the text for a variety of approaches to music learning. Instructors are encouraged to incorporate concepts and experiences most appropriate for their students' particular goals. For example, although the chapters on listening and creativity appear late in the book, items from these chapters will be beneficial if introduced earlier, in conjunction with other activities. The section on the voice, included in the Appendix, will be of utmost importance to some classes and should be introduced early in the learning sequence for those classes.

Explanations are included in the text to minimize note taking in class time, thus allowing more time for student/teacher active involvement in musical experiences.

The main goals of the text are to help the student

1. Learn music fundamentals such as note values, meter and key signatures, pitch names, chords, and so on.
2. Develop an understanding of music concepts such as beat, meter, syncopation, melodic direction, form, mode, and so on.
3. Consistently learn theoretical aspects of music fundamentals in conjunction with aural experience.
4. Participate in aesthetic experiences.
5. Increase involvement in music through singing and playing of melodic and harmonic insturments.

Getting Started in Music is organized with a variety of provisions for musical experiences. The tape, the music, the rhythm drills and examples in the text, and the instrument instructional materials focus on these experiences. Many chapters of the text include analysis of music in regard to seven elements: rhythm, melody, harmony, form, tempo, dynamics, and timbre. Analysis leads to aural experience of the music, to performance of the music, or both.

The performance media included are the voice, keyboard, autoharp, guitar, and recorder. In classes with these instruments available, it is possible (and recommended as a challenge) for the student to explore the musical elements using all the instruments included. Adults with little musical background may concentrate on only one instrument for producing melody, and another for producing harmony, as aids to understanding the concepts presented. Large classes and those with no available instruments can incorporate singing as a regular performance opportunity. Listening should be part of every class, no matter what the other participatory involvements. Choices are provided so students and teachers can select their best alternatives. In addition to singing, listening, and playing, opportunities are provided for the student to read, write, create, and move to music.

These resources are provided as components of *Getting Started in Music:*

1. The text with twelve chapters explaining relevant concepts and providing exercises to strengthen the student's musicianship.
2. A tape with musical illustrations to help the student understand the concepts more fully through aural involvement.
3. Music notation for analysis and performance.
4. An appendix that includes supplementary materials, answers to questions asked in the text, reference charts, a keyboard facsimile and an instrument section with instructions for voice, autoharp, guitar, keyboard, and recorder directly related to discussions in the text.
5. A teacher's manual available on request from the publisher. This supplementary

book includes discussion of how different groups of students may use the text. Sample tests that may be used as study aids by the students are also in the teacher's manual.

The student should read about concepts in the main text, apply the discussion to music selections, listen to related items on the tape, and follow performance instructions in the appendix when required. Liberal use of paper clips will help the student locate supplementary materials in the music section and the appendix.

The music section is arranged in alphabetical order. Because some melodies have more than one set of words, a music index has been added at the end of the book to facilitate finding different versions of the piece. The music index also includes selections shown in the text. A list of the names and numbers of the instrumental sections that mention the piece appears under each selection that is so mentioned.

The large dot (●) in the margin is there to alert you to the expectation that you will be instructed to carry out an overt response (clapping, singing, writing, answering, or the like).

Although students should work through many parts of the text independently, group participation with a teacher's help is recommended. Teachers are needed to help students ascertain correct musical and written reponses.

Getting Started in Music was strengthened by its use with students at three tertiary institutions, the University of Oregon, the University of the Pacific and Western Australian College of Advanced Education, with their supportive and complementary environments. I am grateful to the students who made helpful comments and who asked perceptive questions. The final product benefited from their involvement and from contributions made by cooperating teachers who used, and then discussed, the materials with me: Chris Anderson, Wendy March, Barry Palmer, Alan True, Sandra Williams, Mary Lou Van Rysselberghe. Edmund Soule was a source of inspiration in dealing with both editorial and musical matters.

University of the Pacific faculty members were generous in contributing to the tape (Joan Coulter, William Dehning, William Domink, Wolfgang Fetsch and Carol van Bronkhorst) and the text (Joan Anderson and Terry Mills), as were University of the Pacific students who played on the tape (Paul Kimball, Mary McKean, Jody McComb, Jean Neven, Ed Powell, Tim Roberson, Coleman Sholl and Karen Wilson). Marge Dehning (Stanislaus State), Victor Steinhardt (University of Oregon), and Hope Harrison (Klamath Falls Union High School) cheerfully gave time and talent. My husband, Nelden Ward, gave me the gift of time by taking on many reponsibilities that otherwise would have been mine.

Before "getting started," read the table of contents to ascertain the general plan of the book. Find and follow the directions for identifying the selections on the tape (Appendix, p. 234) as you listen to it. This book is most effective when all its resources are used.

CHAPTER 1

ELEMENTS OF MUSIC

This chapter will help you understand the *constituent* and *expressive elements* of music. Although the elements will often be considered separately for purposes of definition and clarification, they are inseparably interrelated in their ultimate roles of contributing to the art we know as music.

The constituent elements—*rhythm, melody, harmony,* and *form*—are present in most types of music you will encounter. Constituent elements may be likened to the basic building blocks of music. They are affected by the expressive elements while still maintaining their integrity.

The expressive elements—*tempo, dynamics,* and *timbre*—help add variety and contrast to music. They lend themselves to creative performance.

RHYTHM

The movement of sound through time is called rhythm. Concepts contributing to an understanding of rhythm are those related to the contrasts of regular and irregular, strong and weak, long and short, and equal and unequal.

- To help you understand these concepts, try these activities:

   1. *Regular and irregular.* Create a regular beat by tapping your foot so the sound of each tap is an equal distance from the next one (! ! ! ! ! ! ! !).

Contrast the regular beat with an irregular one in which the taps are not equally spaced (! !! ! !!! !).

2. *Strong and weak.* Alternate a strong hand clap with the weak sound of your forearms striking each other. After doing a series of strong claps alternating with weak forearm strikes, switch to one strong clap, followed by two weak forearm strikes. Keep the spaces between the clap and strikes equidistant.

3. *Long and short.* Create a long humming sound with no break. Contrast it with a series of short humming sounds.

4. *Equal and unequal.* Contrast the equal sounds of the chanted "murmur" with the unequal sound of a pseudo-sneeze. Say "murmur murmur kachoo kachoo." Notice that both syllables of "murmur" are equal in length; the syllables of "kachoo" are unequal with the first syllable being shorter than the second. These equal and unequal syllables are related to *beat divisions*. They can be superimposed over a regular beat if you choose to say them that way, or they can be chanted irregularly. Say them with both a regular and an irregular beat for an added contrast.

```
murmur   murmur    kachoo    kachoo
!        !         !         !
murmur             murmur    kachoo   kachoo
!                  !         !        !
```

These words used only two syllables for each beat. Beats can also be subdivided into three: "merrily" is a word with three syllables that can be chanted to show division of the beat into *three* equal parts. Contrast the equal syllables of "merrily" with the unequal syllables of "intellect."

```
merrily    merrily    merrily    merrily
!          !          !          !
intellect  intellect  intellect  intellect
!          !          !          !
```

Rhythm patterns combining the contrasts of long/short and equal/unequal are used in melodies and harmonies as well as with rhythm passages standing alone. They are related to regular/irregular and to strong/weak, and are superimposed over the basic rhythmic structures caused by them.

Most of the rhythm you hear in contemporary music is built upon a series of regular beats called the *steady beat*. Most of the music you will experience in this text will have a steady beat. It is easier for the beginner in music to perceive music that has regularity of rhythm.

Because you will be working with music having a steady beat, that music will also have *meter* that is constant. Meter refers to the grouping of a strong beat followed by one or two weaker beats that creates *sets* of steady beats. In most of the music you study with this text, you will be working with meter that remains constant throughout the piece. You should be aware, however, that musical pieces are not always confined to one meter throughout. It is possible to change meters within a composition.

When you tap your foot regularly in time with a piece of music, you are responding to the underlying pulsation, or the steady beat of that composition. A nonmusical illustration of a steady beat is the ticking of a clock. If music used only the steady beat, it would not be very interesting! To maintain variety in music, rhythm patterns are superimposed over the beat. Such patterns are often repeated, or stated only once. Patterns are used with

1. the rhythm of the melody.
2. the rhythm of the harmony.
3. the rhythm of percussion instruments or sounds made by parts of the body, such as clapping, clicking, tapping, thumping, and so on.

• Find the response section (Tape 1). This section demonstrates repeated rhythm patterns. Respond with the music playing on the tape:

1. When you hear the claves (the first instrument playing in the response section) clap along with it on the steady beat. Even when other instruments begin to play, continue to clap the steady beat with the claves.
2. As soon as you are confident in keeping the steady beat, try to produce rhythm patterns related to the steady beat. Slap your thighs with the harmonic rhythm as played by the piano. Notice that even though the notes played by the piano change, the rhythm pattern is consistently repeated.
3. Tap the melodic rhythm as played by the recorder. Notice that even though the recorder pitches change, the rhythm pattern repeats itself.
4. Use either percussion instruments or environmental objects (easily accessible sound-producers found around you, such as pens, keys, spoons) to reproduce five more patterns illustrated on the tape by the following instruments (in order):

   a. tambourine
   b. woodblock
   c. bongo
   d. triangle
   e. xylophone

• Listen to Tape 2 for an example of irregular rhythm (Gregorian chant). Rhythm is generally predictable and regular, but this music does not have a regularly recurring beat. In the case of Gregorian chant, the lack of regularity helps one to identify it. Instead of the systematic grouping of sounds according to their duration, as is heard in the previous items on the tape, the rhythm of Gregorian chant follows the natural stresses of the words.

In contrast to Gregorian chant, much music uses not only a steady underlying beat but also a grouping of steady beats in sets of twos or threes or combinations of twos and threes. This grouping, called *meter,* is caused by stress (accent) being given to the first beat in each group:

<u>1</u> 2 3 <u>1</u> 2 3

    or

<u>1</u> 2 <u>1</u> 2.

- As you listen to "Hallelujah!" (Tape 20), alternate a clap (for the strong beat) with a forearm strike (for the weak beat) to find the meter of two.

- As you listen to "Orchestra Song" (Tape 13), use one clap followed by two forearm strikes to find the meter of three.

- Find the meter of a piece of music of your own choosing that has a steady beat. Is it in two or three? Create a brief rhythm pattern to accompany your music. Your pattern should be related to the steady beat (regular) and should match the grouping of the meter (with its strong and weak beats), but should also demonstrate the variety made possible by the use of long/short and equal/unequal rhythmic contrasts. Repeat the pattern as you listen to the music. Be analytical; does your pattern fit with the music you selected? Do the accents of the meter in your piece correspond with the important notes of your pattern?

A rhythm pattern repeated throughout a piece is called a *rhythm ostinato.* Rather than explaining that a musical pattern will be repeated many times in succession, it is more direct to use the word *ostinato* when that effect is desired. In a rhythm ostinato only the rhythm is patterned, whereas the *melodic ostinato* incorporates a pattern of pitches as well as of rhythm.

- Create a rhythm ostinato to go with "Semper Fidelis" (Tape 8). Follow these steps in creating the ostinato:

  1. Find the steady beat as you listen to the piece.
  2. Clap or tap with the steady beat.
  3. Find the strong/weak beats to determine if the meter is two or three.
  4. Use long/short and equal/unequal rhythmic ideas to create a pattern that fits with the steady beat and the meter of the piece. The pattern should match the rhythmic emphasis demonstrated by the meter. In other words, your pattern should emphasize the strong beats of the music you are hearing.

- Create two other rhythm ostinatos to accompany two different musical selections chosen by you. (Your teacher may ask you to collect musical examples on tape for class sharing in assignments like this.)

PITCH

The elements of both melody and harmony are related to pitch. The word *pitch* refers to identification of individual musical sound in relationship to other individual musical sounds in a tonal arrangement proceeding from low to high, or high to low. Exact pitch is determined by the frequency or number of vibrations per second of the sound.

MELODY

Although *melody* can be defined as a succcession of musical pitches, it is crucial to note that an integral part of melody is rhythm. The notes of a melody vary according to both pitch and duration. The rhythm concepts already introduced apply to melodies as well as to independent nonmelodic patterns. The element of form applies to melody also. Repetition and contrast of sections of melodies help contribute to their unique characteristics.

- Whistle or hum a song you know. It is unlikely that you would whistle or hum something other than the melody, since that identifies the song.
- Listen to the Gregorian chant again. The succession of single notes of the chant is a melody, although not an easy one to remember.
- Listen to Tape 3. Pearl Bailey sings the melody of "Takes Two to Tango."
- Practice singing a melody you like.
- Listen to Tape 4. William Kendall, a tenor, sings the melody of "Ev'ry Valley" (Handel) accompanied by a symphony orchestra.

  Pitch characteristics of melodies include

  1. *Direction.* The pitch of a melody may go up, go down, or stay the same. The notes for the first words of "Ev'ry Valley" (Tape 4) clearly move in an upward direction; the notes for the "Horn" (Tape 13) stay the same; those for "feelin' of romance" (Tape 3) move in a downward direction.
  2. *Range.* The melody may have a wide or narrow spectrum of notes ranging from low to high.
  3. *Position.* The melody may be performed using notes of high pitches or it may be *transposed* to notes of low pitches. As long as the intervals between the pitches remain consistent, the melody may be performed at different places within the total pitch continuum.

4. *Intervals.* The distance between the pitches of the melody may be

    a. *Steps.* When this is true, the melody moves in a stepwise fashion from one note to the next adjacent one. The pitches go in a downward direction using steps with the words "Do the dance of love" on Tape 3.

    b. *Skips.* Intervals larger than steps may be small skips, such as those at the beginning of the clarinet part of the "Orchestra Song" (Tape 13, "The clarinet, the"). Notice that steps follow these small skips ("clarinet makes doodle, doodle, doodle").

        Large skips occur when pitches leap from one to the other. See if you can hear some spectacularly large skips in "Bravour, Variations on a Theme from Mozart" (Tape 17).

HARMONY

At least two different pitches must be sounded simultaneously to produce *harmony*. *Chords* result from the simultaneous sounding of three or more different pitches. A *chord progression* results from chords being produced successively.

Depending upon the *texture* of the piece, harmony may be the result of

1. *Vertical structure:* chords connected to and supportive of the melody (*homophonic*).

- Listen to an illustration of homophonic harmony ("Bring Me Little Water, Silvy," Tape 9).

    or

2. *Horizontal structure:* chords created by simultaneously sounding melodies (*polyphonic*).

- Listen to an illustration of polyphonic harmony ("Orchestra Song," Tape 13), created when all the instruments play together. *Rounds* are also examples of polyphonic harmony.

To review the concept of texture in music that you have heard: There is no harmony with the Gregorian chant; the melody is unaccompanied (*monophonic*). The symphony orchestra accompanying the tenor soloist in "Every Valley" provides homophonic harmony as does Pete Seeger's guitar in "Bring Me Little Water, Silvy" and the group accompanying Pearl Bailey in "Takes Two to Tango."

Listeners sometimes hear modern music and say it doesn't have harmony. This suggests a confusion in terms. Some contemporary music may not be *consonant,* that is, it may not have harmony meeting the expectations of an individual, but it still has harmony, two or more pitches sounding together. *Dissonance* is a term for harmony that produces a sensation of unrest, disturbance, or instability. Consonant harmony is stable; it lacks the sense of tension and disruption caused by dissonance. Dissonance and consonance are opposites. As music has developed historically, dissonances have gradually been perceived as more consonant. Listeners become accustomed to sounds that were previously considered dissonant. Because of changing attitudes and individual reactions, equating consonance and dissonance to ''pleasant'' and ''unpleasant'' is not entirely satisfactory. Even though the overall concept of a piece of music generally is that of consonance or dissonance, the two contrasting qualities can both be present in varying degrees in any one piece of music.

- Listen to the illustrations. Tape 5, 6, and 7 showing different kinds of harmony.
  1. ''Sixty-seventh Psalm'' by Charles Ives (Tape 5) is dissonant.
  2. ''Danse Sacrale,'' is the climax of ''The Rite of Spring'' by Stravinsky (Tape 6). In its premier performance it was regarded as so dissonant that people fought in the aisles of the concert hall while the orchestra played. Audience members disagreed violently on its acceptability. Today ''The Rite of Spring'' has become a regular part of orchestral concert literature.
  3. ''Country Gardens'' by Percy Grainger uses harmony that is consonant (Tape 7).
- Find another example of consonant harmony.
- Find another example of dissonant harmony.

FORM

Form relates to the organization of music, its shape or structure, the arrangement of the elements in their unique musical relationships. It is perceived in terms of repetition and variety. Short pieces can be analyzed according to *phrases* that are the same or different. Phrases are short sections of music that end with a feeling of pausing or stopping. They are generally comparable to a sentence or a clause in language. Phrases end with *cadences,* which consist of a combination of melodic, harmonic, and rhythmic factors that combine to give a sense of stopping or pausing. The stop often is the end of a piece or section. The pause implies that more music will follow. (This use of the word *cadence* is not to be confused with its use when referring to the beat of music in a march or a dance.)

A song with two different phrases can be labeled *AB* form; two phrases that are the same can be labeled *AA* form; two phrases that differ in minor details only can be labeled *AA'*. The letters provide an abbreviated way to describe the structure of the piece.

Another way of describing form is to use the words *binary* and *ternary*. Binary form (*AB*) occurs when the music is in two contrasting sections. Ternary form (*ABA*) occurs when the music has three sections; the third is a repetition of the first.

Although the beginning student may analyze the form of a piece of music in small pieces, even measure by measure, it is advisable to develop the ability to look at the total composition as soon as possible in order to ascertain its overall structure.

- Sing "Old MacDonald" after you find it in the music section of this book. (Although there is an index for the music section at the end of the book to help find songs with several sets of words, most of the songs can be located easily because they are in alphabetical order.)

Did you recognize any repetitions in the melody? How many times did you sing "ee-i-ee-i-o"? Compare the sound of the music before the first and last times you sing "ee-i-ee-i-o." Both the music and the words are the same in these parts of the song. Compare the music just before the second "ee-i-ee-i-o" with the two phrases for the words "Old MacDonald had a farm." The words are different, but except for one extra note to accommodate the words, the music is the same. Form in music should not be determined by the words, even though the music sometimes changes to match the words. Look at the music alone to determine the form of a song.

What is the music like for "With a chick-chick here, chick-chick there, Here a chick, there a chick, Everywhere a chick-chick"?

You are right if you decided it was different from the music for the other parts of the song. An efficient way to represent the form of this piece is to say it is *AA'BA*. These letters indicate that the third part is different from the other three parts. The second part differs from the first and last parts only slightly, so a prime mark is used next to the letter of that phrase to indicate it is slightly different. The cadences at the end of the *A* phrases imply full stops. The cadence at the end of the *B* phrase hardly pauses. It seemed to hurtle into the last phrase.

- Place the letters on your copy of "Old MacDonald" to show the analysis of its form.

- After you have analyzed "Old MacDonald" as directed here, compare the placement of your letters with the analysis in the Appendix.

- Listen to Pearl Bailey on your tape (3) again. What is the form of the song she sings? (The answer is in the Appendix. Please don't look until you have tried to identify the form by yourself!)

TEMPO

The speed at which a musical composition is played is called its *tempo*. Italian terms are used universally to indicate varying degrees of tempo as well as changes of speed in musical compositions. Sometimes words in the language of the country in which the music is written or used are substituted for the Italian terms. The tempo directions are placed at the top left of the page, over the beginning of the music notation. If tempo changes are made in the music, the descriptive words are introduced where the effect is to take place.

This nonmusical illustration may help you understand the meaning of the word tempo. Most heartbeats are steady. Close the opening to one of your ears to hear your heart beat, or find your pulse in your neck or on your wrist. How fast is the beat? Run in place for a minute; then listen to your heartbeat or feel your pulse again. Is the beat faster? Is the beat still steady? The consistent spaces between the beats are still there, but the spaces are now smaller. The tempo is faster. Changing tempo in music means that the speed of the steady beat becomes faster or slower.

Normal heartbeat   !   !   !   !   !   !
Heartbeat after running !

- Listen to Tape 8 for music with a fast tempo ("Semper Fidelis" Sousa.)

- Listen to music with a slower tempo, Tape 5 ("Sixty-seventh Psalm" Ives.)

There are many gradations of tempo. In some music the tempo changes during the piece. A table of tempo marks appears in the Appendix.

- Find a piece of slow music.

- Find a piece of fast music.

Be careful to use "fast" and "slow" and terms like them to describe the speed of a piece of music. These terms should not be used to describe "long" and "short" notes. The durations of the notes will retain their relationships to each other, but they will become faster and/or slower depending on the tempo of the piece. No matter what the tempo, the longest notes will still be the longest notes, the shortest notes will still be the shortest notes even when all of them are speeded up or slowed down. Their values are relative rather than absolute.

DYNAMICS

Degrees of loudness and softness used in music are called *dynamics*. Compositions may be at a certain dynamic level throughout; they may use subtle or abrupt dynamic contrasts.

Many abbreviations, such as *f* and *p,* are used in place of Italian words to describe dynamic variations. They are generally placed below the melodic notation. A table of dynamic marks is in the Appendix.

The Stravinsky "Danse Sacrale" (Tape 6) illustrates music with variety in dynamics. Listen especially for sudden, loud accents.

• Describe dynamic variations in a piece of your choice.

TIMBRE

Tone color or quality of sound is called *timbre* (pronounced "tamburr"). Distinguishing timbre characteristics identify the voice or instrument creating the sound. Although, in general, a certain timbre is associated with an instrument or voice classification, variation is usual within the classifications because of individual characteristics and usage. Two people singing the same pitch will have differences in timbre. An oboe and a trumpet playing the same pitch will have contrasting timbres. The relative presence or absence of overtones (*harmonics*) in the sound determine the timbre.

• Listen to Tape 18, 11, and 12 to hear the timbre of a *string, woodwind,* and *brass* instrument, respectively.

    1. *Violin.* "Modere" by Ravel (Tape 18).

    2. *Clarinet.* "Zart und mit Ausdruck" by Schumann (Tape 11).

    3. *Trumpet.* "Concerto in E-flat Major" by Haydn (Tape 12).

• Explore timbre differences made possible by different uses of your voice. Can you produce these effects: nasal, husky, strident, breathy? Compare your effects with those of a friend. Does your voice have characteristic timbre that distinguishes it from your friend's voice when you both try to produce new effects? A tape recorder is a useful tool in this exercise to help you gain perspective on your particular vocal timbre.

MUSIC CHECK

You should be able to define, identify, and illustrate musically:

CONSTITUENT ELEMENTS	STEPS
RHYTHM	SKIPS
MELODY	CHORD
HARMONY	MONOPHONIC
FORM	HOMOPHONIC
EXPRESSIVE ELEMENTS	POLYPHONIC
TEMPO	CONSONANCE
DYNAMICS	DISSONANCE
TIMBRE	PHRASE
BEAT	CADENCE
OSTINATO	BINARY
METER	TERNARY
PITCH	

CHAPTER 2

NOTATION: VISUAL REPRESENTATION OF MUSIC

Learning to read music gives the prospective musician independent access to music. Although songs are often transmitted from one person to another by aural means, learning to interpret notation can save time by expanding repertoire in an efficient way. It enables the reader to bring to life music that is unavailable on records or tapes or through another "live" performer. This chapter introduces the basic visual symbols that represent music.

Reading music is the ability to interpret written notation. The notation represents regular and irregular, strong and weak, long and short, equal and unequal, melodic direction, high and low, intervals, combinations of sounds, patterns, phrases, repetitions and contrasts, fast and slow, loud and soft, and other components of music. Soon you will be challenged to use symbols for all the elements of music at the same time. Before combining them, learn some of the symbols for components of the elements separately.

RHYTHM

Rhythm is shown by notes representing how long or short the sound will be. The longest sound in general use is shown by the *whole note* (𝅝). The rhythm names of the notes indicate the length of sound and their mathematical relationships to each other. A sound half as long as the whole-note is shown by the *half note* (𝅗𝅥). The *quarter note* (♩) is half as long as the half; the *eighth note* (♪) half as long as the quarter; the *sixteenth* (♬) half as long as the eighth. If progressively shorter notes are needed, they are formed by adding flags to the stem (♪, ♪) and named by doubling the number (32nd, 64th, and so on). Practically speaking, notes shorter than sixteenth-notes appear infrequently in music for beginning music students.

The round part of the note is called its *head* (○), the perpendicular line is the *stem* (|), the curved line attached to the stem is the *flag* (﹨).

Notes with flags are often joined together so they are easier to read. These are eighth-notes: ♩♩ These are sixteenth-notes: ♩♩ The straight horizontal line used to join the notes in place of the curved flag used with single notes, is called a *beam*.

The separate notes shown so far have their stems on the right side, going up. Notes are generally written this way when their heads are on, or lower than the middle line of the staff. (The staff is a set of five parallel lines used to show pitch placement.)

Note heads on, or higher than, the middle line have their stems going down on the left side.

Shorter notes, placed above the middle line, have stems going down, but their flags and beams, like those of the lower notes, are on the right of the stem.

An exception to the rule of stem direction occurs when two vocal parts are placed on one staff with stems up for the higher part, and stems down for the lower part.

Silence is important in music, too. The absence of sound is indicated by *rests*. The *whole-rest* (▬) is the longest silence commonly used in music. Notice it is attached to the bottom of a line, usually the fourth line of the staff. (Call the bottom staff line number one, and count up to find line four.) The names of rests correspond to the names of the notes, similarly demonstrating their relative values. The *half-rest* (▬), half as long as the whole-rest, sits on top of a line, usually the third staff line. The *quarter-rest* (♩), half as long as the half-rest, is not easy to draw as precisely as it appears in printed music. Think of the quarter-rest as a backward, elongated "Z" when you make one. The *eighth-rest* (♪), half as long as the quarter-rest, is like a seven starting with a large dot. To make progressively shorter rests, add lines with large dots similar to the top of the eighth-rest to the left of the main part of the rest (♪, ♪) and name them by doubling the number (16th, 32nd, and so on).

- Complete this chart to show the comparison of notes and rests. (Answers are in the Appendix.)

	notes	rests
whole		
half		
quarter		
eighth		
sixteenth		

- Chant this old rhyme to help you learn how to use notes and rests.

    Pease porridge hot, Pease porridge cold,
    Pease porridge in the pot, Nine days old.

- Say the rhyme again, clapping a steady beat as you say it.

    Pease porridge hot,   Pease porridge cold,
     /   /   /   /   /   /   /   /
    Pease porridge in the pot, Nine days old.
     /   /   /   /   /   /   /   /

Notice that every syllable does not have a clap mark (/). If you use quarter-notes to represent the steady beats or claps, you must add eighth-notes where two syllables appear within the time span between two steady beats:

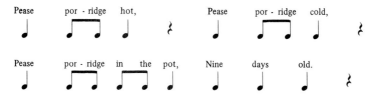

- Find three places with no word or syllable above the quarter-note. Circle the quarter-notes with no matching syllable. Since the usual way of saying "hot," "cold," and "old" gives no indication that these words should be elongated (such as by saying "ho-ot"), there is no need for the note under these words to be lengthened. Instead, put corresponding rests in place of the extra quarter-notes.

- Clap the rhythm of the words indicated by the notation as you say the rhyme again. Be sure to show the rests by *separating* your hands emphatically rather than clapping.

  Rhythm syllables are often used to help students learn the rhythmic relationships of notes. This chart gives rhythm names for notes and rests.

Rhythm Syllables

♪	ti	♾	si
♩	ta	𝄾	sa
𝅗𝅥	ta-a	▬	sa-a
𝅝	ta-a-a-a	▬	sa-a-a-a

The rhythm for "Pease Porridge Hot" with rhythm syllables is:

ta	ti	ti	ta		sa
ta	ti	ti	ta		sa
ta	ti	ti	ti	ti	ta
ta	ta		ta		sa

- Say the syllables in the same rhythm you previously chanted the rhyme. If you need help later with more advanced combinations of rhythm syllables, check the Appendix for the Rhythm Syllable Chart.

- Put notes under these automobile names to show the rhythm of the words.

Datsun	Volkswagen	Ford
Colt	Subaru	Buick
Chevrolet	Volvo	Honda
Oldsmobile	Chrysler	Audi
Pontiac	Cadillac	Lincoln-Mercury

If your answers differ from those given to you in the Appendix, consult your instructor to see if you have devised an acceptable alternative matching the rhythm of your speech.

- Use rhythm syllables to match the automobile names.

The notation below is the visual representation of the rhythm patterns you clapped at the beginning of your tape:

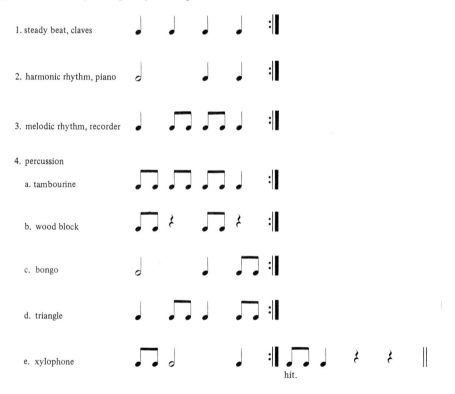

1. steady beat, claves

2. harmonic rhythm, piano

3. melodic rhythm, recorder

4. percussion

   a. tambourine

   b. wood block

   c. bongo

   d. triangle

   e. xylophone

hit.

- Clap the patterns, looking at the notation and listening to the tape. Begin with the steady beat (number one), then clap the harmonic rhythm (number two) and so on.

   The repeat sign (:‖) normally tells you to play or sing the pattern or section of the music once more. In this case, repeat the patterns as many times as the tape does. Pattern number one is repeated throughout the response section of the tape. You will be required to clap or play each of the other patterns four times instead of the normal two times indicated by the repeat sign.

   Show rests by moving your hands away from each other emphatically. Show half-notes by holding hands together; but still show the pulsation of the longer note with your clasped hands.

- Clap the patterns with the tape as you say the appropriate rhythm syllables. As soon as you can perform the rhythm patterns accurately, clap or play them (using nonpitched percussion instruments) without the tape. Form an ensemble with other people playing or clapping patterns other than the one you are performing. Find musicians to join your ensemble who can play the piano, recorder, and xylophone to recreate the parts you have heard on the tape. Music for these parts is in the music section of this book (Response Section, Additional Parts).

- Practice additional rhythm drills by clapping, saying the rhythm syllables, and playing them on nonpitched percussion instruments, or on sound makers that are readily available (such as two pencils striking each other, a pen striking a book, a spoon striking a glass, and so on):

- After you have played or clapped these rhythm patterns a line at a time, play them consecutively with no stop or hesitation from one line to the next unless a rest has been indicated.

- Play or clap them next with another person starting on line two while you play line one, both of you moving to the next line until you have played them all.

- As you become more independent, add players on other lines until your ensemble is composed of people playing all the different lines. Be careful to maintain accurate rhythmic relationships throughout the exercise.

PITCH

Pitch is shown in notation by the position of the note head on the *staff* ( ). The staff is made up of five parallel lines. It is used to show the position of the notehead as the determiner of the highness or lowness of the sound. *Highness* in music notation refers to the top of the staff; *lowness* refers to the bottom of the staff.

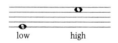

The first two words of "Ev'ry Valley" (tape 4) illustrate the sound of a melody going from low to high. Notice that the orchestra begins the introduction with the same melodic fragment going from low to high.

To read a melody, it is necessary to look at the note to see the

1. *rhythm,* as shown by the stem, beam, or flag, and whether the note head is empty or filled.
2. *pitch,* as shown by the placement of the note head.

The position of the note head itself is the only determiner of the highness or lowness of the sound.

One staff is often used alone, depending on the instrument(s) or voice(s) using it to realize the notation. Two staves, each containing five parallel lines, may be joined together for instruments with wide ranges, such as keyboard instruments, which use both staves simultaneously. Also, the upper staff can be used by high voices or instruments while the lower staff is used by low voices or instruments.

Notes higher or lower than those represented within the staff are shown by ledger lines above or below the staves.

Each note on the staff has a letter name. Only the first *seven* letters of the alphabet are used for these names, so the position of the note on the staff is necessary to help define its exact sound.

The position of a note refers to its placement on the line or in the space of a staff, counting from the bottom up. Line two indicates the second line from the bottom.

A special symbol at the beginning of each staff, called a *clef,* is also necessary to identify the note locations:

treble clef sign

bass clef sign

Although these signs are commonly called the *treble* and *bass clefs,* they are more precisely identified by the names *G-clef* and *F-clef.* The G-clef shows the location of the G on the second line. This information helps you determine the names of all the other notes. Notice that the G-clef cuts through the second line of the staff four times.

Notice, too, that the clef circles the second line as if to emphasize its importance. You will observe that clef signs in music books use curved and shaded lines. Artistic drawing of the clef sign is attractive, but not essential. It is essential to be accurate in placing the clef sign so the note "G" is in its proper location.

• Practice making the G-clef sign until you can do it easily.

When placing notes on the staff, put them *on the line* or *in the space*. This music terminology is different than the directions applied to writing or printing the alphabet:

Written letters sit on the line, but notes on the line have the line going through them. Notes in the spaces are placed with no line running through them.

Ascending consecutive notes alternate lines and spaces.

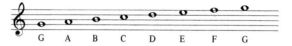

Beginning with the note "G" on the G-clef, this staff shows how the notes look going up in pitch using only the first seven letters of the alphabet.

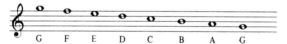

Consecutive notes descending also alternate lines and spaces, but use the seven letters of the alphabet in reverse order.

• In the treble clef, draw ten notes in spaces and ten notes on lines.

• Name the notes you have drawn.

Students sometimes find memory aids (*mnemonics*) valuable in helping them remember note names quickly. The lines of the treble clef (E, G, B, D, F) may be remembered by thinking of *Elephants' Great Big Dusty Feet*.

The spaces of the treble clef spell the word *FACE*.

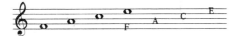

The bass or F-clef shows the placement of fourth line F.

This clef sign begins with the large dot on the F line, curves up before cutting down through the F line, then, after stopping just below the second line, uses two more dots, one on either side of the F line.

Note names with the F-clef follow the same order as those with the G-clef, but they are in different places on the staff. Lines and spaces going up from F are:

Lines and spaces going down from F are:

- Practice making the F-clef sign until it is easy for you.

- In the bass clef, draw ten notes in spaces and ten notes on lines.

- Name the notes you have drawn.

Memory aids that may be helpful to you in remembering bass clef note names are *All Cows Eat Grass* for the spaces, and *Gentle Babies Don't Fight Alligators* for the lines.

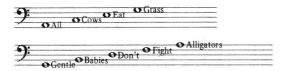

Mnemonics that you make up may be even better than the ones shown above, but the best thing to do is to learn the notes thoroughly so that their names come easily without memory aids.

- The notes on the staff below spell words. Find the words by naming the notes. (Answers are in the Appendix.)

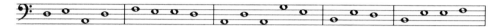

- Put notes on the staff over the letter names given below. These pitches are from a song you may know. Be sure to draw a G- or an F-clef at the beginning of the staff before you place the notes. (Answers in Appendix.)

The moveable *C-clef* is used much less often than the F- and G-clefs. Its most frequent use in music today is with orchestral instruments such as the viola, when it is called the *alto clef,* or cello and bassoon (for their high ranges), when it is called the *tenor clef.* Its indentation shows the location of middle C.

Historically, the C-clef has been used to avoid using ledger lines.

Ledger lines extend the staff above or below for higher and lower pitches. Lines and spaces alternate as they do within the staff.

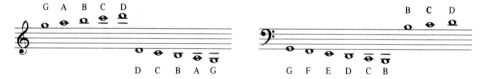

When notation is needed to show high or low pitches, the notes are spaced away from the staff using short lines drawn as if the staff were being extended beyond its usual five lines. It is important to space the ledger lines the same distance from each other as the lines of the staff are from each other. Ledger lines must be used to show notes in spaces as well as on lines; they are used only between the notes and the staff.

Middle C is one of the most often used ledger lines. It gets its name because it is in the middle, between the G- and F-clefs. Middle C is placed as follows in relationship to the G- and F-clefs.

When two staves are joined together, middle C should come precisely between the two, theoretically. Actually, it is never placed that way. Extra space is allowed between the two staves to make it easier to distinguish the notes on two separate five-line staves, rather than having ten lines so close together that it is difficult visually to separate their lines. Middle C is located near one of the staves.

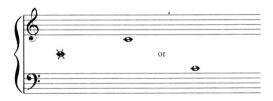

- Identify these notes.

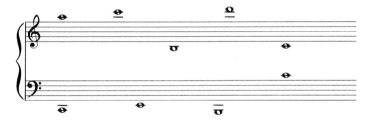

(Answers are in the Appendix.)

The octave sign (*8va*) may be used with high or low notes to avoid ledger lines. The word *octave* means eight notes, the distance between one pitch letter name to the next pitch having the same name. The octave sign followed by a broken line over the G-clef staff means that all the notes under the broken line are to sound an octave higher:

The octave sign followed by a broken line under the F-clef means that all the notes over the broken line sound one octave lower:

- Write these notes with ledger lines to show the same pitches:

- Write these notes with the octave sign (8va) instead of ledger lines to show the same pitches. (Answers in Appendix.)

TEMPO

Tempo is indicated on a musical score by words and by metronome markings. Although tempo words may be in English, they are generally in Italian. Many of these words will be introduced to you in association with the music you use. Start by finding the meaning of two tempo words on the Tempo Marks chart in the Appendix: *allegro* and *andante*.

- Compare the Telemann "Triste" (Tape 16) with Grainger's "Country Gardens" (Tape 7). Which of these selections is played allegro? Which is played andante?

The abbreviation *M.M.* sometimes appears at the beginning of a piece to show metronome markings. M.M. stands for *Maelzel's metronome,* named after the man who invented it. The metronome is a musician's tool that emits a regular click to show the steady beat. It is sometimes electric, sometimes handwound like a clock. The beat can be adjusted so the tempo can be changed. M.M. ♩ = 60 means that when the metronome is set at 60 clicks per minute, each click corresponds to a quarter note or its equivalent. The metronome marking is sometimes shown without M.M., using only ♩ = 60. Some metronomes are marked with words corresponding to the numbers to show how many beats per minute correspond to the Italian words.

DYNAMICS

Dynamics are generally indicated by abbreviations showing gradations of loudness and softness. Although the Italian word for soft is *piano,* that dynamic level is most often shown by using the letter *p.* Very soft, *pianissimo,* is *pp.* Even softer than that is *pianissississimo, ppp.* Find the meaning of *mp* on the Dynamic Marks chart in the Appendix. Also, study the Gradations of Dynamics chart following it.

• After listening to ''Semper Fidelis'' (Tape 8), decide on an appropriate dynamic marking for it.

• Determine the dynamic marking for ''Bring Me Little Water, Silvy'' (Tape 9).

MUSIC CHECK

You should be able to define, identify, and illustrate musically:

RHYTHMIC VALUES OF NOTES AND RESTS	HIGH AND LOW SOUNDS
WHOLE, HALF, QUARTER, EIGHTH, SIXTEENTH	LEDGER LINES
RHYTHM SYLLABLES	OCTAVE SIGN
REPEAT SIGNS	TEMPO MARKINGS, INCLUDING M.M.
PITCH NAMES IN BOTH TREBLE AND BASS CLEFS	DYNAMIC MARKINGS
G-, F-, AND C-CLEFS	

CHAPTER 3

USING
NOTATION

This chapter presents opportunities for you to develop concepts presented in the first chapters of this book and to add new ones. Songs and instrumental excerpts are used to help you apply your knowledge of music fundamentals. Many music concepts are of negligible value if they are perceived intellectually only, without developing aural perception. You should play, sing, or listen to these musical materials. If it is impossible for you to perform them because of factors such as lack of musical instruments or size of class, concentrate on development of your listening skills as your teacher presents the musical illustrations.

This chapter provides directions for students who will learn to play the materials on piano, recorder, autoharp, or guitar. These instrumentalists should follow the directions in condensed print. If you are not going to play the music, skip the condensed print directions. If your class sings the song examples, use portions of the voice section of the instrument book as needed.

This chapter is organized around selected pieces of music. Below each title is a list of terms that will be introduced or amplified in the discussion to follow. The elements of music needing clarification will be consistently addressed in the context of the song or instrumental excerpt.

Hot Cross Buns

KEY SIGNATURE, KEY OF G

SHARPS (♯), FLATS (♭)

METER SIGNATURE, $\frac{4}{4}$

MEASURE, BAR-LINE, BEATS, RHYTHM PATTERNS

PITCHES G, A, AND B

G CHORD

FORTE, MODERATO

Rhythm:

- Apply your knowledge of note values to clap this rhythm pattern.

Melody:

- Name the notes below:

(Answers are in the Appendix.)

Form:

Do you see repeated patterns in either the rhythm or pitch examples above?

- Circle the patterns even if they consist only of three notes.
- Use letter *A* to label the first pattern, and any like it; use *B, C,* and so on, to label other patterns.
- Check the placement of your circles and labels in the Appendix.

Tempo:

What does *moderato* mean? (Put a paper clip on the tempo chart in the Appendix to help you find tempo term definitions quickly.)

Dynamics:

What does *f* mean?

- Find the notation in the music section for "Hot Cross Buns."

Notice these items that appear first as you look at the notation:

1. The *key signature*. The *sharp* (♯) immediately after the G-clef sign is on the F line. It tells you that all F's should be altered and that the piece is in the key of G. Sharps (♯) or *flats* (♭) after the clef sign tell what key the piece is in, and make up the key signature. The key is important because it affects specific notes of the melody if the altered notes are included in the melody. (In this piece, there are no F's in the melody, so the key does not require the musician to alter any melody notes.) It also indicates the harmonies that should be used to support the melody. The name of the key tells the center of tonality, sometimes called the "key tone," "home tone," and "tonic," to which other notes relate as the most important pitch. The key signature will help you select and construct chords. It appears on every line of notation.

2. The *meter signature*. The numbers following the key signature make up the *meter* (or *time*) *signature*. The top number tells how many steady beats there are in one measure. It documents the recurring sets of accented and unaccented beats. The bottom number tells the kind of note that gets one beat. The meter signature appears only at the beginning of a piece unless it changes.

Rhythm:

In this piece, the meter is four; there are four steady beats in each measure. The strongest pulse will be felt on the first beat of the four.

- Clap on the first beat, strike your forearms together on the other beats as you count meter created by a series of steady beats grouped in sets of four: (1 2 3 4 1 2 3 4).

Measures are formed by vertical lines cutting through the staff.

The vertical lines are called *bar-lines* (or bars). A measure occupies the space between two bar-lines. Even though no bar-line appears at the beginning of a piece, the space between the clef sign and the first bar-line can also be a measure. Each measure (with the possible exception of the first and last measures, which may be incomplete) contains the number of beats indicated by the top number of the meter signature.

- How many measures are in "Hot Cross Buns"? (Answer is in the Appendix.)

- Count 1 2 3 4 as you clap this rhythm. Be sure to hold the half notes through as you show their pulsation.

When the bottom number of the meter (time) signature is four, it tells that the quarter-note gets one beat. Imagine that four stands for ¼ or a quarter-note. If a 2 were on the bottom it would stand for ½ or a half-note. Notice that as you counted 1 2 3 4 in the illustration above, the quarter-note got one count or beat. How many beats did the half-note get? How many beats did the eighth-note get?

- Fill in quarter notes to equal notes shown in the left column.

(Answers are in the Appendix.)

- These examples all use the ⁴⁄₄ meter signature. The top number tells you there are _____ beats in a measure; the bottom number tells you the _____ note gets one beat. (Appendix.)

From now on, look for answers in the Appendix when questions or exercises are followed by the word *Appendix* in parentheses.

- Write four beats in the correct places for each measure of these examples. After you have checked the placement of your beats to see if they are correct, count them aloud while you clap the rhythm patterns. As you count, give extra emphasis to the first beat.

(Appendix.)

- Now, say the rhythm syllables for the patterns.

So far, even though the name of this chapter is "Using Notation," you have not integrated it with music. You have looked at it, answered questions about it, and clapped rhythm patterns. The next step is to put the musical package together as the notation shows. "Hot Cross Buns" was chosen as your first piece because you probably know it.

1. If you can already play an instrument, use it to play "Hot Cross Buns".

2. If you do not play an instrument, or if you wish to learn to play another one, turn to either *Keyboard 1* or *Recorder 1*.

3. If you want to learn more than one melodic instrument, play both *Keyboard 1* and *Recorder 1*.

4. After you have played the melody, return to this chapter.

Melody:

- Sing the melody of "Hot Cross Buns" using the words.

- Sing the melody using the letter names of the notes.

Notice the numbers and syllables written under the melody. They are included as aids for two systems of learning to sightread vocally through perceiving relationships between pitches. The numbers are assigned to notes according to the key of the composition. (In this introductory discussion, keys referred to are all major keys.) The key name, in this case G, is numbered one, its next highest neighbor is numbered two, the next highest, three, and so on. The numbers used are from one to seven; if higher or lower notes are needed, the numbers are used over again, corresponding with the pitch names. Unlike pitch names that remain constant, the numbers change according to the key. Thus, when you move out of the key of G into a new one, such as C, number one will be used to represent C, number two D, and so on. The idea of using the numbers in this way is to establish aural relations between the pitches of any key to make it easier for the student to hear, read, and relate the sounds. One–two–three in any key will have the same relative sound even though the exact pitches will be higher or lower depending upon the key.

- Sing the melody using the numbers.

Solfège is a system in which syllables (*do, re, mi, fa, so, la, ti*) are used in the same way as the numbers in the previously described system: *Do* is the name of the key-note G, *re* is A, *mi* is B, and so on. These syllables come from a Latin source and were originally the first part of Latin words. Many musicians prefer to use them instead of numbers because they are more musical to sing. If you were to use the *fixed do* system, *do* would always be C, *re* would be D, and so on. However, in the United States, the *moveable do* (*do* is always the name of the major key) is most often used. This text uses the moveable do.

- Sing "Hot Cross Buns" using the syllables.

If you and your teacher decide to use the syllables and/or the numbers to help you with vocal sightreading, continue to use them with the pieces as they are introduced even when specific instructions are no longer given to you. In using either system, it is necessary first to get the sounds of the note relationships (*intervals*) into your ear, to recognize them in the notation, and then to apply them to new situations by reading the notation, hearing the sound internally before you produce it. Whether you decide to use numbers or syllables, the system you use must be practiced consistently and accurately to be effective.

If you choose to work with numbers, be careful to differentiate between the numbers used to represent pitches, and the numbers used to represent counting of beats.

If you choose to work with syllables, be careful not to confuse *ti* as assigned to the seventh syllable in solfège, with the "ti" assigned to represent eighth-notes when using rhythm syllables.

Harmony:

It is easy to provide a harmonic accompaniment for some pieces, especially those like "Hot Cross Buns," which uses only one *chord*. (A chord is a combination of three or more notes.) The letter G near the beginning of the piece tells the instrumentalist to play a G chord (spelled G-B-D.) The absence of any other chord symbol in the piece means that the G chord is repeated throughout.

1. If you already can play a harmony instrument, use it to put one G chord with each measure of "Hot Cross Buns."
2. If you don't play a harmony instrument, or want to learn another, turn either to *Keyboard 2, Autoharp 1,* or *Guitar 1.*

Lady, Come

PITCHES C AND D, SEQUENCE

- From now on, as each new piece is introduced, find it in the music section. Mark it with a paper clip or rubber band for ease in finding it as needed.

Rhythm:

- What is the meter signature for "Lady, Come"? _____ It tells you there are _____ beats in a measure and the _____ note gets one beat.

- Write the correct numbers under the notes to show the proper locations of the four beats in each measure. Be careful, the numbers already written under the words refer to the pitch, not the meter.

- Use rhythm syllables to show the appropriate length of the notes.

- Clap the notes as you count the four beats for each measure.

- Say the words for this piece as you clap the rhythm.

Melody:

- What pitches appear in "Lady, Come" that were also in "Hot Cross Buns"? What pitches were not in "Hot Cross Buns"?

- Identify all the pitches of "Lady, Come" using letter names.
  - Play "Lady, Come," turning to *Keyboard 3* or *Recorder 2* if you need help.

- Sing "Lady Come," using words, pitch names, syllables, and numbers. Notice that since this piece is in the key of G (as was "Hot Cross Buns") the relationship of the words, syllables, and numbers remains the same.

Form:

How many measures are in "Lady, Come"? Find three measures with the same rhythm. Do any of them have the same melody? Measures one and two are *sequential:* They have different pitches, but the same melodic shape and rhythm. Measures one and four also have melodies that are related: Measure four is measure one *inverted* (upside down).

Harmony:

"Lady, Come" requires only the G chord to accompany the melody.

- Play the G chord either at the beginning of each measure or on counts 1 and 3 of each measure.

Dynamics:

- Choose a dynamic marking from the chart in the Appendix for this piece to show how loudly you think it should be performed.

Tempo:

- Choose a tempo marking from the chart in the Appendix to show how fast you think this piece should be performed.

- Sing the melody using both the tempo and dynamic markings you have selected.
    - Use the tempo and dynamic marking you have chosen as you play the melody.
    - Sing the melody as you play the chordal accompaniment.
    - Enlist the aid of friends or family to put the melody and harmony together. If you can, play the melody and harmony together using the piano.

Are You Sleeping?

ADDING "AND" ("TI") FOR EIGHTH-NOTES, PITCHES E AND LOW D, ECHO SONG

Rhythm:

- Write the time signature for "Are You Sleeping?" here: _____. How many beats are in each measure? _____ What kind of a note gets the beat? _____ You have probably written: The time signature is ⁴⁄₄, there are four beats in each measure, and the quarter-note gets one beat. Those are correct answers.

- Write the count for each measure of this rhythm pattern. When counting eighth-notes, add "and" for the second eighth-note ("1 and 2 and," etc.)

- Count as you clap the rhythm pattern. Be sure to hold the half-notes and clap twice on beats showing two eighth-notes.

- Say the rhythm syllables for each note as you clap the rhythm.

- Say the words as you clap this rhythm pattern.

Melody:

There are two new notes in "Are You Sleeping?"

- Write the names of all the notes under the staff below.

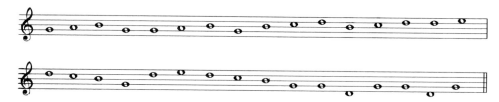

Which of these notes were not in "Hot Cross Buns" or "Lady, Come"?

- Play "Are You Sleeping." Turn to *Keyboard 4* or *Recorder 3* if you need help with the new notes.

Harmony:

How many different chords are needed to accompany "Are You Sleeping?"

- Sing the melody as you accompany yourself on your chordal instrument.

Form:

- Find measures in "Are You Sleeping?" with exactly the same melody and rhythm. Did you find a pattern of repetition in this piece? It is a good example of an *echo song:* Each measure is repeated throughout.

Dynamics and Tempo:

- Use the charts in the Appendix to help you choose appropriate tempos and dynamics for this song.
- Sing "Are You Sleeping" using the expressive markings you have chosen.

    - Practice "Are You Sleeping?" until you can play it accurately. Play it with other people as often as you can so you have the experience of hearing melody and harmony together. Use the piano to play melody and harmony together if you can. Vary tempo and dynamics when you wish to change the interpretation of the piece.

Introductions or Beginning Pitches:

When you sing, it is crucial that you begin the melody on the correct pitch. If you are to sing with other people, unless you all begin on the correct pitch, you will probably each select your own keys, with dissonant results. Even when you sing alone, unless you establish a reasonable starting pitch, you may find yourself singing portions of the song using unreasonably high or low areas of your vocal range. There are several ways to find the correct starting pitch:

1. The most direct way is to play the beginning pitch on a fixed pitch instrument, such as a keyboard or recorder. Match the pitch with your voice before starting the melody; listen to make sure you are singing the same note you are playing. If you have difficulty in matching one pitch, it may be helpful for you to hear the first phrase before beginning to sing. Be careful to give yourself the first pitch again before you begin, especially if the phrase you have heard does not end on the pitch you need.

2. Play, or have someone else play, an introduction to the song. The introduction should give the tempo of the piece, its style, and the key. If the introduction is harmonic only, you will have to find the beginning pitch by ear, relating the starting pitch to the chordal construction of the introduction. If the introduction is both harmonic and melodic, the melody of the introduction can end on the starting pitch for the beginning of the song.

3. Use a combination of 1 and 2: Play the starting pitch first, then use an introduction to add attractive elements that will enhance the beginning of the piece.

Be consistent in giving attention to starting pitches, especially if you think of yourself as an uncertain singer. See the Voice section of the Appendix for additional discussion of singing as a mode of musical expression.

An introduction to "Are You Sleeping" can be as simple as using the guitar, piano, or autoharp to play four G chords in the tempo you wish to sing the song. If the four chords do not clearly indicate the starting pitch to you, play the starting pitch alone before beginning the introduction.

The Bird's Song

D7 CHORD, ALLEGRO, MF

Apply what you know about music to this new piece.

Rhythm:

- Use as many of these techniques as you need to be accurate in performing the rhythm patterns below.

  1. Write the counts in their proper places for each measure. Clap the rhythm saying the counts evenly.

2. Write rhythm syllables ("ta," "ti" and "ta-a") under the appropriate notes. Clap the rhythm as you say the rhythm syllables accurately.

3. Find the notation for "The Bird's Song" in the music book. Say the words for the song showing the rhythm indicated by the notation.

(As you continue to learn new music, use as many of the techniques of counting, writing, clapping, using rhythm syllables, and rhythmic speaking of words as you need to help you be rhythmically accurate. Devise alternatives to clapping to generate rhythmic interest and keep your hands from becoming tired. Tapping, clicking, and using percussion instruments or sound producers found in your environment are some of these alternatives.)

Melody:

- Write the letter names for these notes under the staff below. Write the numbers, then the syllables, with G as "1" or "do."

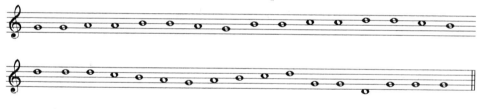

(Appendix.)

- Sing and/or play "The Bird's Song" with accurate rhythm and pitch.

Harmony:

"The Bird's Song" is in the key of G, as were the previous songs in this chapter. Notice it has the same signature (F-sharp) at the beginning of each line. The reasons for staying in this key for so long are to give the instrumentalists practice in playing the chord(s) in that key, and to give singers using solfège or numbers ample opportunity to locate the symbols they are using.

Look at the chord symbols above the melody line. Instead of having only one chord for this piece, there are two: G (spelled G-B-D) 𝄢 and D7 (spelled D–F♯–A–C) 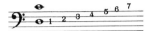 The 7 in the D7 chord symbol indicates that instead of only three notes in the chord, four notes are to be used. The 7 means that the additional note is seven notes away from the bottom note (*root*).

1. For help with chords, turn to *Keyboard 5, Autoharp 2,* or *Guitar 2.*
2. Before adding the D7 to the piece, play the G chord at the beginning of each measure. If you accidentally play the G chord where the symbol says D7, you will notice a dissonance.
3. Play the G and D7 chords at the places indicated by the symbols above the melody.
4. Use repeated chords between the chord symbol indications. In the first measure, play two G chords, then two D7 chords on the steady beat with four beats in a measure. In the second measure, play four G chords. In the third measure, play two G chords and two D7 chords. If a new chord is not indicated in the next measure, you should continue playing the last chord shown.

Form:

- Find repeated rhythm patterns in ''The Bird's Song.'' Divide the song into two-measure phrases. Are any two-measure melodic passages repeated? Can you find sequences?

   The rhythm of the first two measures is the same as the rhythm of the second two measures. The shape of the melody of these two phrases is the same, but the notes are different; the second phrase is higher. These two phrases are sequential. Sequences are often used in music. There can be many more than just two phrases involved in sequences. Their general characteristics are:

   1. The rhythm is either exactly the same, or very similar.
   2. The melody has the exact, or very similar shape.
   3. The notes used in the melody are not the same. Repeated passages are not sequential since they use the same notes.

Tempo:

What does *allegro* mean?

Dynamics:

What does *mf* mean?

- Put all the elements together to play and sing ''The Bird's Song.''

A-Hunting We Will Go

ANACRUSIS, PICK-UP OR UPBEAT, DOTTED HALF-NOTE, C CHORD

Rhythm:

Sometimes it is necessary to use a note longer than a half-note and shorter than a whole-note. A dot placed immediately after the half-note indicates that half the value of the half-note will be added to it. Thus, if the value of the half-note is 2, the dot will add 1. If the value of the half-note is 1, the dot will add ½. This rule applies to any note: A dot following the note adds half its value.

The value of a note is determined by the meter signature. What is the meter signature in the rhythm example below? _____ The upper number tells you there are _____ counts or beats in each measure. The lower number tells you the _____ gets one count. Since a half-note is twice as long as a quarter-note, it gets two counts. When the half-note has a dot after it, it gets three counts.

- In the example below, write "1 2 3" under each dotted half-note.

Notice that the first dotted half-notes are followed by quarter-notes. Write "4" under these quarter-notes. They complete the four counts needed for each measure of this rhythm pattern.

Notice that the last dotted half-note is not followed by a quarter-note. Can you find the missing fourth count of the last measure?

The missing fourth count is at the beginning of the pattern. Write "4-and" under the first two notes of the pattern. These two eighth-notes form an incomplete measure. Many pieces begin with incomplete measures. An unaccented note (or notes) in an incomplete measure at the beginning of a piece is called an *upbeat, anacrusis,* or *pick-up.* The anacrusis is used when the rhythmic emphasis for the first note or notes is less than that required for the following one. The first beat of the measure, the strongest one, is saved for the note requiring the greatest emphasis. Music is an orderly art; the remainder of the incomplete starting measure will be found somewhere else, at the end of either the piece or the section.

- Write the numbers for the correct count under the notes not already marked in the preceding pattern. Be sure to use "and" or "+" for the second eighth-notes when the eighth-notes are shown in sets of twos.

- Keep a steady beat as you count and clap the rhythm pattern. Be sure to clasp your hands and show the pulsation of three for the dotted half-notes.

- Write "ta" and "ti" under the appropriate notes above. Use "ta-a-a" for the dotted half-note.

- Clap the rhythm pattern above as you say the rhythm syllables aloud.

- Say the words for this rhythm pattern aloud as you clap the rhythm.

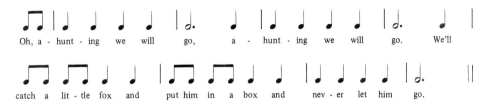

The following example by Schubert shows the dotted half-note used in the introduction to the first movement of his *Unfinished Symphony* (No. 8).

- What is the difference between this meter signature and the one for "A-Hunting We Will Go"? This one shows that there are _____ beats in a measure, and the _____ note gets one count.

- Write three counts under each measure of the examples below. After you have placed the counts, check them for accuracy, then count aloud as you clap the rhythm patterns. Emphasize the first beat of each measure to strengthen the feeling of the meter grouping the beats in sets of three. (Appendix.)

- Say the patterns using rhythm syllables. A dotted half-note will be "ta-a-a." If you are not sure of other rhythm syllables, check the chart in the Appendix.

Johann Strauss, Jr., used the ¾ meter signature in his waltz "On the Beautiful Blue Danube." Since his melody contained notes that were worth four counts, and since in ¾ meter there can only be three counts in a measure, Strauss needed a means to make the dotted half-note sound for one extra beat. His solution was to use a *tie* (⌒) to join the dotted half-note to the quarter-note in the next measure:

When two or more notes on the same pitch are tied together (joined by a curved line), the notes following the first note are not sounded anew, but their value is added to that of the first note for the total number of counts on that pitch. Ties can only be used to connect pitches that are the same: They are not to be confused with *slurs,* curved lines that join notes of different pitches indicating that they are to be played or sung *legato* (smoothly joined together).

- Count and clap these examples that use tied notes.

(Appendix.)

- Say the rhythm syllables for the examples above. The dotted half-note tied to the quarter-note will be "ta-a-a-a." Be sure to say "sa" for the quarter rests.

  The second theme from the overture to Mozart's *Marriage of Figaro* uses the dotted half-note in another meter.

- The meter signature ¢ stands for ²⁄₂. That means there are _____ beats in the measure, and the _____ gets one beat. If the half-note gets one beat, what will the dotted half-note get? _____

- Write the count for each note in the left column when there is a meter signature of $\frac{2}{2}$:

(Appendix.)

- Write two counts below each measure of the examples below. After you have placed the counts, check them for accuracy, then count aloud as you clap the rhythm patterns. Use "one-uh and-uh" for ♩♩ ♩♩.

(Appendix.)

Melody:

You have previously used all the notes of the melody for "A-Hunting We Will Go." Decide whether or not you need the practice of writing letter names, syllables, or numbers under the melody to help you sing it accurately. Write as much or as little as you need.

- Sing or play the melody, being careful to keep the rhythm steady.

- Write the letter names for the notes under the Schubert, Strauss, and Mozart examples above.

Harmony:

• What is the key signature for "A-Hunting We Will Go"? _____ How many different chords are needed to accompany the melody? _____ Name the chords.
_____

> • Turn to either *Keyboard 6*, *Autoharp 3*, or *Guitar 3* for help in learning to play the new chord.

Form:

• Find repeated rhythm patterns in "A-Hunting We Will Go." Are the pitches the same for the repeated rhythm patterns? Is the shape of the melody the same?

• Identify two sequential patterns. (Appendix.)

Dynamics:

Are dynamics marked for "A-Hunting We Will Go"? If none are marked, you can determine the dynamics you think are appropriate for the music.

• Put a dynamic mark on this piece using a symbol from the chart in the Appendix.

• Sing or play the piece with the dynamic intensity you have selected.

Tempo:

• Sing or play "A-Hunting We Will Go" using the tempo indicated in the music notation.

Good News

c AND ¢ TIME SIGNATURES

Rhythm:

The sign c sometimes appears instead of the usual numbers for the meter signature. It stands for $\frac{4}{4}$. Note the difference between it and the ¢ with a line through it in the Mozart example. The addition of the line signifies the pulsation of 2 rather than 4 in the measure even though the notes may have the same general appearance.

• Review what you have learned so far by clapping the rhythm for "Good News."

Expression:

- Select tempo and dynamic markings for this piece.

Form:

- Circle measures in this piece that are the same. Debate this statement: Since the phrase with the words "Good news, the chariot's comin'," occurs three times, and since the music for each of those repetitions varies only slightly, the form of this piece is *aa'ab*. (The mark used next to letter *a* for the second repetition indicates a slight variation in each phrase.)

Melody and Harmony:

- Sing the melody.

  - Play the accompanying chords as you sing the melody.

It's Raining

LOW E, KEY OF C, C CHORD

Rhythm:

- Clap or tap the rhythm of the piece before you sing or play the melody.

Melody:

How many different pitches are used in this traditional children's song? Name the notes you have not used in previous pieces in this chapter.

If you cannot play these new notes, turn to *Keyboard 7* or *Recorder 4*.

Some of the pieces in your music book such as "It's Raining" have numbers over the melody to show which fingers of the right hand to use when playing the keyboard.

Harmony:

"It's Raining" is in a different key than the one you have used in previous pieces. There are no flats or sharps at the beginning of the staves. The piece is in the key of C. Notice that only one chord is shown at the beginning of the piece, the C chord. Instrumentalists have already played this chord in "A-Hunting We Will

Go," but it was in an inverted position on the keyboard. The C chord used in the key of C will be in root position (C–E–G rather than G–C–E).

root position   inverted position

If you are playing autoharp or guitar, you need not change what you are doing. If you are playing a keyboard instrument, you should now learn the C chord in root position for "It's Raining." For help in playing the C chord in root position, turn to *Keyboard 8*.

Expression:

● Write dynamic and tempo indicators at the beginning of this piece. Play and sing it using the tempo and dynamic instructions you have written. Choose different expression indicators to use as you play and sing the piece again. Determine which of them are most suitable for your interpretation of the music.

Orchestra Song

¾ METER SIGNATURE; G7 CHORD

TIMBRE OF FRENCH HORN, TIMPANI, CLARINET, TRUMPET, VIOLIN, BASSOON

PHRASES

MIDDLE C, LOW AND HIGH F

CHORD PROGRESSION

SIXTEENTH-NOTES; CONCERTO

SLURS

DOTTED NOTES, DOUBLE-DOTTED NOTES

STACCATO/LEGATO

The next six pieces with instrument names are part of the "Orchestra Song." Some of them are much easier to perform than others. The easiest is probably the "Horn," part one. Before you consider individual characteristics of sections of the "Orchestra Song," look at them as contributing parts of one piece. Answer these general questions:

1. Are all the sections in the same key?
2. What key are they in?
3. What meter signature is used?
4. Analyze the forms of each section. Notate the form with letters under each section.

5. How many different chords are needed to accompany this piece?

6. Compare the placement of chord changes in all the sections.

7. With what pitch does each section begin?

8. Which of the sections begin with an anacrusis? (Appendix.)

- In preparation for realizing the rhythm of the "Orchestra Song" sections, count 1 2 3 as you clap these rhythm patterns.

- Label the rhythm pattern with the name of the section having a matching rhythm.

  Which of the patterns above match this phrase from Mozart's Minuet in F?

- Say the rhythm patterns using the rhythm syllables.

- Say the rhythm patterns using the words of their corresponding texts.

  Now look at the unique characteristics of each of the instruments in the "Orchestra Song."

Horn

How many different pitches are used in the "Horn"? Give yourself the pitch from a stable pitch producer such as the piano, recorder, or pitch pipe, and sing the "Horn."

- Write the beats for each measure under the notes, beginning with "3" for the first note.

  - If you need help in playing the G7 chord, turn to *Keyboard 9, Autoharp 4,* or *Guitar 4.*
  - Accompany yourself as you sing the "Horn" part of the "Orchestra Song."

You may comment on the limited interest in a part with only one note. Orchestra and band players sometimes complain about uninteresting parts written for the French horns, especially in pieces for beginners. Listen to Tape 13 to hear the "Horn" part of the "Orchestra Song" played by a French horn. Then listen to an attractive French horn solo that is not so easy to play (Tape 14). At the beginning of *Till Eulenspiegel's Merry Pranks,* you hear a brief section played first by the strings, then by the clarinet, then the French horn.

Pictures of the instruments you hear in the "Orchestra Song" are found in Chapter 12.

Drum

How many different pitches are used in the "Drum"? Which note has not been used in other pieces in this chapter?

If you need help to play it, turn to *Keyboard 10* or *Recorder 5.*

- Write the beats under the notation.

- Count and clap the rhythm before you sing or play the melody.

If you sing the piece with chordal accompaniment, listen to the changing chords. The order in which they are used is called the *chord progression.*

  - Play the chordal accompaniment as you sing the melody.
  - Play and sing the melody and the accompaniment for the "Drum" at the same time a friend plays and sings the "Horn."

This part was written with the timpani in mind. The timpani, or kettledrums, differ from most other drums because they can be tuned to specific pitches by increasing or decreasing the tension of the drumhead (membrane covering the open end of the kettle). Since the word *drum* is used to describe many types of percussion instruments, the word *timpani* should be used to describe those that play discernibly different pitches. Listen to the timpanist playing the "Drum" (Tape 13), and then a solo for timpani (Tape 15) in the percussion section of *The Young Person's Guide to the Orchestra.*

Clarinet

- Write three counts per measure in their appropriate places under the notation for the "Clarinet."

- Tap steady beats while you say rhythm syllables for the notes of the "Clarinet."

    How many different pitches are used in the melody of the "Clarinet"? Which of them have not been included in songs used in this chapter?

    - If you need help in playing these notes, refer to either *Keyboard 11* or *Recorder 6*.
    - Play the melody using accurate rhythm.
    - Sing the melody for the "Clarinet" while you accompany yourself on the keyboard, autoharp, or guitar.

- Sing the melody for the "Clarinet." When you find that you can sing it accurately and confidently, sing it while other musicians sing the "Horn" and the "Drum." Switch parts. Try not to be dependent upon large group experiences only; endeavor to carry each part alone. Use numbers and syllables as well as words.

- Listen to the clarinet playing this part of the "Orchestra Song" (Tape 13). Then listen to the clarinet playing Movement I from "Phantasiestücke" (Tape 11) to identify the clarinet sound in a different context.

Trumpet

- Circle the sixteenth-notes in this part. Notice that all the sixteenth-notes here are on the last half of the first beat of the measure in which they occur. When you count these measures, use "and-uh" for the sixteenth-notes.

Sixteenth-notes can occur on the first part of the beat ♩♩♩ or on the last part (1 - uh and) of the beat as shown above; or they can comprise the entire beat ♩♩♩♩ (1 - uh and - uh) Even though the examples shown in parentheses use beat 1, the sixteenth-notes can be used with any beat.

- Write the beats in the appropriate places for these rhythm patterns.

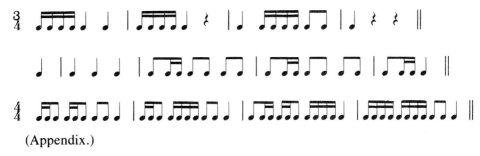

(Appendix.)

- Count as you clap the rhythm patterns.

- Say the rhythms with rhythm syllables. Use tu tu for the sixteenth-notes.

- Count, clap, and use rhythm syllables with these themes:

Rossini, theme from
"William Tell Overture"

Scarlatti, Sonata in G

(Appendix.)

- Count as you clap the rhythm for the "Trumpet."

- Review the pitch names in the melody, then play and sing it with correct rhythm.

    - Sing the melody as you play the chordal accompaniment.

    - Play the chordal accompaniment as classmates sing two or three parts of the "Orchestra Song."

- Listen to the trumpet play this part (Tape 13). Then listen to the "Andante" of the Haydn Trumpet Concerto (Tape 12). A *concerto* is a piece written for solo instrument with orchestra accompaniment. It usually provides the instrumentalist with a chance to demonstrate great *virtuosity* (exceptional artistic and technical skill).

Violin

- Count and clap the rhythm for this part.

- Say the rhythm syllables as you tap the steady beat.

    The curved lines under or over selected notes in the "Violin" are called slurs. They show that more than one note is to be used with one word or syllable. The first slur, over "ring," shows that two notes go with the first part of the word "ringing." The second slur shows that four notes are to be used with "love-." How many slurs can you find in the "Violin"? A slur helps you produce a smooth (legato) melodic line.

- Say the words using a pulsation in your voice to show the notes joined by the slurs.

• Name the new notes in this melody.

  • For help in playing them, turn to *Keyboard 12* or *Recorder 7.*

• Sing the "Violin" with care in matching the correct number of notes with each word or syllable.

• Listen to the violin play this part (Tape 13), then listen to the sound of the violin in "Modere" (Tape 18). After a brief piano introduction, the violin (high) and the cello (low) play the first theme together.

Bassoon

You have used dotted half-notes in other pieces. The dotted note used in the "Bassoon" part is a *dotted quarter*. The rule for the use of the dot is the same: It adds half the value of the note preceding it. When writing these dots, put them in spaces so the line of the staff does not obscure them.

The dot appearing to the right of the note is not to be confused with a dot appearing either under or over a note head: ♩ or ♩. The dot to the right adds half the temporal value of the note; the dot over or under the note is a *staccato* mark, indicating the note is to be separated or detached. Staccato is the opposite of legato.

The time signature indicates that the quarter-note gets one beat. The dot following the quarter-note adds half its value or half a beat. Hold the dotted quarter-note for one and one-half beats. Notice that an eighth-note follows the dotted quarter-note in this part. This combination is often found in music. It makes it easy to count:

```
♫  ♩.     ♪
1  and  2      3  and
ti  ti  ta  —  i  ti
```

The half beat unused by the dotted note is used by the eighth-note following the dotted quarter-note.

• Count and clap the rhythm for the "Bassoon." Be sure to clasp your hands and show the pulsation for the extra half beat of the dotted quarter-note.

• Say the words as you tap the steady beat.

• Use dotted quarter-notes followed by eighth-notes to show the notation for these words. As you say them, be sure to elongate and emphasize the syllables preceding the dashes.

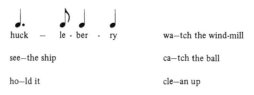

huck — le - ber - ry   wa—tch the wind-mill

see—the ship   ca—tch the ball

ho—ld it   cle—an up

(Appendix.)

- After you write the beats per measure in the correct places, count and clap these patterns.

(Appendix.)

Some of the rhythm patterns above match the following excerpts:

Gounod, first theme from
"Ballet Music, Faust," Act V

Allegretto

Schubert, first theme from first
movement, "Unfinished Symphony"

Allegro moderato

Tchaikovsky, finale to
first act, "Swan Lake"

Andante

Schumann, "The Happy Farmer"

Allegro

- Put the number of the matching rhythm pattern after the composer's name: Gounod _____, Schubert _____, Schumann _____, Tchaikovsky _____.

    Tempo marks are of great importance in interpreting music.

- Clap the rhythms of the excerpts reflecting the influence of the tempo marks.

    A note followed by a dot may substitute for two notes tied together. For example, a dotted quarter-note is the equivalent of a quarter and an eighth tied together, since the dot, representing half the value of the quarter, has the value of an eighth-note.

- Draw *one* note to equal these tied notes.

- Draw *two* notes to equal these dotted lines.

(Appendix.)

    Double-dotted notes are used less frequently than single-dotted ones. Double dots elongate the note they follow by three-quarters of the original value of the note: The first dot adds one-half the original value of the note; the second dot adds one quarter of the original value of the note. If a quarter-note (♩) is worth one beat, the dotted quarter-note (♩·) is worth one and one-half beats, the double-dotted quarter note (♩··) is worth one and three quarter beats.

- Fill in these equations:

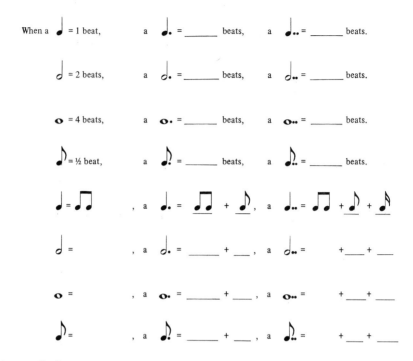

(Appendix.)

    When you use dotted notes, be sure to hold them out for their full value. If composers do not want the extra length, they will use rests instead of the dots, as Mozart did in "Eine Kleine Nachtmusik."

- Clap and use rhythm syllables to show the differences in sound between these examples using either dotted notes or rests.

(Appendix.)

What new pitches are notated in the "Bassoon"?

• If you need help in playing the new notes, turn to *Keyboard 13* or *Recorder 8*.

• Listen to the sound of the bassoon playing its part in the "Orchestra Song" (Tape 13). Then listen to it playing a more challenging composition, "Triste" (Tape 16).

• Sing the "Bassoon" part as you play the chord progression.

• Review singing and/or playing all the parts of the "Orchestra Song." As you gain confidence, involve other performers until you are one of six parts playing and singing together. Have some musicians play the melody along with the singing. Because the key is the same, the chord progression is the same, and the melodies are compatible, these parts can be used together to create consonant polyphonic harmony.

• Listen to the instruments play these parts together (Tape 13). Notice that the cadences in the "Orchestra Song" are much more clearly defined when the instruments play together.

African Noel

²₄ METER SIGNATURE, SYNCOPATION, TIES, REPEAT SIGNS,

DOUBLE BARS, F CHORD, CHANGING DYNAMICS AND TEMPOS

You have used all the notes in this melody. Review them to be sure you remember them.

Although the "African Noel" uses a new meter signature, the principle for using it is the same. How many beats are in each measure? _____ What kind of note gets one beat? _____

An example of *syncopation* is found at the end of the third measure. Unexpectedly, the pattern of two eighth-notes followed by a quarter-note, established in the first two measures, is broken when a fourth eighth-note is introduced at the end of the third measure and then tied over into the fourth measure.

No - el   No - el.

The result is that the second syllable of the word "Noel" begins on the last half of the second beat in measure three instead of on the first beat of the fourth measure as might be expected. This rhythmic emphasis in an unexpected place produces syncopation, which is generally caused by a displacement of rhythm or meter. How many examples of syncopation can you find in this piece? (Appendix.)

What do you call the curved lines in "African Noel"? These curved lines, ties, are used to join together notes having the same pitch. When properly written, they curve from one note *head* to the other.

- Check the curved lines used in "African Noel." Do they all join notes of the same pitch? _____ How many ties can you find? _____

What composer have you read about in this text that used ties to make a note longer than would fit into a measure?

How many beats should be given to the last "-el" of the "African Noel"?

- State the differences between the tie and the slur. What are the similarities?

- Count, clap, and use rhythm syllables with the following examples that use tied notes:

Vivaldi, third movement of the
"Concerto in A Minor"
for Viola d'Amore

Rameau, Minuet No. 1

Wagner, first theme from the
overture to "Die Meistersinger"

Observe the repeat signs of the "African Noel." Not only is the first line repeated; the second one is also. The repeat sign (:‖) at the end of the second line refers to the one at the beginning of the second line (‖:). Notice that the dots inside the repeated section are to the right of the double bar for the beginning of the repeated section and to the left of the double bar for the end of the repeated section. The dots are on the side of the double bar next to the material to be repeated: ‖:   :‖ When there is no initial repeat sign, as at the beginning of the first line, it is understood that the repeat goes back to the beginning of the music.

Do not confuse the *double bar* (‖) at the end of the piece with a repeat sign. Double bars with no dots indicate the end of a piece or section. They do not indicate repetition.

In what key is "African Noel?"

What chords are used to accompany it?

The chords for "African Noel" are the three most commonly used chords for the key of C. Since the key is named "C," call the C chord Roman numeral I. Count from C to F, with C as I, to find that the F chord is Roman numeral IV. Count from C to G7, with C as I, to find that the G7 chord is Roman numeral V7. Many pieces can be performed using only the I, IV, and V7 chords, although they may not be in the same key. The idea of numbering chords is transferable from one key to another.

• Identify the chords to correspond to these numbers in the key of G. Be sure to number the name of the key as I, then count through the alphabet to find the chord name.

I chord

IV chord

V7 chord

(Appendix.)

As you analyze musical selections in the future, look at the relationships of the chords you use. The I, IV, and V7 chords make up a family of often-used chords. Keyboard players especially must look at the key to determine if the chords are to be used in root or inverted positions.

• For help with the new chord, turn to *Keyboard 14, Autoharp 5,* or *Guitar 5.*

• Play the chordal accompaniment as you sing the melody for "African Noel."

Many different dynamic levels are shown in this piece. Use them as you sing and play the piece. Are you making an obvious difference between the various dynamic levels?

• Begin the "African Noel" andante. Accelerate until you are singing and playing allegro at the beginning of the fourth line. At the end of the fourth line, ritard so your tempo is andante by the end of the piece.

- Use drums or empty containers, such as cottage cheese holders, coffee cans with plastic lids, or oatmeal boxes, to add percussion sounds to "African Noel." Use patterns like these at first:

- Make up your own patterns.

- Notate at least three original patterns here that you can play as percussion parts for "African Noel."

Alphabet Song

RHYTHM CHANGES TO MATCH TEXT, *ABA* FORM, VARIATIONS

In what key is the "Alphabet Song?" _____

- Play the chord progression as it occurs in the piece.

- Count and clap the rhythm of the melody.

- Say the words in rhythm.

- Two sets of alternate words appear under the "Alphabet Song." Write the rhythm as it must be adjusted to match the rhythm of each of these two sets of words.

- On a blank piece of staff paper, write the correct rhythm and the melody for one set of these words. Be sure to write the words under the corrected notation.

  - Play the melody.

  - Sing the melody with chordal accompaniment.

  The "Alphabet Song" is a clear example of *ABA* form.

- Bracket and label the three parts of the song.

- Find repeated patterns within one of the parts of the song.

- Compare the cadences for each phrase. Which cadence is the least definite? (Appendix.)

  Composers often use familiar songs as themes for elaborate compositions. Mozart used the French song "Ah! Vous dirai-je, Maman" as the theme for one of his piano compositions. Adolphe Adam borrowed the same theme and used it in a brilliant series of variations for soprano. The form of this composition is *theme and variations*.

- Listen to Tape 17. Do you recognize the theme? How many times is it used? What kinds of changes do you hear in the variations?

- Assign different tempo and dynamic marks for versions of this song using three different sets of words.

- Play and sing the different versions of the song with classmates, family, and friends, using not only the various expression marks you have chosen but also different timbres for each version. For example, use only voices and guitars for one version, autoharps and recorders for another version, piano only for another version. For one version, consider adding the percussion instruments you need in "African Noel." Create original rhythm patterns for them to play that are appropriate for the interpretation you have chosen for the "Alphabet Song."

Ten Little Indians

F SHARP, *ABAC* FORM

Rhythm:

- Clap the rhythm of the first two measures. How many times can you find that rhythm repeated in the piece?

- Clap the rhythm pattern that is different.

- Clap the rhythm of the entire piece.

Melody and Harmony:

The new note in "Ten Little Indians" is F-sharp. Because the piece is in the key of G with the sharp (♯) appearing on the F line, all F's are to be sung and played one half step higher than the F without the sharp. This applies to low F's as well as high F's, even though the sharp appears only on the top line in the key signature.

- Circle all the F-sharps in the melody to remind you where they are.
    - If you do not know how to play an F-sharp, refer to *Keyboard 15* or *Recorder 9*.
    - Play the melody using the correct rhythm.
    - Sing the melody as you play the chordal accompaniment.

Form:

This piece is a good example of *ABAC* form.

- Label each of the phrases of "Ten Little Indians" with the appropriate letter to show its form. How long is each phrase of the melody? _____ What makes the last cadence seem more final than the others? (Appendix.)

Tempo and Dynamics:

- Choose appropriate dynamic and tempo markings to show your interpretation of this piece.

Timbre:

- Choose percussion sounds to add to the Indian atmosphere of this piece.

- Write two rhythm patterns here for the percussion instruments to play.

- Listen to Tape 21 to hear an authentic American Indian song performed with a rattle.

SUMMARY

The purpose of Chapter 3 is to help you begin to use notation. You are developing basic concepts necessary to get you started in music.

- Before you turn to Chapter 4, review the concepts and skills you have developed so far by singing and playing these pieces. If they have ostinatos or ensemble parts, practice the parts by yourself, then play and sing them with other musicians.

"Auld Lang Syne"   "Polly Wolly Doodle"

"Dance in a Circle"   "Shroom Song"

"The Muffin Man"

Be sure you can answer these questions about each of the pieces:

What is the key of the piece?

What is the form?

How many different chords are used?

What is the meter signature?

(Appendix.)

- You should be able to anticipate sound by looking at notation. Identify these excerpts:

If you do not know their names, sing or play them. (Appendix.)

MUSIC CHECK

You should be able to define, identify, and illustrate musically

KEY SIGNATURES OF G, C

SHARPS, FLATS

METER SIGNATURES OF C $\mathbb{C}$ $\frac{2}{4}$ $\frac{3}{4}$ $\frac{4}{4}$

MEASURES

BAR-LINES

BEATS

RHYTHMIC AND MELODIC PATTERNS

PITCHES FROM MIDDLE C TO HIGH F IN THE TREBLE CLEF

CHORDS: G, D7, C, G7, F

DYNAMIC MARKINGS: F, MF

TEMPO MARKINGS: MODERATO, ALLEGRO, ACCELERANDO, RITARD,

   ANDANTE

SEQUENCE

SYMBOLS FOR: ♩, ♪, 𝅘𝅥, 𝅝, ♫, 𝅗𝅥., 𝅘𝅥., 𝄽, 𝄾, 𝄼, 𝄺

DOTTED AND DOUBLE-DOTTED NOTES

ANACRUSIS, UPBEAT, OR PICK-UP

ROUNDS

TIMBRE OF: FRENCH HORN, TIMPANI, CLARINET, TRUMPET, VIOLIN, BASSOON

PHRASES

CHORD PROGRESSION

CONCERTO

SLURS AND TIES

LEGATO/STACCATO

SYNCOPATION

REPEAT SIGNS

DOUBLE BARS

VARIETY OF FORMS

VARIATIONS

CHAPTER 4

METER

While it is important for you as a beginner to deal with written and intellectual aspects of music, the most significant part of your learning should continue to be making and listening to music. This chapter is intended to broaden your abilities and increase your perception of musical qualities related to meter. Read the materials, listen to the music recommended, and do the activities described.

Meter is the grouping of steady beats in sets of twos (*duple meter*) or threes (*triple meter*) or combinations of twos and threes. The grouping is caused by stress being given to certain beats on a regularly recurring basis:

<u>1</u> 2 <u>1</u> 2 <u>1</u> 2 <u>1</u> 2

    or

<u>1</u> 2 3 <u>1</u> 2 3 <u>1</u> 2 3

Music may be perceived with either regular *or* irregular metrical organization. Most of the music used in this text has regular meter. Some music, however, uses irregular meter, or changes meter so frequently that it is difficult to find the meter, or uses expressive devices such as *fermatas* (holds), *accelerandos* (tempo directions to become faster), and *ritards* (tempo directions to become slower) that impede the regularity of the meter. Examples of music in which the meter is not obvious are found on your tape: Gregorian chant (Tape 2), *The Rite of Spring* (Tape 6), *Trio in A Minor* (Tape 18), *Prelude to the Afternoon of a Faun* (Tape 19), *Djamu the Dingo* (Tape 22).

Listen to them for contrast with the examples of regular meter described in the remainder of this chapter.

By this time, you can probably tell the meaning of both numbers of the meter signature easily. Although there is no rule specifying which numbers can be used for the top of the meter signature, in common practice the ones that appear most often are 2, 3, 4, and 6. The pulsation of music, if it has a regular meter. can be narrowed down even more: to either two or three, or to multiples of two or three. Even though music will be written with a variety of top numbers in meter signatures, and conductors will conduct the music using patterns related to those numbers (shown in these diagrams), listeners often do not hear the differences represented by the meter signatures or the conducting patterns. The differences between two beats in a measure and four beats in a measure, or between a six and two sets of three are not always obvious.

Conductor's
Patterns

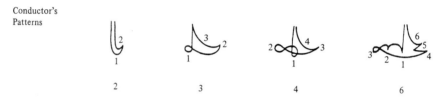

2   3   4   6

- To feel duple meter, alternate a handclap with an arm-strike. (Strike your right forearm with your left wrist.) This will give you a feeling of a strong beat alternating with a weak beat. It shows how the beats are grouped in sets of two.

As you find the grouping of beats in music, remember that the tempo of each piece of music is unique; beats may be faster or slower depending upon the characteristics of the music. The constant item in music with regular meter is the steady repetition of the beat. A piece with duple meter enables you to clap/strike evenly with no extra-long holding of the clap or strike to give it an uneven movement.

- These pieces are examples of music with duple meter. Clap/strike evenly as you listen to them. Count 1–2 as you clap/strike, assigning count 1 to the clap, or the strongest beat.

    Tape 4. "Ev'ry Valley"
    Tape 7. "Country Gardens"
    Tape 11. "Phantasiestücke"

- Change from duple to triple meter: Follow one clap with two strikes for a meter of three. Count 1–2–3 evenly as you clap/strike/strike with emphasis on the first count. Continue to count and clap as you listen to these pieces with a meter of three.

Tape 15. "Young People's Guide to the Orchestra"

Tape 16. "Triste"

- Use Tape 4, 7, 11, 13, 15, 16, 20, and 23 with a variety of physical responses to show their meter:

    1. Stamp your foot for the first beat, clap your hands for the following beat or beats.

    2. Use a combination of other body percussion sounds such as thigh slapping (sometimes called *patschen*) and finger clicking to show the strong and weak beats.

    3. Use nonpitched vocal sounds to show the strong and weak beats. Be sure they are soft enough that you can still hear the music.

    4. Move with the music using a large step to show the strong beat and a small step(s) to show the weak beat(s).

    5. Make note here of another way you devise to show strong and weak beats with your body.

- Use percussion instruments to show groupings of meter. Listen carefully to your choices to be sure that the stronger instruments are used for the first beat. For example, use a large hand drum for the first beat and a triangle for the weaker, or secondary beat(s). If percussion instruments are not available to you, substitute sound producers that are available either in your home or in your classroom. For example, strike a large wastebasket for beat one; tap a pencil or pen for the secondary beat(s). Produce these metrical patterns alone and in ensembles.

- Write the names of instruments or other sound producers you use to make meters of two and three in the tempos indicated.

    In two

        A. Allegretto

        B. Lento

    In three

        C. Largamente

        D. Vivace

    - Add pitch components to the instrumentation you have just created. Decide how many instrumentalists will be needed for the ensembles you develop.

        1. Add a piano improvisation on the black keys to A.
        2. Add a vocal improvisation to C.
        3. Use a recorder or barred percussion instrument with B and D.

    Improvise on the instrument you have selected in a style that is compatible with the rest of the ensemble.

- Select two pieces (one with a meter of two and one with a meter of three) that you can sing or play on a melody instrument. (Pieces in four can be used, too, considering four as a form of duple meter, two plus two.) Add body sounds, percussion instruments, or other sound producers to these pieces to enhance their metric organization as you sing the melody. Write the names of the pieces you have chosen to arrange:

In two:

In three:

SIMPLE METER

So far, all the pieces you have sung and played in this text have been in *simple meter;* their basic beat has been normally subdivided into two pulsations:

Quarter-notes have been assigned the beat; they have the potential of being subdivided into two eighth-notes.

Half-notes have been assigned the beat; they have the potential of being subdivided into two quarter-notes.

• Fill in the blanks to check your understanding of simple meter:

In $\frac{4}{4}$ meter, the _____ note gets the beat and may be subdivided into __2__ _____.

In $\frac{2}{2}$ meter, the _____ note gets the beat and may be subdivided into _____ _____.

In $\frac{6}{8}$ meter, the _____ note gets the beat and may be subdivided into _____ _____.

In $\frac{3}{16}$ meter, the _____ note gets the beat and may be subdivided into _____ _____.

(Appendix.)

Home on the Range

• Find the notation for "Home on the Range." There are two versions, the one you need now is the one marked Andantino with a meter signature of $\frac{3}{4}$. It is an example of simple meter.

• Chant the words as you clap/strike the triple meter.

• Sing or play the melody. You have not previously used the key of F in this text. All B's must be flatted.

• Recorder players should consult *Recorder 10* for help with note fingering.

The Wild Colonial Boy

Rhythm:

For the first time in this text, you will analyze a song whose meter signature uses an eight for the bottom number. This means that the eighth-note gets one beat. When this happens, the quarter-note gets _____ beats, the dotted quarter-note gets _____ beats, the dotted half-note gets _____ beats, the half-note gets _____ beats. How many beats are in each measure? _____ (Appendix.)

- Clap the rhythm of "The Wild Colonial Boy" as you count six beats in each measure.

- Use rhythm syllables to say the rhythm of the melody.

- Say the words as you clap the melodic rhythm.

- Clap and count, these examples in $\frac{6}{8}$:

- Apply rhythm syllables to the examples above.

- Write six beats in their proper places in each measure for this excerpt from Offenbach's "Barcarolle" in Act II of *Tales of Hoffman*.

- Count and clap the rhythm. Match the rhythm of "Barcarolle" with one of the rhythm examples above.

Melody:

"The Wild Colonial Boy" is in the key of D.

- Name the two sharps in the key of D.

  - Before you play the melody, turn to *Keyboard 16* or *Recorder 11* for help in finding C-sharps. Be sure to play sharps for all F's and C's, not just the ones on the sharped line or space of the key signature.

- Sing the melody.

Harmony:

- Name the chords used in the chord progression for "The Wild Colonial Boy."

  - Turn to *Autoharp 6, Keyboard 17,* or *Guitar 6* for help with the new chords.
  - Practice the chord progression D–G–A7–D, giving eight beats to each chord, then four beats, then two beats. As soon as you can change chords and keep a steady beat, sing the melody with the chords changing in the appropriate places to accompany the melody.

Form:

- Compare the song's phrases to determine its form. Label the phrases with letters to show the form. (Appendix.)

Tempo:

- Practice "The Wild Colonial Boy" until you can sing or play it allegro.

Dynamics:

- Vary the dynamics according to your interpretation of the the words in the different verses.

- Complete this diagram to help you confirm your understanding of note relationships in ⁶⁄₈ time when counted with six beats in a measure:

Note	Value in $\frac{6}{8}$ time
♪ (sixteenth)	
♪ (eighth)	
♩ (dotted quarter)	
♩ (half)	
♩. (dotted quarter)	
♪. (dotted eighth)	

(Appendix.)

COMPOUND METER

Compound meter occurs when the beat is subdivided into three equal parts. The following examples show a 6 as the top part of the meter signature, but the pulsation of the listener's response will be as if it were a 2. "The Wild Horseman" by Schumann shows a clear pattern of two sets of three eighth-notes making up a measure counted in two. It is not counted in six because the rapid tempo of the piece makes it too unwieldy to try.

• Write the two beats per measure under the notation above. (Appendix.)

The following illustrations of compound meter are all from "Semper Fidelis" by Sousa (Tape 8).

- Write six beats in the proper places in each measure as if it would be counted in six rather than two.

- Count and clap the themes slowly with six beats in each measure.

- Listen to Tape 8, trying to count six beats in each measure. You will find that the music is too fast to count that way.

- Without referring to the notation, try to find a pulsation of two beats. It is much easier to respond to the feeling of two than it is to try to respond in six.

- Under the six beats you have already written, write two beats for each measure. In doing this, note that there will be three eighth-notes for each beat. This is a good example of compound time. (Appendix.)

- Listen to Tape 8 again, responding to the pulsation of two, and try to locate each of the four themes shown above.

Compound time occurs with meter signatures other than ⅜, also. In this example in ⁶⁄₄, the quarter-note is indicated as the note to get the beat, but because of the feeling of the meter, each of the two beats/measure will be given to a dotted half-note.

"Liebestraum"
Liszt

Poco allegro

"Jesu, Joy of Man's Desiring" by Bach is in compound time. How many beats are there in each measure? _____

The "Pastoral Symphony" from *The Messiah* by Handel is in compound time. How many beats are there in each measure? _____

(Appendix.)

Decisions on whether the composition is to be counted and conducted in simple or compound meter are based on the feeling of the rhythmic pulsation, the performance style, and to a large extent, on the tempo.

- Complete this diagram to help you confirm your understanding of note relationships when a ⅜ piece is counted with two beats in a measure. The ♪. gets one beat.

(Appendix.)

Home on the Range

- Find your copy of "Home on the Range" with a meter signature of §.

     The rhythm of this version of "Home on the Range" looks different from the version you used in ¾. The tempo is different, also. Pieces written in different ways reflect differing interpretations. In the § version, the tempo is faster; the rhythmic feeling will be in two, with beat one receiving greater stress than beat two.

- On your copy of "Home on the Range" in §, write numbers 1–6 in their appropriate places in the measure as if the piece were marked Largo. (Appendix.)

- Play or sing it as though the conductor were using the conductor's pattern of six in a slow tempo with primary emphasis on beat one, and less emphasis on beat four.

- Under your counts in six, write counts 1 and 2 as though the conductor were leading a fast tempo with only two beats in a measure. (Appendix.)

- Play or sing "Home on the Range" quickly with the feeling of only two beats in the measure.

The Wild Colonial Boy

- Sing or play "The Wild Colonial Boy" in compound meter using a faster tempo than you did previously.

     - Add pitched percussion or recorder parts to the melody.

The Cuckoo

     The meter signature of this piece tells you there are _____ beats in each measure and the _____ note gets one beat.

- Say the words in rhythm as you clap/strike the meter of the piece. Be sure to clap on the first beat of the measure. When you reach the beginning of the fourth line, you see three *fermatas* (⌢) over the notes. The fermata tells you to hold the note longer than usual. Use your discretion to determine how long you want to hold the note under each fermata.

     Beethoven uses fermatas at the beginning of the first movement of his Fifth Symphony.

Listening to several conductors' interpretations of Beethoven's Fifth is likely to show that notes under the fermata are held for varying lengths of time depending upon the individual's interpretation.

- Say the words for "The Cuckoo" aloud, in rhythm, as you tap the rhythm.

- Tap the rhythm as you say the words to yourself.

The key signature for this piece is one you have used before. The single sharp in the key signature is _____. Do you remember the name of the key with one sharp?

- Play the melody on either the recorder or the piano. The numbers over the notes of the piece tell you which piano fingers to use to make it easier to play. Use the recorder fingering chart (*Recorder 12*) if you need to find new notes. Be especially sure to play the F-sharp accurately.

- Play the chords for "The Cuckoo" on your harmony instrument.

- Sing the melody as you accompany yourself on your harmony instrument.

- Change the style of your harmonic accompaniment. On the first beat of every measure play the lowest note of your chord alone. Play the rest of the chord on your second and third beats. This will give you an "oom-pa-pa" effect.

- Play or sing this piece using three different dynamics. Write the dynamic marking you prefer here. _____ Do you like playing it with the same dynamics throughout?

- Select an appropriate tempo marking for this music. Write what you have chosen here: _____

The Frogs

What is the key of this piece?

What does its meter signature tell you?

What kind of rests are used in this piece?

In the sixth measure of "The Frogs, a number 3 is written under the first three notes of the measure: ♪♪♪ (In another piece you may find the 3 written above the notes or with a slur: ♪♪♪ The meaning is the same.) It tells you that the three notes form a *triplet*. They receive the amount of time usually given to two notes. Without the triplet sign, only two eighth-notes would be used for that beat. The triplet makes each of these three eighth-notes shorter than they would normally be.

The triplet does not change the meter from simple to compound; it only changes parts of the rhythm in simple meter.

- Say the words to "The Frogs" in rhythm, keeping a steady beat.

- Play or sing the whole piece.

- Write the tempo and dynamics you prefer on your music.

- Clap and count the rhythm of these examples:

- Use rhythm syllables with them. Say "tri-ple-ti" for the triplet.

Over the River and Through the Wood

- Before singing or playing this piece, review the meaning of the meter signature with an eight on the bottom for a piece that is performed slowly. For the slow piece there will be _____ beats in a measure. The _____ note will get one beat. Fill in the blanks in this chart.

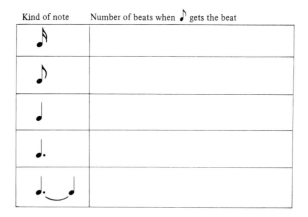

(Appendix.)

- Chant and clap the words and rhythm of "Over the River and Through the Wood" as if it were to be performed slowly. Then chant and clap it reflecting the tempo marking of Allegro.

    This piece sounds better in compound time (counted in two rather than six).

- Fill in the blanks of this chart for compound meter:

Notes	Number of beats when $\frac{6}{8}$ is counted with two beats in a measure
♪	
♩♩♩	
♩ ♪	
♩.	
♩. ⌒ ♪	

(Appendix.)

What does the key signature for "Over the River and Through the Wood" tell you?

- What is the song's form? _____ (Appendix.)

- Play and sing the melody.

  - Add chords to accompany the melody.

  - Use ♩ ♪♪ ♪ with the chordal accompaniment to heighten the sense of traveling in a horse-drawn sleigh.

SONG ANALYSIS

From now on, you will be expected to be independent in analyzing the musical material you play and sing. Make a habit of asking yourself the same kind of questions this book has posed for you about the pieces. To help you with systematic analysis, use the Music Analysis Sheet (*MAS*) from the Appendix. It lists appropriate considerations for you. Along with the MAS is a Music Analysis Sheet Elaboration to help you learn how to use the sheet. This text will continue to point out new or unusual features of the songs. In addition to responding to the specific questions raised in the text, fill out a Music Analysis Sheet (*MAS*) for each new piece. For your convenience, duplicate a number of the sheets from the form in the Appendix. As you become skilled in musicianship and thorough in your approach to music, your practiced routine of looking carefully at all aspects of the composition should eventually free you of the necessity of continuously writing this information. Use the *MAS* until you have your routine memorized.

- Use the *MAS* from the Appendix to help you play and/or sing these songs. Be especially perceptive of the metrical analysis of each piece.

El Jarabe

Watch the sharps. In addition to the accidentals written in the melodic line, be sure to play/sing the sharps indicated by the key signature.

A problem that may arise as you continue to play the recorder is that pieces may use notes below the range of the instrument. Do not let this limitation affect your choice of materials. Rather than avoid a piece if it has notes lower than your recorder can play, consider alternatives such as these suggested for "El Jarabe."

Find the one place where a note lower than the recorder range appears in the melody. If you are not sure what the lowest recorder note is, check the fingering chart in *Recorder 12*. Look at the notation for the soprano recorder (appearing above the fingering diagrams), not for the alto recorder (which appears below the diagrams).

Among the options you have for taking care of this problem are:

1. Play the melody or another instrument, such as the keyboard.
2. Play it on the recorder, but sing or leave out the note that is too low.
3. Play the first five notes of the second phrase an octave higher.

4. Transpose it to a higher key. Since the low note is only a half step below the range of the recorder, play everything one half step higher. This puts the piece in the key of A flat with the starting pitch on E-flat. In order to transpose it still higher, play all the notes of the piece one whole step higher. The transposition done this way puts you in the key of A with the starting pitch on E. Transposition is difficult, but not impossible. It requires the harmonizing chords to be transposed as well. This fourth alternative is not the best solution here, but may be the best solution for pieces that are easier to transpose.

Returning to "El Jarabe" as written, the last four phrases seem to be in a different key than the first four phrases. Play the A7 and D chords as if you are in the key of D for the last four phrases, then return to the key of G for the Da Capo al Fine.

The *D.C al fine* (fee-nay) at the end of the notation stands for the Italian "Da Capo al Fine." It means: Go back to the beginning; the piece is not finished. Play until *Fine*, the end.

There is one slur in the piece. To review, depending on your performance medium, the slur tells you to

1. Sing one word or syllable with more than one note.
2. Play smoothly from one note to the next on the keyboard.
3. Tongue only the note at the beginning of the slur on the recorder.

- Use this rhythm with your chordal accompaniment for "El Jarabe":

Summer Is A-coming In

This song dates from the thirteenth century. What sharps does it require? How many ties can you find in "Summer is A-coming In"? _____ How many slurs are there? _____

- Play or sing this piece with attention to the meter signature and the tempo marking.

Yankee Doodle

Although the meter signature of "Yankee Doodle" is ⅔, the notation *appears* the same as if it had a ⁴⁄₄ signature. In Allegro, ⅔ indicates that the piece should be performed with a brisk tempo and a strong feeling of two beats in a measure.

What kind of note gets one beat? _____
What kind of note gets half a beat? _____
What kind of note gets three quarters of a beat? _____

- Write two beats per measure in their appropriate places under each measure of "Yankee Doodle." (Appendix.)

    - Use this rhythm with your chordal accompaniment of the verse: ♩ ♩ Switch to ♩ ⏜ for the chorus. Play your chordal accompaniment with a different rhythm of your own choosing.

Yellow Rose of Texas

Sometimes ¢ appears in the meter signature instead of ⅔. The meaning is the same. How many beats are in a measure of this piece? _____ What kind of note gets one beat? _____ What kind of note gets half a beat? _____ What kind of note gets three quarters of a beat? _____ What kind of note gets one and a half beats?

_____ What kind of note gets one quarter of a beat? _____ What kind of note gets three eighths of a beat? _____ (Appendix.)

- Tap the rhythms of these examples:

First theme, "Overture" to the
Marriage of Figaro, Mozart

"Sailor's Dance,"
Purcell

Three kinds of dotted notes appear in the "Yellow Rose of Texas": ♪. ♩. ♩. To help you perceive their length, review the rule you used previously telling you how long to hold a dotted note. Then, draw the correct dotted note next to the tied note it matches.

(Appendix.)

- Clap the rhythm of the melody.

- Sing the melody of the "Yellow Rose of Texas."

   - Accompany yourself on a chordal instrument.

Bela Bimba

- Name the sharps in the key signature.

- Say the rhythm of the piece using rhythm syllables.

   - Play the accompaniment with a single chord note on beat one and at least two chord notes on beats two and three.

Shoo, Fly

Syncopated passages are often caused by a combination of a short note on the accented beat followed by a long note on the unaccented beat. The combination of the eighth-note and the quarter-note with the words "shoo, fly" illustrates this type of syncopation.

- Circle all the syncopations in this piece.

    What is the meaning of *D.C. al Fine?*

    What is the ending word of "Shoo, Fly"? (Appendix.)

    When you play and sing "Shoo, Fly," be sure to put extra emphasis on beat one of each measure. Playing chords on beat one only will help make a strong first beat.

This Train

- Circle syncopated passages in this melody before you play it.

- Find accidentals in the melody. These flats alter the tonality of the piece. They are often called "blue notes." When you hear reference to the "blues" or a "blues singer," it is probably because of the altered tonality associated with Afro-American music, particularly jazz. In this piece, the blue notes occur on the third and seventh steps of the scale.

    How long should the dotted quarter-note tied to the quarter-note be held?_____ What is the difference between the tie and the slur? (Appendix.)

SUMMARY

Many pieces of music use duple or triple metrical groupings. Approaching meter from a purely intellecutal perspective will probably not give you the sensation of meter. Review the songs in this chapter. As you play and sing them, do you feel the groupings? Whether clapping their rhythms or singing or playing them, stress the first beat of the measure. Contrast these regular meters with the irregular feeling of selections on your tape (2, 6, 18, 19, 22).

- Devise an arrangement for at least two songs using nonpitched percussion instruments to emphasize their metric grouping.

MUSIC CHECK

You should be able to define, identify, and illustrate musically:

METER	SIMPLE METER
METER SIGNATURE	COMPOUND METER
$\frac{2}{4} \frac{3}{4} \frac{4}{4} \frac{8}{8} \frac{3}{2} \ ¢ \ c$	FERMATA
NOTE VALUES IN DIFFERENT METERS	TRIPLET
CONDUCTOR'S PATTERNS	D.C. AL FINE
PATSCHEN	SLUR/TIE
TEMPO INDICATORS	SYNCOPATION
ALLEGRETTO, LARGAMENTE, LENTO, VIVACE	BLUE NOTES
DOTTED NOTES IN DIFFERENT METERS	

CHAPTER 5

THE KEYBOARD

Whether or not you intend to use the keyboard as a performing medium, it can be a helpful tool to further your understanding of theoretical concepts related to music. The keyboard is especially useful because it gives visual reinforcement of aural concepts. It also gives tactile reinforcement of musical concepts and provides attractive ways for the beginning music student to create. Even if you have chosen to play chordal accompaniments on autoharp or guitar, be sure to use the keyboard to help you understand selected concepts identified in this chapter. The keyboard will help you hear the sounds described, see the organization of whole- and half-steps in scales and chords, and feel spatial relationships.

There will be times when you cannot be at a real keyboard. For those occasions, pictures of the keyboard have been provided in the Appendix. One is a plain keyboard; the other shows the names of notes. Use this aid only when you cannot be at a real keyboard. Its limitation is the absence of sound to reinforce the musical concepts presented.

NOTE NAMES AND LOCATIONS

Notice that the black keys are grouped in alternating sets of twos and threes. The pattern of two and three black keys sets helps to locate note names on the keyboard. Find the set of two black keys nearest the middle of the keyboard. The white key to the left of this set is called *middle C*. The white key to the left of any black set of two on the keyboard is always C.

Middle C is shown on the keyboard picture above.

- Write C on all the other appropriate keys in that picture.

- Play all the C's on the keyboard you use for practice. Many keyboards available for student use today are smaller than the traditional keyboard with 88 keys. No matter what the size of the keyboard, C will always appear to the left of the black key set of two.

The white keys to the left of the three black key sets are F's.

- Label all the F's on this keyboard.

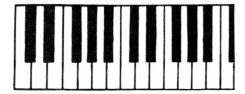

- Play all the F's on your keyboard.

Since you already know that musical pitches are named by letter names from A to G, and that they follow each other either forward or backward, you should be able to figure out the names of all the keys on the piano. (Try to label them with no help. If you need to check, use the keyboard picture in the appendix with the names written on the keys.)

- Label all the D's on this keyboard.

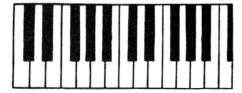

- Play all the D's on your practice keyboard.
- Label all the G's on this keyboard.

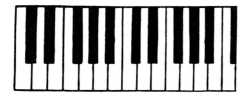

- Play all the G's on your practice keyboard.
- Label all the E's and F's on this keyboard.

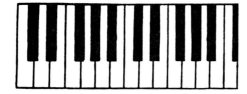

- Play all the E's and F's on your practice keyboard.
- Label all the A's and B's on this keyboard.

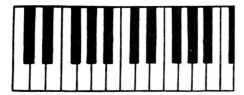

- Play all the A's and B's on your practice keyboard.
- Label and play the notes indicated on this keyboard.

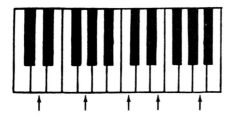

OCTAVES

When you played all the notes having a common name on the keyboard, you were playing *octaves*. Beginning at the bottom of your keyboard, play the lowest D, the next highest one, and so on. You are playing successively higher octaves. The word *octave* is derived from *octa,* or ''eight.'' If you count the bottom D as number one, then count each of the note names up to and including the next highest D, that note will be number eight, or an octave higher than the first D.

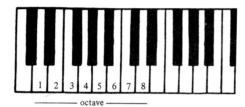

SHARPS AND FLATS

In learning note names on the keyboard so far, you have played only white keys. Black keys are often used. They may be indicated by *flat* (♭) or *sharp* (♯) signs. The black key directly to the right of middle C is called *C-sharp*. It sounds a half a step higher than C. (Another name for half-step is *semitone*.)

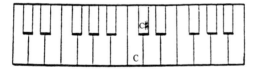

- Label the rest of the C-sharps.

- Find all the C-sharps on your keyboard. They will be in octaves, or eight notes apart.

- After you have played the C-sharps alone, then play all the C to C-sharp combinations on the keyboard, listening for the half-step difference in pitch going up.

- Label all the F-sharps on this keyboard.

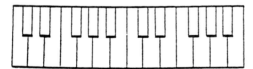

(If you are not sure, refer to the keyboard picture in the Appendix.)

- Play all the F-sharps on your keyboard.

- Play all the F to F-sharp combinations listening to the half-step difference in pitch.

- Label all the black-note sharps on this keyboard.

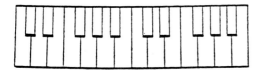

- As you play all the black keys on your keyboard, say their sharp names aloud.

A black key may also be named in relation to the white key on its right; then it is called a *flat* (♭). This note is D-flat. It sounds a half-step lower than D.

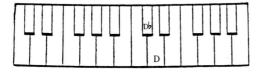

- Play all the D-flats on your practice keyboard.

- After you have played the D-flats alone, then play all the D to D-flat combinations, listening for the half-step difference in pitch going down.

- Label all the black-note flats on this keyboard.

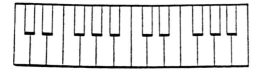

- As you play all the black keys on your keyboard, say their flat names aloud.

ENHARMONIC SPELLING

You are probably aware that the note you played and called D-flat was called C-sharp earlier. Two different names for the same key are called *enharmonic spellings*. C-sharp is to the right of C and D-flat is to the left of D, but the key you play on the keyboard for both of them is the same.

- Write two names for each black key on the keyboard pictured here.

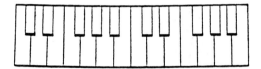

HALF-STEPS (SEMITONES)

- Play C, then C-sharp. The difference in sound between the two notes is half a step, the space on the keyboard between two adjacent keys. The C-sharp sounds a half-step higher than C. Play D, then D-flat. The difference in sound is a half-step. The D-flat sounds a half-step lower than D.

- Play D to D-sharp. Listen carefully to get the half-step sound in your ear. Play D to D-flat. Notice that the sound of D to D-sharp is a half-step going up. The sound of D to D-flat is a half-step going down.

- Play F to F-sharp, then G to G-flat. Listen to the sound of a half-step going up, then a half-step going down.

- With the same aural attention, play G to G-sharp, A to A-flat, A to A-sharp, B to B-flat.

  All the sharps and flats you have been playing are from white to black keys. Sharps and flats can also be from white to white keys. Notice on your keyboard there is no black key between E and F. In order to have an E-sharp, it is necessary to use F as the note one half-step above E. Although this does not happen a great deal, learn it now, so you are accurate even in its infrequent use.

- Label all the E-sharps on this keyboard.

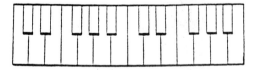

- Play all the E to E-sharp combinations on your keyboard. As you play them, listen to the half-step sound from E to E-sharp.

  Just as F is used for E-sharp, E is used for F-flat.

- Label all the F-flats on this keyboard.

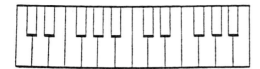

- Play all the F-flats on your keyboard. Listen to the sound of the half-step as you play from F to F-flat.

- Find other places on the keyboard where white keys must be used for flats and sharps.

- Label all the B-sharps on this keyboard.

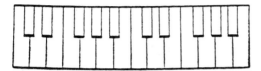

- Play all the B's followed by B-sharps, listening for the half-step sound.

- Label all the C-flats on this keyboard.

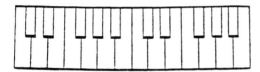

- Play all the C's followed by C-flats, listening for the half-step sound.

CHROMATIC SCALE

A *scale* is a series of musical pitches in ascending or descending order. If you play all the half-steps on your keyboard consecutively, you will play a *chromatic scale*.

- Play the chromatic scale and listen for the sounds of the half-steps.

- Find and listen to a recording of Rimsky-Korsakov's "Flight of the Bumblebee." Its melody uses chromatics extensively. Find recordings in libraries (public, school, or friend's) and record shops. Purchases of attractive recordings for your own continuous use are long-term investments for your listening enjoyment.

- Play the chromatic scale again, then write it on the staff beginning with middle C. As you write the ascending notes, mark all the names of the black keys as sharps (♯). As you write the descending notes, mark all the names of the black keys as flats (♭). Even though you call the notes by the letter name *followed by* the flat or sharp (A-sharp, E-flat, and so on), when writing music, write the flat or sharp sign *in front of* the note (♯♩ ♭♪).

- Continue writing this upward chromatic scale for one octave only. (Appendix.)

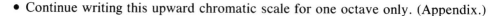

- Play the chromatic scale until your ear can identify its unique sound.

- Continue writing this downward scale for one octave only. (Appendix.)

- Play the downward chromatic scale until your ear can identify its sound.

    This example shows how Liszt used a chromatic scale in his first theme from the "Grand Galop Chromatique" for piano.

- Write a one octave chromatic scale going up, then down, beginning on G. (Appendix.)

- Begin this chromatic scale on E. (Appendix.)

WHOLE STEPS (WHOLE-TONES)

Music frequently uses whole steps (whole-tones) as well as half-steps (semitones). *Whole steps* are composed of two half-steps. To determine a whole step, be sure there is one key between two adjacent keys. For example, from C to D is a whole step because C-sharp (D-flat) is between them. From E to F is not a whole step because there is no key between them.

- On the keyboard picture below, identify the spaces between the marked notes as being either whole steps (W) or half-steps (H) As you figure out what they are, play them on your keyboard, listening to their different sounds.

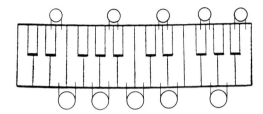

(Appendix.)

All the whole steps you have identified so far have been from white key to white key. Whole steps can also be from black key to black key, such as from F-sharp to G-sharp. They will be whole steps as long as there is a key between them. In this case, the key between them is G.

- Label the whole and half steps in the picture below. (Appendix.)

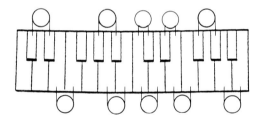

- Play the whole and half steps, listening for their differences.

Whole steps can also occur between a white key and a black key. A whole step up from E is F-sharp. The key between them is F.

- Label the whole and half steps in the picture below. Play them, listening for their differences. (Appendix.)

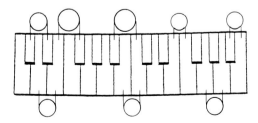

In summary:

Half-steps can occur between a white key and a black key, a black key and a white key, or a white key and a white key. A half-step is present if there is no key between the two named keys.

Whole steps can occur between a white key and a white key, a black key and a black key, a white key and a black key, or a black key and a white key. One key must be present between the notes of the whole step.

- Review whole steps and half-steps by labeling the intervals (spaces between the notes) in this picture either with a W (whole) or H (half) and listening for their differences as you play them. (Appendix.)

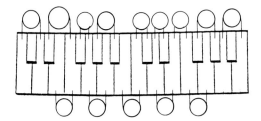

WHOLE-TONE SCALE

A contrast to the chromatic scale (which uses all half-steps) is the *whole-tone scale* (which uses all whole steps.)

- Finish writing this whole-tone scale. Be sure to end with the same key you started on, only an octave higher.

How many notes are in a whole-tone scale? (Appendix.)

- Play the whole-tone scale. Listen to it as you play to help your ear identify it.

- Finish writing these whole-tone scales. It may be easier for you to write them if you play as you write. Be sure to play them after you have finished writing. Keep the same accidentals you start with; i.e., if you use a sharp or a flat in the scale, continue to use the same sign. Don't mix sharps and flats in the same scale.

(Appendix.)

- Listen to the Debussy *Prelude to the Afternoon of a Faun* (Tape 19). One of the factors contributing to this composer's originality is his use of pentatonic, chromatic, and whole-tone scales.

ACCIDENTALS

In addition to flat or sharp signs, the following signs can be used to alter notes: *natural* (♮), *double flat* (♭♭), *double sharp* (×). All these accidental signs affect notes of the same pitch within the same measure, but not notes of the same name in different octaves.

If a flat or sharp has been used in a piece but subsequently is not needed, the note can be returned to its original condition by canceling the flat or sharp through the use of a natural sign (♮). This example shows the natural sign being used after a note that had been sharped. The natural indicates that the note following it will be an F instead of an F-sharp as it was at the beginning of the measure.

This example shows the natural sign being used after a flat. The natural indicates that the note following it will be a B instead of a B-flat as it was at the beginning of the measure.

Because the natural sign removes flats and sharps, it can alter a pitch by indicating it is to be a half-step higher or lower than it was previously. Notice in this illustration that the effect of the natural on the G-sharp is to lower it one half-step, the effect of the natural on the A-flat is to raise it one half-step.

A natural sign can also cancel a sharp or flat indicated in the key signature. Because this key signature says that the B is to be flatted, it will be played that way unless the natural is inserted in the notation. The effect of the natural on the key signature is only for one measure. If the effect of the natural is desired for more than one measure, it must be inserted in all measures where needed.

This example ("Für Elise," Beethoven) shows the insertion of the sharp in two different measures, then the cancellation of the sharp by use of the natural.

The natural sign is used *in* a key signature only when there is a change of key. The use of the natural then is a reminder that the flats or sharps of the previous key signature have been superseded by the new key signature.

A *double flat* (♭♭) lowers a pitch one whole step; a *double sharp* (×) raises it a whole step. These signs are used infrequently. Both the double flat and the double sharp can be canceled by a natural.

• Name these notes.

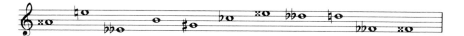

(Appendix.)

Sharps, flats, naturals, double flats, or double sharps used within the notation of a piece of music are called *accidentals*. This term does not apply to the signs when they are used in a key signature.

• Write and play these notes in the treble clef:

G♯   D♭   A×   C♭♭   F   B♯   E♭   G♭♭   D♯   A♭   C♯   G×

● Write and play these notes in the bass clef:

C♭   A𝄪   D♯   E♭♭   A♯   B♭   C♯   A♭   G♭♭   C𝄪   D♭   F♯

● Label these notes on the keyboard picture below:

B♭♭ F𝄪 D♯ C♭ A♮ F♭♭ E♯

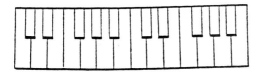

MUSIC CHECK

You should be able to define, identify, and illustrate musically:

NOTES ON THE KEYBOARD	ACCIDENTALS
HALF AND WHOLE STEPS	SHARPS
SEMITONES AND WHOLE-TONES	FLATS
SCALES	NATURALS
CHROMATIC	DOUBLE FLATS
WHOLE-TONE	DOUBLE SHARPS
	ENHARMONIC SPELLINGS

CHAPTER 6

MAJOR SCALES AND KEY SIGNATURES

This chapter deals with tetrachords and major scales (how to build them, their use in selected pieces) and key signatures (their formation, ways to name them, order of sharps and flats).

Scales are arrangements of pitches with predetermined relationships to each other, into ascending or descending order. You have used chromatic and whole-tone scales. The arrangement of the component pitches of the chromatic scale sharply contrasts with the arrangement of the whole-tone scale pitches. The major scale that you are about to study provides another contrasting arrangement of pitches. Once you become familiar with the arrangement of pitches in any given scale, that familiarity will help guide you to recognize correct pitches of melodies based upon the scale. This recognition of appropriate pitches within the context set up by the scale transfers to melodies that are not arranged in the order of the scale. The scale summarizes tonal relationships within given keys.

MAJOR SCALES

The *major scale* is used much more frequently than the chromatic and the whole-tone scales. It incorporates both whole and half steps. As an introduction to the major scale, put both hands on the keyboard with the shortest finger of each hand on C's an octave apart.

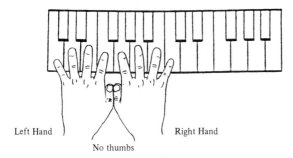

Left Hand   Right Hand

No thumbs

In order to play the major scale now, *do not use your thumbs*. Play four con-secutive notes with your left hand beginning with the little finger, then four con-secutive notes with your right hand beginning with the forefinger. After you have played the C major scale up, reverse the use of your fingers, and play the C major scale down.

You have just played a *tetrachord* with each hand. *Tetra* means "four"; you played four notes with each hand.

You can play every major scale by combining two tetrachords in this way, but C is the only major scale using no black keys. The problem in other major scales is the correct placement of the black keys. Remember that there will be a whole step between all your fingers except those marked in this picture. Each hand will put one half-step in place in the scale. Each hand plays that half-step between the third and fourth notes of its tetrachord.

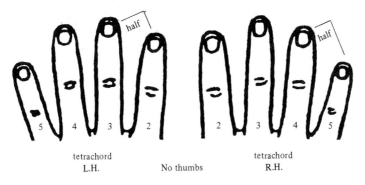

tetrachord   tetrachord
L.H.   No thumbs   R.H.

- Put your left little finger on an F. Begin playing up the scale with white keys under your first three fingers. To put a half-step next, you must use a black key, B-flat. Play it with your left forefinger. The next note, C, a whole step away, is played with your right forefinger. Continue with your right hand playing up the scale. You will not need another black key because there is already a half-step between E and F on the keyboard (the third and fourth notes of this tetrachord.) Practice playing the F major scale with four fingers of each hand until it is comfortable to play and easy to find. For consistency in playing the two tetrachords of a major scale, do not use your thumbs. Pianists, practicing to gain skill in playing scales, use many fingerings that include the use of the thumb and fingers crossing over or under each other. Since the purpose here of playing scales is to determine the location of the half-steps in the tetrachords of major scales and not to develop playing skill, be consistent in using four fingers only to develop the concept of tetrachord major scale building.

Notice that the sound of the third tone of the scale is pulled by the half-step into the fourth tone. The same pull is felt by the seventh tone toward the eighth tone of the scale. The third and seventh tones *lead into* the fourth and eighth tones of the major scale. When one puts two tetrachords together to form a major scale, it becomes evident that the major scale has a half-step between the third and fourth and seventh and eighth degrees of the scale. All other steps of the major scale are whole ones. This is true of every major scale.

- Listen carefully as you play to help your ear learn to identify the major scale.

- This is what the F major scale you have been playing looks like when notated.

/\ shows the half steps

- Put your left hand little finger on G. Figure out by sight and sound how to play the G major scale. After you can play it easily, finish writing it. Check to be sure that half steps are between steps three and four and steps seven and eight of the scale and that all other steps of the scale are whole ones. When writing major scales, be sure that all note names are used once, except for the key name (used at the beginning and the end), and that only flats or sharps are used in one scale. *They cannot be mixed.*

(Appendix.)

- The D scale has two sharps. Begin playing it with your left little finger on D. After you are satisfied with the sound, finish writing it.

SINGING MAJOR SCALES

Do not rely solely on the keyboard to help you with the sight and sound of music. Practice *singing* the scales in several different ways. At first you may want to play as you sing to give you confidence. As soon as you can, try singing without playing the notes on the keyboard.

- Sing the C major scale as you play it. First sing the numbers of the scale tones, then the syllables.

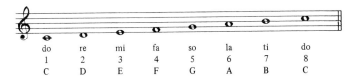

- Sing the letter names of the C major scale. Notice that (as with the songs previously introduced using numbers and solfege) as you sing different scales, the numbers and syllables remain the same, but the letter names must be changed according to the scale you are singing.

- Sing both the F and G major scale using numbers, syllables, and letter names. (Appendix.)

    The syllables and numbers retain the same relationship as in the scale, even when they are used in a melody with different order or in a different major key.

- Sing the following melodies using numbers, syllables, and letter names. Note that the first piece is in the key of C and the second is in the key of G.

do do do re mi mi mi re do re mi do
1 1 1 2 3   3 3 2   1 2   3   1

mi mi fa so so fa mi fa so mi
3   3   4   5   5   4   3   4   5   3

so so
5   5

- Sing "Row, Row, Row Your Boat" using numbers, syllables, and letter names by ear. It starts on "1," "do," or "C."

  Scales sometimes begin on black keys. In building these major scales beginning on black keys, follow the same procedure as when building major scales starting on white keys. Use four fingers of each hand. Be sure there are half steps only between the top two notes of both tetrachords. Another way of saying this important rule: *Half-steps will occur between the third and fourth degrees and between the seventh and eighth degrees of the major scale.* Be sure that *either* flats or sharps are used when writing a major scale. Both are not used in the same major scale.

- After drawing a treble clef sign, begin writing a scale using flats by drawing a flat in front of the B note in the space under the first ledger line below the treble staff. Continue to write the correct notes of the B-flat major scale as you play it. Listen to the sounds of the individual pitches, determining their relationship to the accurate total *sound* of the scale.

- Sing the B-flat major scale using numbers, syllables, and letter names. (Appendix.)

  So far, you have played, sung, and written scales in the treble clef. When you sang them, you may not have sung the pitches exactly where they are written. For example, a man singing an F scale written in the treble clef may not be able to sing it in his normal voice. He may have to sing the scale an octave, or perhaps two octaves, lower than written. Changing octaves to suit your individual voice is generally recommended, but also strive to stretch your vocal capability to avoid being a lazy singer. Both women and men often erroneously think they cannot sing high pitches. In fact, they may only need practice to expand their ranges. Men should experiment with singing in falsetto to develop additional range capacity. (Further discussion of vocal techniques and capabilities appears in the *Voice* section of the Appendix.) Even though the following scales are to be written in the bass clef, sing them in the range most comfortable for you.

- Using the tetrachord approach, write and play these major scales in the bass clef. Also sing them using syllables, numbers, and letter names. Use flats when black keys are needed for the first three scales. Use $\wedge$ to show the placement of the half-steps in the scales.

Eb scale

Ab scale

Db scale

- Use sharps when black keys are needed for these scales.

A scale

E scale

B scale

(Appendix.)

Lullaby Round

Melody:

Some music uses complete major scales for melodic lines. "Lullaby Round" uses

1. a complete descending C major scale (with some repeated notes).

2. an incomplete descending C major scale (with some repeated notes).

3. an incomplete ascending C major scale.

• Find and label each of these scales and parts of scales in the "Lullaby Round." (Appendix.)

Finding the key of "Lullaby Round" is easy. When you look at the beginning of the staves for this piece, you will notice that there are no flats or sharps there. This helps tell you that the piece is in the key of C. Remember that the *key of C has no flats or sharps in its signature.*

Rhythm:

What does the meter signature tell you about this piece? Review the meaning of the dot after a note. The first two notes are the equivalent of one quarter-note. Together they get one beat. Because of the dot, they will be uneven; the first note will receive three quarters of the beat, the second note will receive only one quarter of the beat.

• Count and clap the rhythm for "Lullaby Round."

• Say the words of "Lullaby Round" in strict rhythm. Be sure to hold the half-notes for two full counts. How many measures have exactly the same rhythm? How many measures have the dotted note rhythm? (Appendix.)

• Use rhythm syllables to say the melodic rhythm.

These examples show uses of the dotted eighth-note followed by a sixteenth. Two examples also include the dotted quarter-note.

• Count and clap the rhythm of the examples. Add pitch to the rhythm either independently, or with the help of your teacher.

"Minuet in G"
Beethoven

"Nocturne in E Major"
Mendelssohn

"Prelude in A Major"
Chopin

First theme, "Overture"
to *Dido and Aeneas*
Purcell

Form:

Are any measures of this piece exactly the same? How many measures have the same rhythm? What is the form of this piece? (Appendix.)

- Play the melody of "Lullaby Round" in the key of C. Put your hands in the same position you used to play the C major scale in tetrachords.

- Transpose the melody of "Lullaby Round" to the key of D by moving your hands to the tetrachord positions for the D scale.

- Sing "Lullaby Round" using syllables, numbers, and letter names. Use the keyboard to help you sing accurately if you need it.

Harmony:

After you have learned to play and sing the melody accurately, enlist other musicians to perform this piece with you as a round, using the entrances indicated by the numbers above the melody at the beginning of each measure. Note that up to nine independent entrances are shown.

Philippine School Song

This song is in the key of _____. Its meter signature says that there are _____ beats in a measure and the _____ note gets one beat. The piece begins on beat _____.

- Clap the rhythm of the piece. Be accurate with silence during the eighth rest.

- Use rhythm syllables to say the rhythm.

Form:

- Circle a repeated pattern.

- Bracket a scale passage that descends regularly except for the inclusion of two extra notes. Underline the two extra notes. (Appendix.)

- What is the form of "Philippine School Song"? (Appendix.)

- Put your hands in the tetrachord position for the C scale. Play the melody of the "Philippine School Song" using both hands.

- Sing the "Philippine School Song" with syllables, numbers, letter names, and Philippine and English words.

- Transpose this piece to the key of F by placing your hands in the tetrachord positions for the F scale.

NAMING KEY SIGNATURES WHEN FLATS ARE USED

When using key signatures, remember that sharps or flats in the key signature apply to all notes with the same name. This is true in all octaves even when the flat is on one line or space of the staff.

This note will be called B-flat even though the flat in the key signature is on the line an octave above.

This note will be called B-flat even though the flat in the key signature is on the line an octave below.

- Name these notes.

(Appendix.)

Follow this procedure in naming the major key if the piece you wish to play or sing has two flats at the beginning of the staves. Name the last flat (to the right) *fa,* then go down the scale to *do.* You discover that the note for *do* is B, but since there is a flat on the B line, it must be B-flat.

If you called the last flat 4 and counted down to 1, you would also have landed on B-flat.

The use of either of these two methods (syllables or numbers) will help you find the name of the major key when flats appear in the key signature.

In what key is a piece whose key signature has three flats?

In what key is a piece whose key signature has four flats?

(Appendix.)

You may have noticed that when you count from *fa* to *do,* or 4 to 1 to find the name of the major key with flats in the signature, *fa* or 4 is always the last flat to the right, *do* or 1 is always the next-to-last flat. Since this happens in all flat keys (except the key of F with only one flat in its signature), save time by calling the key by the name of its next-to-last flat. This is an accurate short-cut.

- Name these keys.

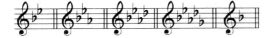

(Appendix.)

NAMING KEY SIGNATURES WHEN SHARPS ARE USED

The key name for a major piece with sharps in the signature is the letter name a half-step up from the last sharp. This key has only one sharp (F-sharp). The letter name one half-step up is G. The key signature is G.

Key of G

- Name these major keys:

(Appendix.)

- Name the keys for these pieces:
    "Skip to My Lou"
    "Holla Hi, Holla Ho"
    "Rocky Mountain"
    "Kum Ba Yah"
    "Old MacDonald"
    "Roll Over"
(Appendix.)

CONSTRUCTING KEY SIGNATURES

You have learned to tell the names of keys whose flats or sharps are shown in a key signature. In the future you may be required to construct a key signature with the name of the key as the only information given to you. Remember, *the key of C has no flats or sharps. All other key names having no flat in the name of the key, EXCEPT the key of F, will be sharp keys.* The names of these sharp keys will all be half a step above the last sharp in the key signature. If you have been asked to tell the number of sharps in the key signature for the key of A, count one-half step down to find that the last sharp in that key is G-sharp. The problem is that with no further information, you don't know how many other sharps are in that key. You need to know the order in which the sharps *always* appear in the key signature.

ORDER OF SHARPS

To help you construct key signatures, memorize the order of sharps. They always appear in the key signature in this order: F, C, G, D, A, E, B. Use the keyboard to help you remember the order in which sharps occur in key signatures. The first sharp to be used in a key signature is F-sharp, the lowest black key in the set of three. The second sharp to be used in a key signature is C-sharp, the lowest black key in the set of two. The order of sharps follows a pattern with the third sharp being the next highest black key in the set of three, the fourth sharp being the next highest black key in the set of two, the fifth sharp being the highest black key in the set of three.

If you wish to determine the order of sharps without the keyboard, start on F-sharp for the first sharp, then count up five note names for the next one (C-sharp), down four note names for the third sharp (G-sharp), up five note names for the fourth sharp (D-sharp), and so on. The pattern is up a fifth and down a fourth.

- Play the sharps in this order. Say their names as you play them.

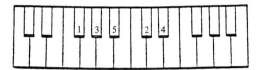

Since you have used all the sharps found on black keys, if you need more sharps for a certain key signature, use white keys. Stay in the same alternating pattern to find the order of all seven sharps.

- Play and name these sharps in order.

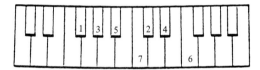

To get back to the process of constructing the key signature in the key of A, you have identified the sharp one half-step lower than the name of a sharp key (G-sharp). Use the order of sharps to help you determine the sharps that preceded that last sharp (F-sharp, C-sharp). Place these three sharps on the staff after the clef sign at the beginning of the line to show the key signature.

This model shows the placement of the sharps for the treble and bass clef key signatures. *Always* place your sharps on the lines and spaces as indicated in this model.

Logically, to show the regularity of the order of sharps, they should be placed like this:

They are never used this way, in spite of the logical arrangement, because the sharps move out of the confines of the staff and become more difficult to read. This illustration is given only to show the regular order. Sharps *never* follow this configuration in the key signature.

To summarize, this is the process to be used in constructing sharp key signatures when the name of the key is known:

1. Find the sharp one half-step below the key name.

2. Find which sharp(s) precede that sharp in the order of sharps.

3. Include the preceding sharps and the sharp one half-step below the key name in the key signature.

4. Place the sharps in the key signature in the correct order of sharps.

• Write these key signatures in the treble clef.

Key of D   Key of B   Key of G

• Write these key signatures in the bass clef.

Key of A   Key of E   Key of C

(Appendix.)

ORDER OF FLATS

All flat keys use a flat in their names except for the *key* of F. Remember from previous discussion, the name of the key when using flats is always *do* or 1. Count up to *fa* or 4 to find the last flat. In all keys except F (with only one flat), the name of the key will be the next to last flat. The order of flats is B, E, A, D, G, C, F. Notice that the order of flats is the reverse of the order of sharps. The first four flats will be easy to remember since they spell the word *BEAD*.

The order of flats follows a pattern on the keyboard also. Notice that the first flat is B, the highest black key in the set of three black keys. The second flat is E, the highest black key in the set of two black keys. The third flat is A, the next highest in the set of three black keys. The fourth flat is D, the lowest in the set of two black keys. The fifth flat is G, the lowest in the set of three black keys.

To find the order of flats without the keyboard, start on B-flat, then count down five note names, up four note names, and so on to find to remainder of the flats. The pattern is down a fifth and up a fourth.

- Play and say these flats in order.

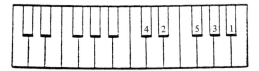

Since you have used all the flats found on black keys, if you need more flats for a certain key signature you must use white keys. Stay in the same alternating pattern to find the order of all seven flats.

- Play and say these flats in order.

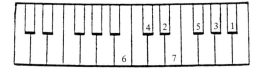

To review:

1. For all flat keys except F (which has only one flat), the name of the key is the next to last flat.
2. Use the order of flats to help you determine the flats preceding the key name and the one flat following it.
3. Place the flats on the staff after the clef sign at the beginning of the line to show the key signature.

This model shows the placement of the flats for the treble and bass clef key signatures. *Always* place your flats on the lines and spaces indicated here.

- Write these key signatures in the treble clef.

Key of E♭   Key of A♭   Key of G♭

• Write these key signatures in the bass clef.

Key of F   Key of B♭   Key of D♭

(Appendix.)

Reminder: All flat keys, except F with one flat, have flats as part of their names. When naming keys, with two exceptions, all keys with no flats in their names are sharp keys. The two exceptions are C with no flats or sharps, and F with one flat.

CIRCLE OF FIFTHS

A way of summarizing the relationship of key signatures to each other and the number of flats and sharps in them is to use a *circle of fifths*. Notice that as your eye moves around the circle clockwise from the top, sharps are added one by one. As your eye moves around the circle counterclockwise from the top, flats are added one by one. They are added in the order previously described.

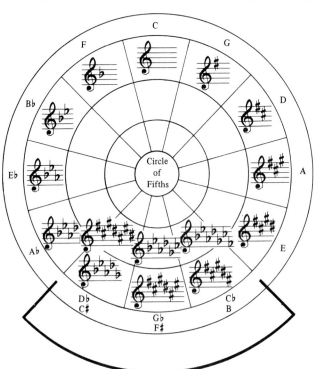

Notice that the distance from the name of a key to its next-door neighbor on the circle is that of a fifth (five note names). *Always count the beginning and ending letters when determining an interval.* From F up to C is a fifth; from C up to G is a fifth, and so on.

Notice at the bottom of the circle the area where the flats and sharps cross over. These relationships are called *enharmonic.* The key of D-flat with five flats is an enharmonic spelling of C-sharp with seven sharps. They look different, but they sound the same and will be played using the same keys on the keyboard.

- Put your hands on the keyboard in the tetrachord position. Play a scale beginning on D-flat. Leave your hands on the same notes and play the scale of C-sharp. The sound should be the same. Write both those scales. They will look quite different.

Key of D♭

Key of C♯

(Appendix.)

Moving in a clockwise direction, notice that the *upper* tetrachord of each scale is the *lower* tetrachord of the next scale.

The octave sign (*8va- - - - -*) is used to indicate that the written notes are to be played an octave higher or lower to avoid ledger lines. Play the notes an octave higher when it appears over the staff; play them an octave lower when it appears under the staff.

- Play all the scales starting with C major and moving in a clockwise direction. Use the tetrachord position with one tetrachord in each hand. As you move to a new key, use the left hand for the tetrachord played by the right hand in the previous key. Depending on where you begin and how many keys are on your keyboard, at some point in the exercise you will run out of notes. When this happens, simply transfer the upper tetrachord to a lower position on the keyboard and continue through the rest of the keys.

• Name the major keys for these signatures:

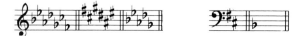

(Appendix.)

Roll Over

What is the key of this piece? (Appendix.)

• Clap the rhythm while you say the words for "Roll Over" rhythmically.

• Place the fifth, third, and first fingers of your left hand on F-sharp, A-sharp, and C-sharp as shown in the picture.

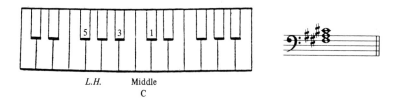

L.H.   Middle
C

Play the notes together to sound an F-sharp major chord. Practice playing the F-sharp major chord on a steady beat.

• Spread your right hand over an octave, from middle C-sharp to C-sharp an octave higher. Your thumb (1) will be on middle C-sharp; your little finger (5) will be on C-sharp an octave higher.

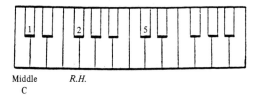

Middle   *R.H.*
C

• Play the melody of "Roll Over" with your right hand. Be careful; the key signature shows that all the notes in this melody are sharps.

• Play the F-sharp chord with the left hand using a steady beat while you play the melody with the right hand. Be sure to get the left thumb out of the way when the right thumb must play the middle C-sharp as part of the melody.

The first and second ending enables economical printing of a piece of music. Normally, the first ending (⌐1¬ :||) and second ending (⌐2¬ ||) contain two differ-ent cadences for a phrase of the repeated section, so the bulk of the printed music can be used twice. "Roll Over" is unusual in that the first ending is used nine times and is longer than the preceding part of the piece. In this case, the "second" ending becomes the tenth ending.

MUSIC CHECK

You should be able to define, identify, and illustrate musically:

MAJOR SCALES	MAJOR SCALE SINGING
TETRACHORDS	MOVEABLE *DO*
MAJOR KEY SIGNATURES	SYLLABLES
ORDER OF SHARPS AND FLATS	NUMBERS
CIRCLE OF FIFTHS	LETTERS

CHAPTER 7

INTERVALS

An *interval* is the difference in pitch between two notes. You have already heard and used many intervals, but have not identified them, visually or aurally. More knowledge about intervals will help you build chords and scales containing intervals larger than whole steps. Practice in recognizing and producing intervals should help you sing and play music accurately.

GENERAL INTERVALS

When naming an interval, be sure to number its first note "one," then count within the scale to the other note of the interval: In the C scale, going up from C to E is a third. Going down from C to G is a fourth.

• Play these intervals on the keyboard as you say their names:

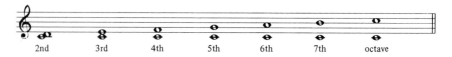

Intervals determined by counting from letter name to letter name are called *general intervals*. When interval names are determined by counting the half-steps they contain, they are called *specific intervals*.

- Determine these general intervals by counting from the letter name of one note to the letter name of the other note in the interval. Be sure to call the first note "one." (Appendix.)

- Name these general intervals. (Appendix.)

INVERSIONS

When intervals are inverted (bottom note is put on top), the relationship of the pitches in the interval is also determined by counting from one note in the interval to the other, calling the first note "one." From C up to E is a third, from C down to E is a sixth. From G up to C is a fourth, from G down to C is a fifth.

The name of an inverted interval can be determined by subtracting the original, noninverted name from the number nine. For example, the third (subtracted from nine) becomes a sixth, the fourth becomes a fifth.

- Play these intervals, followed by their inversions, on the keyboard as you say their names:

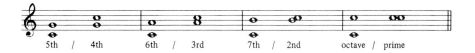

- To check your understanding of inversions, fill out these equations:

  An inverted third = a _____.
  An inverted second = a _____.
  An inverted prime = an _____.
  An inverted fifth = a _____.
  An inverted fourth = a _____.
  An inverted sixth = a _____.
  An inverted seventh = a _____.
  An inverted octave = a _____.

  You determine the accuracy of your answers by totaling the intervals in each equation. If the total is nine, you have given correct answers.

- Next to the intervals on this staff, draw their inversions. Under the intervals, write their names.

(Appendix.)

  The illustrations of intervals and inversions in this chapter so far have been in the key of C major. The principles apply to any major key.

- Check your understanding of intervals by playing and naming these in the key of G:

(Appendix.)

- Identify these intervals, then invert them. Name the inverted intervals also. Name the keys used. (Appendix.)

SPECIFIC INTERVALS

Specific intervals are determined more precisely than general intervals. The number of half-steps within the interval tells whether it is major, minor, perfect, diminished, or augmented.

MAJOR AND MINOR INTERVALS

When describing intervals in an ascending major scale with the lowest tone as the key tone, *seconds, thirds, sixths,* and *sevenths* are called *major* intervals. If any of them are made smaller by a half-step, they become *minor* intervals.

- Play these major intervals, then the interval with the same name made minor by lowering the upper note one half-step. Listen to the difference in their sounds. (Examples given here are in the key of C major. *The same principles apply in other major keys.*)

major 2nd   minor 2nd   major 3rd   minor 3rd   major 6th   minor 6th   major 7th   minor 7th

- Write these intervals in the key of F, using F as the bottom note of each interval. Place the correct key signature after the clef sign. Also, put the appropriate flats from the key signature in parentheses before the notes affected (as reminders). (Appendix.)

maj. 2nd, min. 2nd   maj. 3rd, min. 3rd

maj. 6th, min. 6th   maj. 7th, min. 7th

- Write these intervals in the key of G, using G as the bottom note of each interval. Place the correct key signature after the clef sign. Also, put the appropriate sharps from the key signature in parentheses before the notes affected (as reminders). (Appendix.)

maj. 2nd, min. 2nd   maj. 3rd, min. 3rd

maj. 6th, min. 6th   maj. 7th, min. 7th

When a major interval is *inverted,* it becomes a minor one. The reverse is true also; inverted minor intervals become major ones.

- Play these inversions as you read their names:

major 2nd   minor 7th   major 3rd   minor 6th   major 6th   minor 3rd   major 7th   minor 2nd

- Write these inversions in the key of G. Use the appropriate key signature and the appropriate sharps from the key signature in parentheses (as reminders). Use G as the bottom note of the major intervals. (Appendix.)

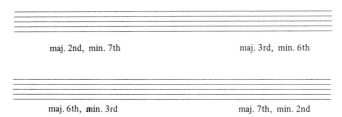

maj. 2nd, min. 7th   maj. 3rd, min. 6th

maj. 6th, min. 3rd   maj. 7th, min. 2nd

- Write these inversions in the key of F. Use the appropriate key signature and the appropriate flats from the key signature in parentheses (as reminders). Use F as the bottom note of the major intervals. (Appendix.)

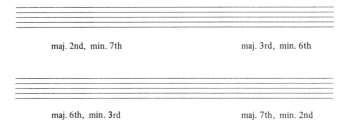

maj. 2nd, min. 7th   maj. 3rd, min. 6th

maj. 6th, min. 3rd   maj. 7th, min. 2nd

- Name the keys. Identify the intervals.

(Appendix.)

PERFECT INTERVALS

Fourths, fifths, octaves, and *unisons* (or *primes*) are called *perfect* intervals. They are never called major or minor.

- Play these perfect intervals, written in the key of C with the key-note on the bottom:

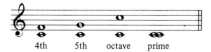

When perfect intervals are inverted, they remain perfect:

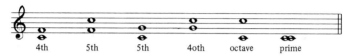

- Write four perfect intervals in the key of D with the key-note on the bottom. Next to them, write their inversions.

(Appendix.)

- Write four perfect intervals in the key of B-flat with the key-note on the bottom. Next to them, write their inversions.

(Appendix.)

DIMINISHED INTERVALS

Both minor and perfect intervals can be reduced by a half-step. When they are so reduced, they are called *diminished* intervals, a term used because the space between the pitches of the interval has been lessened.

- Name and play these diminished intervals. Use "dim" or "o" in naming them.

(Appendix.)

- Name the keys of the following examples; identify the written interval; next to it, notate and name the same interval in its diminished form.

(Appendix.)

AUGMENTED INTERVALS

Perfect and major intervals *increased* by a half-step are called *augmented,* a term used because the size of the interval has been made greater.

- Name and play these augmented intervals. Use "aug" or "+" in naming them.

aug. 6th
or 6th+

(Appendix.)

- Name the keys of the following examples; identify the written interval; next to it, notate and name the same interval in its augmented form.

(Appendix.)

When they are inverted, *augmented intervals* become *diminished* and diminished intervals augmented.

- Play these inversions as you read their names. Be sure to keep accidentals throughout a measure: The sharp in the first chord applies to the F in the second chord as well, because they are both in the same measure. A bar line or a natural sign (♮) is required to remove the sharp or flat if the note is to be played or sung without the accidental.

aug. 4th   dim. 5th   dim. 7th   aug. 2nd   dim. 3rd   aug. 6th   aug. 5th   dim. 4th

- Name the keys of these exercises. Name the written interval. Next to the written interval, notate and name its inversion.

(Appendix.)

Summary of Interval Sizes

1. Minor, half-step smaller than major.
2. Major, half-step larger than minor.
3. Diminished, half-step smaller than perfect or minor.
4. Augmented, half-step larger than perfect or major.

ENHARMONIC INTERVALS

Intervals with different names and different appearances on the staff can *sound* the same. When they do, they are called *enharmonic intervals*. The diminished third sounds like a major second; the diminished fourth sounds like a major third, the augmented second sounds like a minor third; the augmented third sounds like a perfect fourth; and so on. The names of enharmonic intervals depend on the way they are written.

dim. 3rd M2nd dim. 4th M3rd aug. 2nd M3rd aug. 3rd P4th

- Name these enharmonic intervals. Play them.

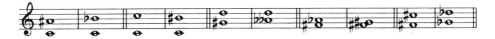

MEASURING INTERVALS IN RELATIONSHIP TO KNOWN KEYS

Illustrations thus far about intervals have been based upon relationships in known keys, with the key-note being one note of the interval. Some of the exercises have asked you to transfer principles to different keys. All of the principles stated about intervals can be transferred to note relationships in any major key.

● Name these major keys, then name the specific intervals.

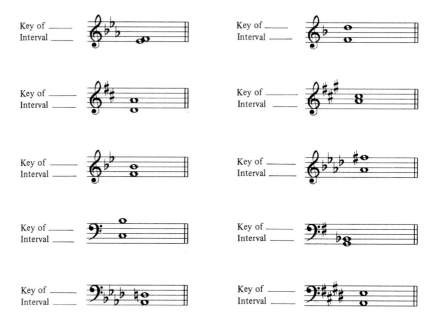

Key of _____
Interval _____

Key of _____
Interval _____

Key of _____
Interval _____

Key of _____
Interval _____

Key of _____
Interval _____

Key of _____
Interval _____

Key of _____
Interval _____

Key of _____
Interval _____

Key of _____
Interval _____

Key of _____
Interval _____

MEASURING SPECIFIC INTERVALS

It is possible to name a specific interval with no reference to key by counting the half-steps that make up the interval. Every specific interval is identified by the number of half-steps contained in it as shown in this chart:

INTERVAL	SIZE
a minor second	= one half step
a major second	= two half steps
a minor third	= three half steps
a major third	= four half steps
a perfect fourth	= five half steps
an aug 4th or dim 5th	= six half steps
a perfect fifth	= seven half steps
a minor sixth	= eight half steps
a major sixth	= nine half steps
a minor seventh	= ten half steps
a major seventh	= eleven half steps
a perfect octave	= twelve half steps

The chart above does not include all the enharmonic spellings that are possible. Nor does it include *compound intervals* that are greater than an octave such as:

10th 12th 9th 11th

- Name these compound intervals. (Appendix.)

- Name these intervals by counting half steps. (Appendix.)

Counting half-steps for large intervals, however, is a time-consuming exercise. Some of the larger intervals can be more easily identified by counting down from the octave (that is, counting one half-step down from the octave for the major seventh, a whole-step down from the octave for the minor seventh, a step and a half down from the octave for the major sixth, etc.).

- Count backwards from the octave to identify large intervals to develop a system that is quicker for you than counting the large number of half-steps in the Interval/Size chart.

(Appendix.)

HEARING INTERVALS

The most musical way to identify intervals is by sound. Constantly involve your ear in developing interval recognition. Some developing musicians find that they can learn the sound of intervals more easily if they relate them to music they already know. You should use examples that are useful to you because you can remember them. The following examples are from music used in this text.

- Play and sing them to learn them both in and out of the context of the songs. A potential problem with memorizing intervals through familiar song intervals is that different contexts may influence your ability to perceive the intervals.

Memory Aids for Learning the Sound of Intervals

minor second between E and F, first two measures of "African Noel"

major second between D and C, next to last measure of "African Noel"

minor third, between F and D, first measure of "America, the Beautiful"

major third, between D and F-sharp, first two notes of "Kum Ba Yah"

perfect fourth, between G and D, last measure of "Are You Sleeping"

perfect fifth, between C and G, first measure of the "Alphabet Song"

minor sixth, between F-sharp and D, next to last measure of "The Cuckoo"

major sixth, between E and C-sharp, first two notes of "Bella Bimba"

minor seventh, between C and B-flat, second measure of "Dona Nobis Pacem"

perfect octave, between D and D, sixth to seventh measures of "The Frogs"

- Analyze the intervals of the "Yellow Rose of Texas." Label the intervals between the melody notes.

(Appendix.)

• Sing the "Yellow Rose of Texas" using numbers, then syllables. Remember, *do* (1) is the name of the key.

So-fa syllables and numbers used consistently help identify the sounds of intervals. The chart below provides *samples* of intervals identified by different syllables and numbers. The intervals are the same ascending and descending. That is, *do–mi* (1–3) is a major third; *mi–do* (3–1) is a major third.

	INTERVAL IDENTIFICATION
minor third	*fa–re* (4–2), *so–mi* (5–3), *re–ti* (2–7), *do–la* (8–6)
major third	*mi–do* (3–1), *la–fa* (6–4), *ti–so* (7–5)
perfect fifth	*do–so* (1–5), *re–la* (2–6), *mi–ti* (3–7), *fa–do* (4–8), *so–re* (5–9), *la–mi* (6–10)
diminished fifth	*ti–fa* (7–11)

In conclusion, subsequent chapters of this book are built on your ability to spell and recognize intervals. Review the sight and sound of intervals by drill with exercises such as the following:

1. Select a specific interval. Write several of the selected intervals on different pitches chosen by you. Sing and/or play the intervals you have written. For example:
   Write major thirds with these notes on the bottom of the interval: D, G, F, B. Play the major thirds you have written on a keyboard. Count the half-steps in each major third you have written. Do they all have four half-steps?

2. Tape-record intervals you play on a keyboard. List the specific intervals as you record them. Play the tape back and identify the intervals as you listen to them without referring to your list. Check your answers with the list to see if you correctly identified the intervals by sound.

MUSIC CHECK

You should be able to define, identify, and illustrate musically:

INTERVALS

    GENERAL

    SPECIFIC

    INVERSIONS

    ENHARMONIC

    MAJOR

    MINOR

    PERFECT

    DIMINISHED

    AUGMENTED

CHAPTER 8

CHORDS

A *chord* is a combination of three or more pitches arranged in thirds. Although the pitches of the chord generally sound simultaneously, a *broken chord* may be used in accompaniments or as part of a melody. The pitches of the broken chord are sounded one after the other, rather than all at once.

So far, you have played chords by placing fingers as directed in the text, or through response to fingering charts and pictures in the instrument book. It is useful for your future musical progress for you to learn how chords are constructed and how they are used.

MAJOR CHORDS

If you have followed the instructions in the instrument book, all the chords you played at the beginning and end of the pieces so far have been major *triads*. (A triad has three different notes, although any of these notes may be used in more than one octave.) It is confusing when analyzing some of the chords because you have not played all the chords in *root positions*. The chords used in the middle of the pieces by students playing the keyboard were often inverted chords; many of the chords used by the guitarists were inverted; it is difficult to determine chord positions on the autoharp because of the nature of the instrument. No matter what your experience has been in playing instruments, you should now look at chords on the keyboard to address both their sound, and their appearance when arranged in root positions.

- Play a C major triad with your left hand.

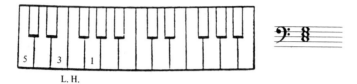

Your little finger (5) plays the *root* of the chord, your middle finger (3) plays the *third* of the chord, and your thumb (1) plays the *fifth* of the chord. The root is both the bottom note of the chord, and the note from which the chord name is derived. The third is three letter names away from the chord root, counting the root as number one; the fifth is five letter names away from the root. The interval between the root and the third is a third, the interval between the third and the fifth is a third. To arrange a chord by thirds, simply skip a letter name between the root and the third; skip another letter name between the third and the fifth.

When traids are in root position, if a root is on a line, the other two notes of the chord will also be on lines. If the root is in a space, the other two notes of the chord will be in spaces.

Chords have different qualities, depending on the size of the thirds in the chord. Unless accidentals are added, the key determines the quality of the chords by influencing the intervallic relationships. To construct chords accurately, it is necessary to stay in the key unless there is a musical reason to change key. Later, as your use of chords becomes more sophisticated, you may construct them with accidentals to meet the requirements of altered chords.

Triads can be constructed on every note of the scale.

For quick identification of chords, *Roman numerals* are used to show the number of the scale-tone upon which they are built. Capitals are used for major chords, lower case for minor or diminished chords. (The raised circle or the letters ''dim'' after the lower case chord symbol indicates a diminished chord.)

Triads built on the first, fourth, and fifth notes of the major scale are major triads. Play these triads and listen to them carefully. The interval from the root to the third of the major triad is a major third (four half-steps.) The interval from the third of the triad to its fifth is a minor third (three half-steps.) Another way to describe the intervallic relationship of the fifth is to say it is a perfect fifth (seven half-steps) from the root.

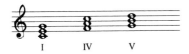

- Write the I, IV, and V triads in root position in the keys of G, F, and D. Write the appropriate key signature at the beginning of the staff. In addition, put flats or sharps in parentheses in front of the affected notes as reminders of the effect of the key signature. Remember that no traid can use both sharps and flats when spelled correctly.

(Appendix.)

Another name for the I chord is the *tonic*. The V chord, often called the *dominant*, is built on the pitch that is five letter names above the tonic. The IV chord, called the *subdominant*, is built on the pitch that is five letter names below the tonic.

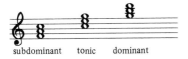

DOMINANT SEVENTH

A *seventh* is frequently added to the V chord to help strengthen the key center. The chord contains a root, third, fifth, and seventh. The number names of the chord notes describe the intervals between them and the root. The third is three notes above the root, the fifth is five notes above the root, and the seventh is seven notes above the root.

The addition of the seventh pulls the ear to a resolution of the dissonance it creates because of its close proximity to the root. It demands that something else follow. The dissonance causes an irresolute stopping place, so the ear anticipates consonance to follow. It demands a *resolution* of the dissonance to a consonant sound. The V7 chord resolves most frequently to the I chord.

- Play these chord progressions in C, G, F, and D with the seventh added to the V chord. Be careful to use the flat or sharp shown in the key signature.

$$V^7 \quad I_4^6 \qquad V^7 \quad I_4^6 \qquad V^7 \quad I_4^6 \qquad V^7 \quad I_4^6$$

INVERSIONS

An *inversion* occurs when notes of a chord are used in positions other than the space-space-space or line-line-line configuration of the root position. Note that the I chord in the examples above is not used in its root position. The change is made to improve *voice leading* (the movement of individual notes from one chord to those of the next chord.) The $^6_4$ next to the I tells the distance from the lowest note of the chord to the other chord notes.

4th   6th

In a $^6_4$ chord, the fifth is the lowest note of the chord. If the third is used as the lowest note, the chord is marked with a 6 alone. This is an abbreviation; it is a $^6_3$ chord (counting from the lowest note to other chord notes in the inversion), but since triads are normally arranged in thirds, it is redundant to use the 3.

3rd   6th

- Write inversions of these major triads. Use accidentals when required. It is important to remember the names of the pitches in the root position chord because when the chord is inverted, even though the original, root position notes appear in different places, they still have the same names. If pitches not in the original spelling are used, the chord assumes a new identity. It becomes a different chord.

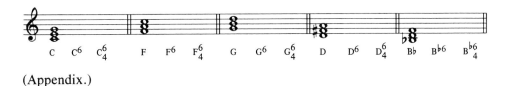

(Appendix.)

Inversions enable the keyboard player to keep notes under the fingers with a minimum of movement from one chord to the other.

- Play these chord progressions with your left hand. The inversions of the V7 are labeled V$\frac{6}{5}$ because of the lower notes' distance from the upper note. If you need help, turn to *Keyboard 2, 5, 6, 8, 9,* and *14* in the Appendix. They show how to play chords with the left hand using inversions of the V7 chord.

The complete V7 chord is spelled with four note names. Often, however, the fifth of the chord is eliminated to improve voice leading or make the progression easier to play.

- Using the same pattern of voice leading that you played above, write V$\frac{6}{5}$-I progressions in D, B-flat, and A major. (Appendix.)

The same principle is used to label inversions of seventh chords that is used to label triad inversions. The numbers next to the chord Roman number or letter name indicate the distance from the lowest note to the rest of the chord tones. Because $\frac{6}{5}$, $\frac{4}{3}$, and 2 establish unique characteristics of these inversions, the numbers in the parenthesis can be eliminated.

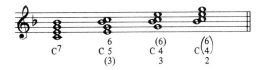

- Write chord inversions as indicated:

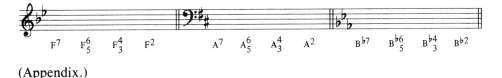

(Appendix.)

MINOR CHORDS

Minor chords differ from major chords in the number of half-steps between the root and the third, the third and the fifth. The major chord is made up of a major third (four half-steps) plus a minor third (three half-steps); the minor chord is made up of a minor third plus a major third. The interval between the root and the fifth of the chord is the same for both major and minor chords.

These chords are minor when used in major keys such as C major:

Other names for the minor chords in a major key are

supertonic (ii), built on the pitch next above the tonic.

mediant (iii), built on the pitch midway between the tonic and the dominant, going up.

submediant (vi), built on the pitch midway between the tonic and the sub-dominant, going down.

As long as you stay in any particular key, you will probably have little trouble in forming chords accurately. However, it is important to know the differences in construction of chords so that you can construct and identify major and minor chords even if you do not know the key.

• Play these major (M) and minor (m) chords. If you see a natural sign (♮) before a note, be sure to take away the flat or sharp previously used with that note. Even though the bar-line removes an accidental, the natural is often used as a reminder, and as a reminder, *may* be shown in parenthesis.

- Write and play these chords. Check their accuracy by sound and sight. Be sure to use natural signs (♮) if necessary. If a capital letter appears alone as the chord name, the chord will be major.

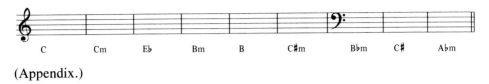

C   Cm   E♭   Bm   B   C♯m   B♭m   C♯   A♭m

(Appendix.)

DIMINISHED CHORD

One chord used in major keys is neither major nor minor:

vii°

This chord is the *leading-tone* or *subtonic chord*. It is a *diminished* chord containing *two minor thirds* and is unstable; it gives little feeling of finality, but pulls toward, or leads into the tonic chord.

subtonic   tonic   supertonic
vii°   I   ii

- Write diminished chords. Be sure they contain two minor thirds.

E°   F♯°   A°   D♭°   B°   G♭°   A♭°   C♯°

(Appendix.)

CHORD NAMES

Names of chords have been given to you as the chords have been introduced. This staff shows the relationship of all these chords as they center around the tonic or key-note.

subdominant   submediant   subtonic   tonic   supertonic   mediant   dominant

- Write the numbers of the chords, then their names. These chords are arranged with their roots in the order of the scale. (Appendix.)

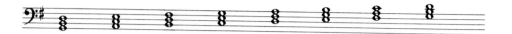

- Number these chords, then write the names of the chords below their numbers. (Appendix.)

SEVENTH CHORDS

You have used the dominant seventh chord (V7). It is important because of its role in establishing the key by resolving to the tonic. It is used more frequently than other seventh chords. The name is given to this chord because it is built on the fifth degree of the scale. It has a major triad with a minor third on top that causes the seventh to be a minor seventh.

Although the dominant seventh can be built on any scale degree, when it is used on any scale degree other than the fifth, it tends to change the key, to *modulate* into a new key.

- Write and play these dominant sevenths. Check their accuracy by sound and sight.

(Appendix.)

Compare the construction of the dominant seventh with other, less frequently used seventh chords.

SEVENTH CHORDS

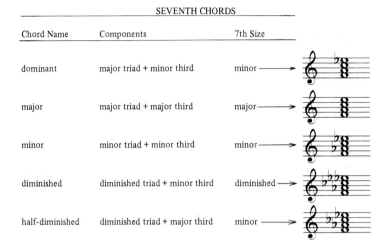

Chord Name	Components	7th Size	
dominant	major triad + minor third	minor ——→	
major	major triad + major third	major ——→	
minor	minor triad + minor third	minor ——→	
diminished	diminished triad + minor third	diminished ——→	
half-diminished	diminished triad + major third	minor ——→	

• Write and play seventh chords as indicated.

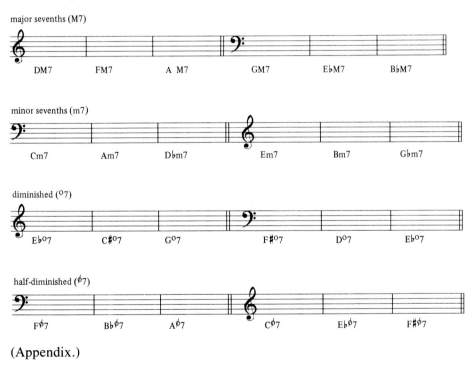

major sevenths (M7)

DM7   FM7   A M7   GM7   EbM7   BbM7

minor sevenths (m7)

Cm7   Am7   Dbm7   Em7   Bm7   Gbm7

diminished (^{o}7)

Eb^{o}7   C#^{o}7   G^{o}7   F#^{o}7   D^{o}7   Eb^{o}7

half-diminished ($^{\phi}$7)

F$^{\phi}$7   Bb$^{\phi}$7   A$^{\phi}$7   C$^{\phi}$7   Eb$^{\phi}$7   F#$^{\phi}$7

(Appendix.)

CHORD PROGRESSIONS

Many melodies can be accompanied using a *progression* of I, IV, and V7 chords. Generally some of these chords are inverted because pitches of the chords do not lead musically from one to the other if root positions are used for all the chords. Use of inverted chords with pitches common to more than one chord remaining in the same octave, and other pitches moving to their closest neighbor in the new chord improves the voice leading. The following example shows a common type of chord progression using inverted F and G7 chords.

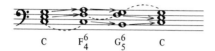

- Write and play the I–IV$^6_4$–V$^6_5$–I progression in F, G, D, A, B-flat, and E using the example above as a model for your voice leading. Write at least half of the progressions in the bass clef. Eliminate the fifth in the V$^6_5$ chord. Show common tones (- - -) and closest neighbors (→).

(Appendix.)

Holla Hi, Holla Ho

- Analyze the form of this piece. (Appendix.)

- Write the chord progression that should be used to accompany the melody. Show common tones (- - -) and closest neighbors (→).

(Appendix.)

- Play and/or sing the melody for "Holla Hi, Holla Ho."

  - Play it on the keyboard or with the recorder. *Recorder 12* contains a fingering chart on which you can look up new notes or fingering for those you have forgotten.

  - Sing the melody while you play the chords on either the autoharp, keyboard, or guitar. *Guitar 7* contains a fingering chart for new or forgotten chords.

• Sing and play the piece using allegro as the tempo indicator. Then perform the piece using andante as the tempo indicator. Which tempo seems more suitable for the piece?

Kum Ba Yah

What is the form of "Kum Ba Yah"? (Appendix.)

• Write the chord progression for this piece.

(Appendix.)

• Sing and/or play the melody for "Kum Ba Yah." Be sure to hold the dotted eighth notes for three-quarters of the beat.

   • Sing the melody while you play the chords on either keyboard, autoharp, or guitar.

• As you sing all the verses of "Kum Ba Yah," vary the dynamics to suit the words. Write the dynamic marking you find most suitable for each verse.

Skip to My Lou

What phrases of this song are musically the same? Which phrases are partially the same? Where is the sequence in this piece? What is the form of this piece? (Appendix.)

• Write the chord progression for "Skip to My Lou."

• Play and/or sing the melody of "Skip to My Lou."

   • Accompany the melody using the chord progression you wrote.

• Select three songs you have used previously in this book. Write chord progressions to accompany them.

As you become familiar with new melodies, analyze chord progressions to accompany them. Thousands of songs can be performed with basic I–IV–V7 progressions. When you become secure in using them, you will probably wish to add or substitute other chords, creating less predictable harmonies.

MUSIC CHECK

You should be able to define, identify, and illustrate musically:

CHORDS

    TRIADS

    MAJOR

    MINOR

    DIMINISHED

    SEVENTH CHORDS

        DOMINANT

        MAJOR

        MINOR

        DIMINISHED

        HALF-DIMINISHED

    ROOT POSITIONS

    INVERSIONS

    NAMES

    NUMBERS

CHAPTER 9

MINOR SCALES AND KEY SIGNATURES

Although major keys are widely used, other means of tonal organization exist to give variety to melodic and harmonic expression. *Minor keys* offer attractive alternatives.

- Listen to "The Young Person's Guide to the Orchestra" (Tape 15), "Triste" (Tape 16), and "Modere" (Tape 18) for examples of music written in minor keys.

    Students faced with music that does not designate whether it is major or minor must learn to discriminate between the two.

- Play or sing "Shalom Chaverim."

    What information is given to you by the key signature for "Shalom Chaverim"? From past experience, it looks like the piece is written in the key of G.

- Try to accompany the melody with a G chord.

    The sound of the G chord clashing inappropriately with the melody provides a clue that the piece is in a key other than the key signature seems to indicate. "Shalom Chaverim" is in E minor, the *relative minor* of G major. Although their key names are three half-steps apart, they share the same key signature. The major *keynote* (also called *tonic* or *home tone*) is three half steps higher than the minor keynote, or, to reverse the relationship, the minor keynote is three half-steps lower than the major keynote.

- Count three half-steps down from G on the keyboard to find the keynote of E minor.

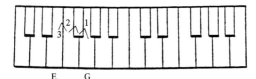

E G

  Even though the relatives share the same key signature, their organization of melodic and harmonic material differs. Differences between a minor key and its relative major include the following:

  1. The minor scale begins and ends on different notes than the major.

  2. The minor uses half-steps in different places than the major.

  3. The minor uses a different chordal structure than the major.

- Play or sing the melody of "Shalom Chaverim" and use an E minor chord to accompany it.

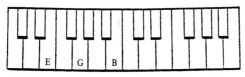

E G B

E minor chord

  Although keyboard pictures are frequently used in this text to illustrate harmonic concepts because they are well-suited for showing note relationships, do not interpret their use as a rejection of the autoharp or guitar for producing harmony. Continue to use the medium you prefer in playing accompaniments to melodies.

NATURAL MINOR

  There are different forms of minor keys. "Shalom Chaverim" is a good example of the *natural* or *pure* minor. It adds no accidentals, so it uses the same pitches as its relative major.

- Write a natural minor scale beginning on E. Like the major scale, the minor uses each letter name consecutively. Include the F-sharp as shown in the key signature. Use ⌒ to show the location of the half-steps in the scale.

The half-steps of the E natural minor scale occur between _____ and between _____.

(Appendix.)

- Play the E natural minor scale. Contrast it with the G major sound.

- Sing the E natural minor scale using pitch names and pitch syllables. To maintain the relationship of pitches with the relative major, call the keynote *la*.

- To consolidate your understanding of relative major and minor using the same key signature, name both the major and minor keys that use these key signatures:

_____ major _____ minor   _____ major _____ minor   _____ major _____ minor

_____ major _____ minor   _____ major _____ minor   _____ major _____ minor

(Appendix.)

The Little Man Who Wasn't There

- Use the Music Analysis Sheet to help you analyze this song.

- Look at the key signature for "The Little Man Who Wasn't There." Play or sing the melody being careful to include the B-flat. What is the key of this piece? You are right if you said D minor. What is its relative major? Play the first measure of the melody with an F chord. Now play it with a D minor chord. What does your ear tell you about using these chords with the first measure?

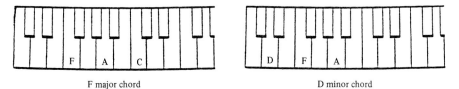

F major chord   D minor chord

- Write the D natural minor scale. Mark the half-steps.

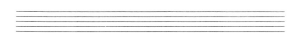

- Check to be sure the placement of the half-steps in the D minor natural scale corresponds to the placement of the half-steps in the E minor scale.

- Review the general rule governing half-steps in the natural minor scale:
  Half-steps in the natural minor scale occur between _____ and between
  _____.
  (Appendix.)

- Describe the outstanding characteristic of the melody for "The Little Man Who Wasn't There." (Appendix.)

- Play a D minor triad on the piano. Move your hand up so the little finger of your left hand is on E, and play a triad with E as its root. Stay in the key of D minor. (That means, be sure to use the B-flat!) Move your hand up so your little finger plays F as the root of the next triad. Continue to move up the D minor scale, playing a triad on each degree of the scale.

- Write the chords you have just played. To insure the correct inclusion of the B-flat, put a flat sign in front of each B that occurs. Put parentheses around the flat (♭) as an indication that you know it is included in the key signature but are reminding yourself it is there.

(Appendix.)

- Practice the chords until you can play them easily.

- Play the chords for F major as you have done for D minor. Be sure to play a B-flat whenever the notation shows a B. Write the chords for F major and number them with Roman numerals from I to vii.

Review the construction of a major chord: The distance from the root (bottom note) of the chord to the third (middle note) is four half-steps, a major third. The distance from the third to the fifth (top note) is three half-steps, a minor third.

Construction of a Major Chord

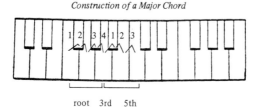

root   3rd   5th

• Analyze the chords of F major. Put an "M" under the number of each chord you identify as major. (Appendix.)

Minor chords reverse the half-step pattern of major chords. The minor chord has a minor third on the bottom, with a major third on top of it.

Construction of a Minor Chord

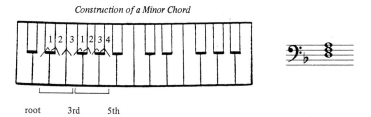

• Identify all the minor chords in F major by putting an "m" under the number of each minor chord. Write the Roman numerals of the minor chords in lower case. (Appendix.)

There should be one chord without an "M" or "m" under its number. If you count the half-steps in the E chord, you will find it has a minor third with a minor third on top of it: This is a *diminished chord*.

Construction of a Diminished Chord

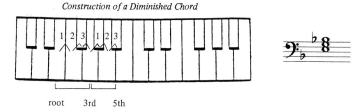

It is called a diminished chord because it is smaller than other chords. The two minor thirds cause the perfect fifth used in other chords to be replaced by a diminished fifth.

• Write the chords for G major. Number the chords with Roman numerals. Identify the chords with "M" for major, "m" for minor, and a raised circle (°) for diminished.

(Appendix.)

Compare the major, minor, and diminished chords for F and G major. Generalize about chords in major keys:

In major keys, chords numbered _____ are major.

In major keys, chords numbered _____ are minor.

In major keys, the chord numbered _____ is diminished.
(Appendix.)

- Analyze the chords for D natural minor, using the same three symbols to show the character of each chord number. (Appendix.)

- Write an E natural minor scale.

- Write a chord over each note of E natural minor. Mark each chord as major, minor, or diminished. (Appendix.)

- Generalize about chords in natural minor keys:

In natural minor keys, chords numbered _____ are major.

In natural minor keys, chords numbered _____ are minor.

In natural minor keys, the chord numbered _____ is diminished.
(Appendix.)

- Play "The Little Man Who Wasn't There" using the chords indicated under the melody.

- Transpose "The Little Man Who Wasn't There" to the key of E minor.

- Transpose it to the key of A minor. Before beginning to play, figure out the name of A minor's relative major. (Appendix.)

Artsa Alinu

Use the Music Analysis Sheet to help you become acquainted with "Artsa Alinu." Analyze its form and clap its rhythm before you begin to sing or play the whole piece. Try to accompany it using a D minor chord. Where do you want to change the chord? Try other chords until you find one you like for the places where you want to use something besides the D minor chord. (Appendix.)

Zum Gali Gali

- Use the chords indicated to accompany the melody for "Zum Gali Gali." Consult *Autoharp 7, Guitar 7,* or *Keyboard 18* if you need help.

What chords did you use to play "Zum Gali Gali"? Were they major or minor? (Appendix.)

HARMONIC MINOR

Not all minor pieces are in the natural minor. Sometimes accidentals are added to strengthen chord progressions, particularly the final *cadences* (endings). The most frequent change is raising the seventh note of the scale to increase the power of the leading tone. Not only does the seventh tone then lead more strongly into the tonic (one half-step away), but also the V7 chord resolving to the i helps set up a stronger key center. Without the raised seventh, the dominant chord is minor. The form of the minor resulting from the raised seventh tone is the *harmonic minor*.

- Write an E natural minor scale. To change it to a harmonic minor, raise the seventh degree of the scale one half-step to a D-sharp. Use ⌒ to show the location of the half-steps.

(Appendix.)

Where are the half-steps in the harmonic minor? Between _____, between _____, and between _____. How many half-steps are between the sixth and seventh degrees of the scale? _____

You should have found half-steps between two and three, between five and six, and between seven and eight. There should be three half-steps between the sixth and seventh degrees of the scale. The interval between the sixth and seventh degrees of the harmonic minor scale is called an augmented second rather than a minor third because it uses consecutive note names. From C to D is a second, from C to D♯ is an augmented second.

- Play the E harmonic minor scale.

- Write a D harmonic minor scale. Use ⌒ to show the half-steps in the scale. Be sure there is an augmented second between the sixth and seventh degrees of the scale.

(Appendix.)

- Play the scale.

- Compare natural and harmonic minor scales. (Appendix.)

  Half steps in the natural minor scale occur between _____

  Half steps in the harmonic minor scale occur between _____

  An augmented second is found between _____ in the _____ minor scale.

- Play and write chords on each note of the E harmonic minor scale. Number them and label them. You will find that the addition of the D-sharp has altered the character of some of the chords. Chord III now has two major thirds in it. Call that chord *augmented* (III+). Chord V has become major, and chord vii has become diminished (vii°).

- Play and write chords on each note of the D harmonic minor scale. Be sure to label each chord. (Appendix.)

- Generalize about chords in harmonic minor keys:

  In harmonic minor keys, chords numbered _____ are major.

  In harmonic minor keys, chords numbered _____ are minor.

  In harmonic minor keys, chords numbered _____ are diminished.

  In harmonic minor keys, the chord numbered _____ is augmented.

  (Appendix.)

  When using the harmonic minor, the V7 is the same as when it is used in major keys. The significant difference is that it is now coupled with a minor tonic chord, so fingering and ear will need to accommodate.

- Analyze, then play the chord progression of the C minor chord to the G7.

- Write, then play these chord progressions.

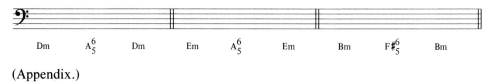

(Appendix.)

MELODIC MINOR

The *melodic minor* is a third form of the minor. It is the only form that is different going up than it is coming down. The melodic minor scale raises its sixth and seventh notes one half-step ascending, then lowers them descending, becoming a natural minor on the way down.

- Write these melodic minors.

Dm

Em

- Label these minor scales. Are they natural, harmonic, or melodic? (The descending part of the melodic minor has been omitted, but it can still be identified by the raised sixth and seventh notes of the scale.)

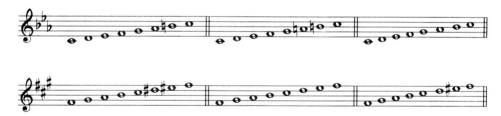

- Write natural, harmonic, and melodic forms of these minor scales.

A minor

G minor

B minor

CIRCLE OF FIFTHS

The *circle of fifths* helps show the logical relationships between the relative majors and minors, their key signatures, and the sharps and flats they use. Minor names are in the outer circle.

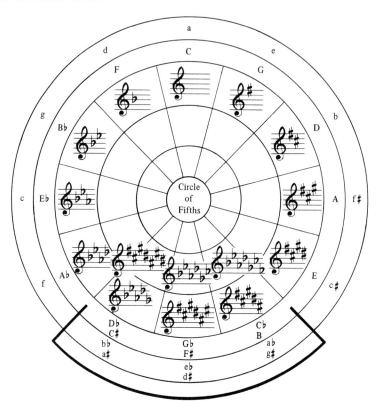

- Use the circle of fifths to help you answer these questions:

  What is the relative minor for these major keys?
  A _____ B-flat _____ D _____ E _____

  What is the relative major for these minor keys?
  Fm _____ A♯m _____ C♯m _____ Gm _____

  Draw key signatures for these major keys:

  E   A   E♭   F

Draw key signatures for these minor keys:

E   G   F♯   B

(Appendix.)

All the Pretty Little Horses

- Practice the chord progressions for this piece. If you need help with keyboard fingering, turn to *Keyboard 19*. The Guitar Chord Chart is *Guitar 7*. If your autoharp does not have the necessary chords, transpose it to a minor key that is close. See *Autoharp 6*.

- After you have analyzed the piece using the *Music Analysis Sheet,* play the melody. If you can sing and play your accompaniment, do so. If you wish to play the melody, invite friends to play the accompaniment with you. What kind of instrument enables you to play both the melody and harmony together?

Hold On

- Practice the chord progressions for "Hold On." Be sure to use the harmonic minor. A clue that this is in the harmonic minor is that the A7 is indicated rather than the Am7. When you play the melody, be careful of the syncopated, anticipated second beat of many measures (such as 2 and 4, where the eighth-note is tied to the half-note).

Erie Canal

Compare the chords of the verse with those of the chorus. What is the key of this piece? _____

The first part of the piece is in D minor; the second part is in F major. If the chords were not written there to help you, you would have to try to figure out the key by considering the possibilities. If you understand the relationship between major and minor keys sharing the same key signature, you have already limited the possibilities as to the key of the song. The single flat in the key signature tells you the piece is in either F major or D minor. When looking at a new song with no chords written in, determine both the major and the minor keys. Recall the notes of the tonic chords for both the major and the minor.

Next, look at the first few and the last few notes of the melody. The first few notes are A, D, and F. When arranged in thirds, these notes spell a D minor chord. They tell you the appropriate chord to use.

The last few notes are A, F, and G.

When you look at the major and minor tonic chords, you see that G is not in either of them, but F and A are in both. Play the melody of the last few measures, then try an F chord with the last melody note. Does it sound all right? Play the last few measures again, but play the D minor chord with the last melody note instead of the F chord. How does that sound? Let your ear be your guide. All pieces do not change from minor to major as this one does, but be prepared for that eventuality. The same procedure used to find the chords for ''Erie Canal'' can be used with other pieces without written chord symbols.

- Play and sing ''Erie Canal'' watching the syncopation, accidentals, and equal (♪♪) and unequal (♪.♪) eighth-notes carefully.

Eency, Weency Spider

- Analyze the key signature of ''Eency, Weency Spider.'' It tells you the song may be in either _____ major or _____ minor. The tonic chord for the major key is spelled _____; for the minor key it is _____.

- Analyze the melody. Does the first pitch of the melody appear in both chords? _____ Consider the eighth-note A at the end of measure one to be a nonchord tone since it is on a weak beat. Does the first pitch of the second measure occur in both the major tonic chord and the minor tonic chord? Since you have discovered that the main notes of the first two measures appear in the tonic chords of both the major and minor keys indicated by the key signature, the most direct way of deciding which chord to use is to try them. Play or sing the melody of the first two measures using a G major chord for the accompaniment, then try the same two measures with an E minor chord. Which sounds best? The key is G major.

- Use the V7 of G major with the next to last measure, moving to G for the last measure.

- Start at the beginning with the G chord, changing only when the sound demands that you do. Use as few chords as possible throughout the piece.

- Write the chords you used over the melody. Check in the Appendix only after you have tried to harmonize the piece all the way through.

I'm a Little Teapot

- Figure out the chords needed for the harmonization of this piece. Change chords as seldom as possible. Check in the Appendix only after you have written your chord choices under the melody.

   The following theme from Haydn's Symphony in G (No. 94, *Surprise*), second movement, shows how a melody sometimes outlines broken chords. The theme can be accompanied by forming chords from melody notes.

- Spell the chords formed by the first two measures of the melody, the third and fourth measures, the fifth and sixth measures, the seventh measure, and the last measure.

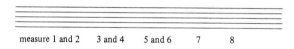

measure 1 and 2   3 and 4   5 and 6   7   8

- Write the chord letter names under the Haydn theme. Play the melody with the chordal accompaniment.

   As you continue to grow in musical sophistication, seek out different modes of musical organization. Music may shift from minor to major as the "Erie Canal" does. It may even use major and minor at the same time. Listen to Ives's "Sixty-seventh Psalm" (Tape 5). The men's voices are singing in G minor, the women's voices in C major.

MUSIC CHECK

You should be able to define, identify, and illustrate musically:

MAJOR	CHORD CONSTRUCTION
MINOR	MAJOR
NATURAL	MINOR
HARMONIC	DIMINISHED
MELODIC	AUGMENTED
RELATIVE MAJOR AND MINOR	DOMINANT SEVENTH
HALF-STEPS IN SCALES	CHORD PROGRESSIONS
AUGMENTED SECONDS IN SCALES	SONG HARMONIZATIONS WITH NO CHORDS INDICATED
CHORDAL ACCOMPANIMENTS	CIRCLE OF FIFTHS INCLUDING MINOR KEYS

CHAPTER 10

PENTATONIC

Pentatonic is the general name given to any scale that has five tones within the octave. There are many pentatonic scales. This text will deal only with the pentatonic scale that avoids half-steps by eliminating the fourth and seventh notes of the major scale.

PENTATONIC IMPROVISATION

If you play on the black keys of the keyboard only, you are using a pentatonic scale. The sounds of these notes, with no half-steps, are so compatible that they generally lend themselves to success in improvising.

- Using the black keys only, create:
    1. A march with a very steady underlying beat. Try to create a sound that trumpets might make as part of the march.
    2. The sound of ocean waves. Use as many notes to create the waves as you can get under your fingers, or use a glissando effect created by gently letting your fingernails (palms up) brush across the black keys.
    3. An accompaniment using your left forearm playing as many black notes as it can cover while your right hand plays a melody in a meter of three.
    4. An accompaniment using your right forearm playing as many black notes as it can cover while your left hand plays a melody in a meter of two.

5. An original composition contrasting monophonic sections (melody with no accompaniment) with homonophonic sections (melody played with accompaniment).

6. A completely original composition.

PENTATONIC ACCOMPANIMENT

Pentatonic songs are easy to play and to accompany. "Get Along Little Dogies" is one of many pentatonic songs for which you can improvise an accompaniment. Begin singing the melody on D-flat next to middle C. Devise an accompaniment using all black keys to sound like horses on the trail. (This sounds different from the white key pentatonic shown by the notation for "Get Along Little Dogies" in this book.)

All songs do not lend themselves to this type of accompaniment. You must analyze the song to see if it is pentatonic before devising an accompaniment. To determine if the music is pentatonic:

1. Name the key shown by the key signature.

2. Identify the fourth and seventh notes of the scale for the key you named.

3. Examine the melody to see if the fourth and seventh notes appear in the melody.

4. Try an accompaniment using only degrees 1–2–3–5–6 of the scale. This is necessary because some melodies may not have degrees 4 and 7 in the melody, but they may still demand a major-key accompaniment because of their particular construction. Use your ear to help you determine this.

- From this list of songs, select those that are pentatonic:

"America"	"Ifca's Castle"
"Go to Sleep"	"It's Raining"
"Hot Cross Buns"	

PENTATONIC SCALES

You used a black-note pentatonic scale when improvising.

- Play a pentatonic scale starting on F-sharp and using the five black keys of the keyboard.

- Write the F-sharp pentatonic scale on this staff.

- Analyze the intervals (half-steps and whole steps) between the pitches of the pentatonic scale. Mark them on the scale you have written. (Appendix.)

  You should have found whole steps between all the pitches of the pentatonic scale except between the third and fourth degrees of the scale. A step and a half occurs between three and four in the pentatonic scale you are using. There are other ways of describing this interval:

  a whole step plus a half-step.

  three half-steps.

  a minor third.

  In a pentatonic scale,

  whole steps occur between _____.

  a minor third occurs between _____.

  half-steps occur between _____.

  (Appendix.)

- Write a pentatonic scale beginning on G.

- Write a G major scale. Cross out the fourth and seventh scale degrees.

  (Appendix.)

  Compare the G pentatonic scale and the G major scale without degrees 4 and 7. If you have written them accurately, they should be the same.

- Play the G pentatonic scale you have written to learn its sound.

- Write and play these pentatonic scales:

  F pentatonic

  E♭ pentatonic

  C pentatonic

  A pentatonic

• Practice singing pentatonic scales using numbers, syllables, and letter names. Use the keyboard to support your singing if you need help in singing accurately. Aim to sing independently as soon as you can.

	1	2	3	5	6
	do	re	mi	so	la
	D	E	F♯	A	B

Go to Sleep

• Analyze the melody of "Go to Sleep." Are any of the measures the same? Can you identify parts of the melody that look like sections of the scale? What scale does it sound like?

• Play the melody on the keyboard. Use your right thumb (1) on the F, your right little finger (5) on C.

• Sing the melody using letter names.

• Sing the melody using numbers.

• Sing the melody using syllables.

  If you need to play the melody as you sing to help you with accuracy or confidence, do so, but try not to become totally dependent on the keyboard. Challenge yourself to sing *a cappella* (voice alone, without an instrument).

• Transpose the melody of "Go to Sleep" to black keys; that is, shift from the white keys where you just read and played it correctly, to the black keys half a step higher.

• Sing the melody in this new key.

• Sing the melody in the new key while you improvise an accompaniment on the black keys. By this time you should have decided correctly that this song is in the pentatonic mode.

• Transpose "Go to Sleep" into the G pentatonic mode. Begin playing the melody on G.

  Look at the key signature for "Go to Sleep." Why didn't you play the indicated flat when you played the piece? Your observation that there is no B-flat in the melody is correct. Why has a flat been written there? That flat is part of the key signature. It helps tell what scale the melody is based on, and what chords can be used to accompany the melody. Some pieces, such as this one, can be in the pentatonic mode but also have a major key signature and can be harmonized with a major tonality. This gives you flexibility in developing different types of accompaniment for the piece.

What is the name of the major key with one flat?

- Play an F chord with your left hand—little finger on F (5), middle finger on A (3), thumb on C (1). Practice playing the F chord with a steady beat.

L.H.

"Go to Sleep" is a piece that can be played or sung with one chord in the accompaniment. Use the F chord on two steady beats per measure while you sing the melody. When you are able to coordinate your singing and chord playing confidently, try playing the melody with your right hand, while the left hand plays the chords.

- Transpose the piece to the key of F-sharp major by raising all the pitches one half-step. Later, you may decide to use more than one chord when playing "Go to Sleep," to give greater variety to the accompaniment.

Roll Over

- Analyze this melody. Is it pentatonic? If so, improvise an accompaniment for it.

Old MacDonald

This piece is in the key of _____. Its meter signature tells that _____. What is its form? _____
(Appendix.)

- Play the melody and harmony of "Old MacDonald" on piano, recorder, autoharp, or guitar.
- After you have played it as written, transpose it on the piano to this key:

- Name the key. _____ (Appendix.)
- Play the melody on the piano using all black keys. Create a black key accompaniment for it.

Rocky Mountain

What kind of rest appears at the end of each phrase of this song?

- Use rhythm syllables to say the rhythm.

In what key is "Rocky Mountain"?

- Try to play both the melody and the harmony in this key. If this is too difficult, transpose the piece up a half-step. This transposition puts the piece in the key of _____. (Appendix.) To transpose the melody, play all the notes one half-step higher than they are written. Move all the notes of the chords one half-step higher, also.

- Play "Rocky Mountain" in the new key on the instrument(s) of your choice. Although you transposed this piece into another key to make it easier to play, sometimes you transpose songs to make singing ranges more suitable.

Swing Low, Sweet Chariot

In what key is "Swing Low, Sweet Chariot"? Does it use all the notes of the major scale? If not, what is missing? (Appendix.)

- Play "Swing Low, Sweet Chariot" as written in your music book, observing the D.C. al Fine. *D.C. al Fine* is an abbreviation for the Italian phrase "da capo al fine" (from the head to the end). It means that you go back to the beginning and continue until the end, which is marked by the word *Fine*. This is not to be confused with *D.S. al Fine* (dal segno al fine) that indicates a repetition starting at the sign (𝄋) and ending at the word *Fine*.

- Transpose "Swing Low, Sweet Chariot" to the black keys starting the melody on B-flat. Are there problems in doing it? Does it sound right?

  - *Roll* (play consecutively) your accompaniment notes from the bottom to the top to sound like a harp for the first two lines *(broken chords)*. Play *block chords* (all the notes sounding at the same time) for the other lines.

Singing on the Old Camp Ground

- Play and sing "Singing on the Old Camp Ground." In what key is it? (Appendix.)

- Play it starting on A-sharp. Can you play it completely on black keys?

Ifca's Castle

- Play and sing "Ifca's Castle." In what key is it? (Appendix.)

The Old Brass Wagon

- Play and sing "The Old Brass Wagon." In what key is it? Would it be easier for you to play it if you transposed it to the key of G? (Appendix.)

Skin and Bones

- Play and sing "Skin and Bones." In what key is it? Would it be easier for you to play it if you transposed it to the key of G-flat pentatonic?

- Improvise accompaniments to pentatonic songs using the keyboard, your recorder, or pitched percussion instruments such as xylophones, metallophones, or glockenspiels. Be careful to choose appropriate tempos and dynamics for your creative work. Because half-steps are missing in the pentatonic mode, it is relatively easy to produce satisfactory harmonizations. Try to create an accompaniment to match the mood of the melody and the words of the songs.

MUSIC CHECK

You should be able to define, identify, and illustrate musically:

PENTATONIC

    SCALES

    IMPROVISATION

    ANALYSIS OF MELODIES

    IDENTIFICATION

CHAPTER 11

CREATING MUSIC

It will take only a few minutes to read the material in this chapter, but if you try the creative activities suggested here, you may find yourself engaged in enjoyable, creative expressions that will make your life increasingly richer. Creative behavior grows, matures, and flourishes if you are willing to take the risk of developing intuition, trying alternatives, and putting together musical ideas that you may not have heard before.

If you are asked to write a symphony, you may not have it ready by tomorrow. If you have never tried to write a symphony, the assignment will be a formidable task. The problem with certain assignments is that they are too large, too unfamiliar, too complicated, to be comprehensible. Yet, doing simpler tasks may eventually result in the completion of a more complicated task, and if you are reasonably successful in the simpler tasks, you may eventually find yourself completing assignments that will amaze even you as you become aware of the advanced level of the product you are creating. Furthermore, you may find that even when no one is giving you assignments to complete, you continue to assume a high degree of self-motivation for using the skills you have developed as vehicles for your creative imagination in ways that may now seem out of the question.

The purpose of this chapter is to help you *begin* to realize some of your potential creative musical ability. You may be relieved to know you won't be asked to write a symphony by the end of the chapter! In fact, the creative activities of this chapter need not be viewed as serious, traditional composition.

They are intended to help you develop an attitude toward creativity that will help you expand your freedom of musical expression.

Creative behavior in music does not necessarily result in an end product. Musical creativity can be a process of dealing with sound in ways that are different. It is not necessary that you produce a product for future use. Musical creativity can be defined, in part, as the human search for organization and re-organization of musical materials in ways that are unique for that individual. The more that an individual practices creativity, the more chance there is that truly unique products may result.

ENVIRONMENTAL SOUND COMPOSITION

- Look around the room. Pick out five sound-producers of any kind. Gather the sound-producers together so you can manipulate them from a central location. See how many different sounds you can produce with each. Devise a variety of ways for producing sound with them. Try striking, rubbing, plucking, tapping, blowing, pulling, tearing (be careful, this is intended for disposable products only), shaking, dropping, pushing, or any other way you can devise to make the sound. Vary the production of the sound. For example, if you are striking the object, vary the intensity of the impact to change the *dynamics*. Change the *tempo* of your striking action. Use different objects as striking implements for variety in *timbre:* hard or soft, large or small, thick or thin, rigid or flexible, single or multiple. It is possible that you have chosen sound-producers that cannot be manipulated by you, such as an animal noise or the household sound of a clock ticking. If the sound cannot be changed by you, how can you include it as part of your composition?

As you experiment with these objects, begin to make judgments about the sounds you are producing with them.

1. Do any of them make sounds you find attractive, unusual, bizarre, horrible, exciting, mundane, beautiful, sickening, sublime?
2. Do some of them have such affinity for each other that they could become part of a unified means of expression?
3. Do some of them contrast in interesting ways so they could be used to develop variety in sound passages?
4. Do some of them demand a higher level of performing skill than others?
5. Could some of them be used at the same time so a thick texture of sound could result from their combination? If this is done, would more than one performer be needed to produce the desired texture?

The questions you are dealing with are questions composers answer in the course of writing music. They are also questions considered by performers involved in improvisation. A main difference between the behavior of the *composer* and the *improvisor* is that the former produces notation for another musician to use to recreate the music. In the past, this distinction was more significant: Because the improvisor creates without notation, it used to be that nothing was left for another musician to use to recreate the music. Today, in the age of electronics, that distinction has become blurred. The improvisor still does not write the music in regular notation for future use, but electronic inventions such as video and audio tape recorders have made it possible to keep a permanent record of the music as it is being made. The recreation of the original work is made possible by having an aural product to study and learn through audible example. In your creative work, keep in mind that recordings are useful options if you wish to pass your musical products on to others. Both the written and the aural model have value. You should try to determine which of these models is your best means of transmitting your own creations if you wish to preserve or share them.

- Now, organize your musical materials. From the five sound-producers you found and the variations you developed with them, select the sound you find most interesting. Decide on a time allotment for the sound to be made.

    1. Within that time allotment, how will you produce the sound?
    2. Does it have melodic potential?
    3. Do you have a rhythmic organization for the sound?
    4. Do you prefer to use more than one sound at a time?

Notice that these questions deal with the elements of *timbre, melody, rhythm,* and *harmony.*

Consider the element of *form.*

1. How much unity do you desire in the composition you are developing?
2. How much variety do you wish to have?
3. Is there a simple song form that will help give you the unity you desire (*AB, ABA, ABACA, ABACADA, ABACABA*)?
4. Would you rather have a *through-composed* composition (one without repeated sections) to allow the variety you seek?

If you need help with organization or in remembering ideas, consider jotting notes to yourself as to the organization of your composition.

1. What do you want to happen first?
2. What next?

3. What stylistic attributes will you include? What will give your composition its own individual characteristics?

4. How do you want the sound produced?

If you make these notes in a thorough enough fashion so that someone else could recreate your intention, you have just written a *score* for your composition. Although a score is conventionally written with notes, rhythms, and so on, an environmental sound composition such as the one you are creating can use non-conventional notation and still effectively transmit the composer's intentions.

- Continue to develop your creative work with environmental sounds until you have a composition you can share with others. The sharing can be done in different ways. Choose one of these:

  1. Write a score that will enable others to recreate your composition.

  2. Perform your composition for other people.

  3. Tape your composition so others can listen to it.

  4. Gather together enough people to make an ensemble to play the composition. Teach them how to play it so it sounds the way you want.

OSTINATOS

Ostinato is a term for a melodic pattern repeated unchanged throughout a composition. The ostinato of the baroque period was often used in the bass part and was called "basso ostinato" or "ground bass." Ostinatos can be used in any part. In addition to melodic ostinatos, rhythmic ones (nonpitched) are also used. They can be instrumental or vocal. The nature of the music to which they are attached helps determine the nature of the ostinato. The key or the chord progressions of the piece must be such that a consistent repetition of the ostinato can take place without creating inappropriate conflict. Ostinatos are found in folk music throughout the world.

- Listen to the didgeridoo ostinato in "Bungalin Bungalin" (Tape 23).

One-chord songs lend themselves to the development of ostinatos. A simple way of creating an ostinato for a one-chord song is to develop a pattern using the notes of that one chord, and words related to the song.

The G chord can be used to accompany "The Frogs." These ostinatos are two of many that will go with it.

- Create two one-measure melodic ostinatos for "The Frogs" using only the pitches of the G chord.

- Create one two-measure rhythmic ostinato to go with "The Frogs."

- Sing or play the ostinatos while someone else sings the melody of the song. (If you are doing this assignment alone, tape the melody, then try your ostinatos with the taped melody.)

- Create at least one ostinato for:

> "Are You Sleeping"
>
> "Lady Come"
>
> "Shalom Chaverim"

Pentatonic songs also lend themselves to the development of ostinatos. Be sure to use only the notes of the pentatonic scale that match the song. Decide whether you wish the ostinato to be played or sung.

- Create a two-measure pattern using the pentatonic scale to play or sing with the melody of these songs:

> "Go to Sleep"
>
> "The Old Brass Wagon"
>
> "Singing on the Old Camp Ground"
>
> "Skin and Bones"
>
> "Swing Low, Sweet Chariot"

IMPROVISATION

If you think of improvisation solely as "making it up as you go along," you do not have the complete picture in mind. It is true that improvisation is a spontaneous activity, but there is almost always a plan connected with it. The plan may be a rhythmic design, a melodic structure, a chord progression, a formal idea, expressive applications, or combinations of all the above. Before embarking on improvisation, have some kind of a scheme in mind. Write it down if you are afraid that you may forget it. Here are suggestions for some things you may plan in advance.

OSTINATO-BASED

Instead of creating an ostinato to go with a song, start with an ostinato. Determine the key, the meter, and the rhythmic and melodic aspects of the ostinato and whether it is to be played or sung. If you are creating this musical experience alone, tape the ostinato so you are free to improvise while it plays. An alternative to taping is for you to play the ostinato while you improvise vocally. Decide whether words are to be part of the improvisation or not. *Scat singers* use syllables effectively, often with no words. The singers don't convey literary meaning through the syllables, but by changing the consonants, vowels, and style, they explore much variety of expression.

• Create two ostinatos with contrasting moods. Improvise in styles matching the moods. Analyze the different techniques you implemented to make the differences in styles.

PITCHED PERCUSSION INSTRUMENTS

School children throughout the world engage in musical experiences using pitched percussion instruments, to a large extent because of the influence of Carl Orff (1895–1982). The evolution of Orff's philosophy of music education resulted in the development of a combination of language, movement, creativity, and playing of instruments that enables beginning musicians to have very musical experiences. Orff encouraged the use of pitched and nonpitched instruments for creative playing. The families of pitched instruments used in the Orff process are the *xylophone, metallophone,* and *glockenspiel.* The xylophone has wooden bars; both the metallophone and glockenspiel have bars made of metal. The bars of the metallophone are heavier and larger so their sounds are different than the high, crisp sound of the glockenspiel.

All the instruments are made with removable bars, so pitches that are unnecessary for a particular piece can be taken off the instrument to avoid striking them unintentionally.

• If you have access to these instruments, use them to create an instrumental composition:
  1. Determine the pentatonic scale you wish to use.
  2. Remove all the bars for notes not in that pentatonic scale.

3. Decide on the mood of the composition.

4. Select the timbre of instrument(s) that enhances the mood you have selected.

5. Set the tempo for the piece.

6. Create an ostinato appropriate for the mood.

7. Decide whether you want more than one ostinato. If you decide on more than one, determine whether they are to be used continuously or alternatively.

8. Decide on the form to be used when creating the melody.

9. As members of the ensemble play the ostinato(s), improvise a melody of your own on one of the instruments, staying in the pentatonic mode and realizing the form you have decided to use.

10. Analyze the components of the ensemble as to their effectiveness in maintaining the mood you desire. Make changes for improvement if necessary.

LANGUAGE-BASED

Creative music can spring from a language base. Because language is easier for many people to handle than is music, association with aspects of language may make music composition easier.

RAP

Start a steady beat, then talk aloud creating rhythm patterns superimposed over the steady beat. A special challenge is to rap creating rhyming phrases.

QUESTION AND ANSWER, MELODIC COMPOSITION

If you are asked to answer a question using language, there is a good chance you can do it. If you are asked to answer the question in several different ways, depending on the question, you probably can do that too. Beginning to create music can be as simple as responding to questions in language. Many musical creations are combinations of smaller musical tasks and inspirations put together in different ways.

• Sing this question with your own melody: "How are you today?" Sing it several times to memorize your melody. Now, make up a singing conversation that you might have with other people. Alternate your question with as many answers to the question as you can devise. The sample conversation below is included only to give you an idea of a possible way to get started. Your conversation could, and should, be longer, have different questions, and have many more answers.

- Carry on musical conversations with other people too. Find a compatible person who will sing questions and answers with you. Try to incorporate the following in your musical conversations:

  1. Answers with beginnings similar to beginnings of questions asked.

  2. Answers with melodies differing from the questions. Note that even though pitches can differ, use of similar language in answering questions may force rhythm to be similar.

  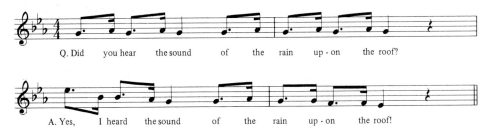

3. Questions with ambiguous cadences followed by answers with a strong sense of completion.

Q. What is your fa - vor - ite col - or?

A. Not one, but or - ange, pink and red.

There is a risk in singing conversations. Because you have to think about music as well as words, your conversation may not be completely coherent. Your melodies may not be masterpieces either, at first. The more you practice, the better they should become because you spend time working on them. These weaknesses in your musical conversation can also be found in some operas in contemporary repertoire. Even the sung conversations of an experienced composer may not be great demonstrations of musicality. (In opera, *recitatives* are used by the composer for conversation as well as narration to move the story ahead. They are usually interspersed between melodious *arias* that often deal more effectively with music than story development.)

Creating musical conversations in this way can be enjoyable and challenging for the musician starting to explore personal creativity.

POETRY

Songs have traditionally been produced by a wedding of poetry and music. Songwriters do not agree as to whether the creation of a song begins with the poetry or the music. Some creative artists write words to fit a piece of music; more often, the music is written to fit the words. The latter procedure begins with poetry.

• Take a short, favorite poem, or create one with a regular meter. (Nonmetrical poetry can also be set to music; find the rhythm of each individual phrase, then proceed with step number three below.)

  1. Say the poem with emphasis on its metrical organization. If it is a measured poem, the meter will emerge.

  2. Clap the strong beats and click the weak beats as you say the poem.

  3. Begin to sing it rhythmically, in a way similar to the musical conversations you developed.

4. Refine the musical phrases. Remember the best ones. Reject ones that you do not like or that you feel are not supportive of the text. Be influenced by the answers to those of the following questions that seem appropriate to your composition. Not all the questions will apply equally to every poem.

    a. Does your rhythm match the rhythm of the poem?

    b. Is there a high point of excitement or emotion in the text?

    c. Does the melody you have created enhance the high point of the text?

    d. Should the pitch be higher, the dynamics louder, the rhythm more intense where the climax of the poem takes place?

    e. Does the poem suggest a formal structure that would benefit from having certain melodic phrases repeated?

    f. Have you a sense of a certain key emerging?

    g. Are you singing in major, minor, pentatonic?

    h. What chords can be used to support the melody?

    i. Do your cadences give a sense of completion or noncompletion that is appropriate for the text?

5. Write your song in music notation or tape its performance.

6. After a period of time, return to your song. Do you like it as it is? Have you thought of changes to improve it?

VARIATIONS

Creativity in music need not always be completely original. You can be creative by making changes in established materials. *Theme and variations* is a popular form that takes a melody (theme) and presents it several times, each time with unique changes.

- Listen to ''Variations on America'' (Tape 10), and ''Bravour—Variations on a Theme from Mozart'' (Tape 17). List ways these composers changed the original songs.

- Sing and play the melodies for ''America'' and ''Twinkle, Twinkle, Little Star'' (same melody as the ''Alphabet Song'').

- Sing and play them with a meter change.

- Change the rhythm of the melody. Add dotted notes, syncopation, and rests where they have not been before.

- Play the melody of "Twinkle" adding *upper neighbors* to the melody. The following is an example of added upper neighbors:

Twin - kle,   twin - kle,   lit - tle   star

- Play the melody of "Twinkle" adding *lower neighbors* to the melody. The following is an example of added lower neighbors:

How___ I   won - der   what___ you___ are?

The last measure of the preceding example shows a different kind of embellishment: The E sounds at first like an upper neighbor, but instead of returning to melody note D, it moves to an F, still further away from the melody. Such an embellishment is called a *passing tone.* Upper and lower neighbors generally return to the melody note from which they departed with no intermediary notes.

- Try other combinations using *passing tones* (nonharmonic notes leading stepwise in the same direction from one note to another member of the chord) and other variations that maintain some relationship to the original melody. The following example illustrates passing tones:

Up___ a - bove___ the   world___ so   high

- Play or sing a variation of either "Twinkle, Twinkle, Little Star" or "Yankee Doodle" combining the techniques you have used to change the melody creatively.

Alternative harmonizations add variety to musical compositions. Any single note of a melody occurs in at least three chords, as the root, the third, or the fifth.

Root   Third   Fifth
 C   Am   F

To give variety to a harmonization, try changing from the original chord to one of the other two possibilities in which the melody note appears. Play and listen to the alternatives suggested here for the first phrase of "Twinkle."

Alternative chords are circled.

- Devise alternate harmonizations for either "Twinkle, Twinkle, Little Star" or "America."

- Select a different melody that you know. Make any changes you wish in melody or harmony to reflect your creativity.

SUMMARY

Creative expression demands a more personal involvement than any other aspect of music making. It is somewhat threatening to think that listeners may not like your creation. It is not realistic to think that everyone will. The most important consideration for you is whether or not you are happy with the creative efforts you make. If you are not, change, revise, invent, until the music you make is acceptable to you. Your efforts may result in breaking traditional rules of composition. Keep in mind that new rules come into being because of creative efforts that expand human acceptance of aural organization. You may find that you are unhappy with some aspects of your creativity. That *may* mean you have violated rules of composition that have been ingrained in your ear because of the culture you are in. If this is true, it will be useful for you to study composition to find more about rules used traditionally and then determine whether your musical creativity is enhanced or inhibited by application of conventions of musical composition.

When you are looking for a really special gift for someone, consider giving music you have created.

MUSIC CHECK

You should be able to define, identify, and illustrate musically:

CREATIVITY

ENVIRONMENTAL SOUNDS

COMPOSITION

IMPROVISATION

CREATIVE ORGANIZATION

WRITING/TAPING

THROUGH-COMPOSED

STYLE

SCORE

SCAT SINGER

OSTINATO

ORFF

    PITCHED PERCUSSION INSTRUMENTS

LANGUAGE-BASED

ARIA

RECITATIVE

VARIATIONS

    UPPER NEIGHBORS

    LOWER NEIGHBORS

    PASSING TONES

    ALTERNATIVE HARMONIZATIONS

CHAPTER 12

LISTENING

Music exists because we are able to hear it, but even when we hear it, we do not always listen to it. All of your associations with music should involve listening. Your music education requires *active listening!* There is a great deal of difference between merely being in a room where music is played and actively listening to the music.

Since the beginning of your work with this text, you have been encouraged to listen. This chapter expands concepts mentioned before and introduces unfamiliar ones to help your listening acuity; it synthesizes concepts already explored and suggests others for your future study. It is likely that many of the concepts have been part of the work done in class with your instructor. Two main perspectives will be developed in this chapter:

1. *Ear-training* for the functioning musician.
   a. melodic dictation
   b. aural analysis
      1) harmony
      2) form
      3) timbre

2. *Music literature* for the educated musician.
   a. cultures
   b. periods

EAR-TRAINING

Even if you listen very well, you cannot always identify what you hear. Ear-training is a process of helping you to identify what you hear and to develop the vocabulary, both in music and in language, to describe it.

You have already been involved in ear-training experiences. You have identified such things as high and low pitches, meters, scales, chords, rhythm patterns, expressive devices, and so on. How fluent are you in translating the sound of music into notation?

MELODIC DICTATION

Perhaps your instructor has already played melodies for you to notate. The process of hearing a melody and then writing it down generally begins with the dictation of melodic fragments of a few measures, gradually increasing to longer phrases as the student develops skill. It is useful for you to be able to write music as you hear it live. When your instructor is not available, work with another student playing or singing melodies for you to notate. Be sure that you know the starting pitch, the key, and the meter when you begin. You are not expected to have *perfect pitch*—that is, the ability to identify the pitch the melody starts on without having it given by a stable pitch producer such as a pitch pipe or an instrument. Once you have the starting pitch, determine the pitches that follow by their relationship to each other. Start with very easy ones such as these.

Progress to more difficult melodies only when you can write the easy ones with facility.

If writing melodies is difficult for you, begin with rhythm patterns only. When you can write the rhythm patterns from dictation, try pitch patterns alone. Finally, put pitch and rhythm together.

You can continue the development of your ability to take melodic dictation by recalling a familiar melody. This requires the use of your *inner ear*. Beethoven had an uncanny ability to use his inner ear. During the last years of his life, when he was writing some of his best music, he was so deaf that he had difficulty hearing the orchestra performing his work. Still, his inner ear enabled him to hear the music in his imagination.

1. Write the melody for "America" ("God Save the Queen") in the key of F. (This exercise is constructed on the premise that you know the song. Substitute another if you do not know this one.)

2. Before writing the pitches, establish the meter signature and the melodic rhythm.

3. The melody begins on *Do,* which is F. Add the pitches of the melody to the melodic rhythm you have noted.

4. Add tempo and dynamic markings.

5. Play the music you have written.

6. If your notation disagrees with the sound you expected, correct it.

7. Compare your writing with the notation of "America" in this book. Play your version and the printed version. If they differ, is the difference because you had a different aural image, or did you notate what you wanted to hear incorrectly?

8. Analyze problems you may have had in order to determine the area(s) in which you need help: meter, rhythm pattern, pitch, or the like.

Some students develop certain musical abilities more quickly than others. If you do not possess the skill of taking melodic dictation immediately, don't give up: your ability can be improved with practice.

- Write the melody of "America, the Beautiful," using the process outlined for "America." The melody of "America, the Beautiful" begins on *so.* Write it in the key of B-flat. When you have finished, compare your work with the score for "America, the Beautiful" found in this book.

- Select two pieces you know well. Write their melodies.

If your inner ear has not developed enough to help you notate familiar music, an intermediary step is to use an instrument to "pick out" the melody before notating it. Use this procedure as an ear-training device until you can notate the music without the aid of the instrument.

AURAL ANALYSIS

You have analyzed songs from printed notation. How much can you tell about music using your ear alone? If you do not have perfect pitch, you are limited in telling exactly what pitches are used, but you can tell a lot about a piece of music without knowing the exact pitches. *Relative pitch* enables you to write melodic dictation because you are aware of the relationships of pitches to each other. *Aural analysis* is dependent upon your ability to perceive what you are hearing about all the elements of music and their relationships.

1. Can you determine the relative tempo and dynamics of what you hear?

2. What timbre(s) are used in the music?

3. What is the meter of the music?

4. What are the rhythmic characteristics?
5. What is its form?
6. What is the harmonic structure?

Notice that the questions posed are similar to those appearing on the *MAS* (Music Analysis Sheet) you have used when looking at song scores. The *MAS* can be used for aural analysis as well. The sections that follow will delve more deeply into some of the elements of music in order to increase your ability to analyze music aurally.

Harmony

The songs in this text, for the most part, use *vertical harmony*. That is, the songs have melodies with chordal accompaniment to go with them. Vertical harmony is also called *homophony*. The F and C7 chords used with the melody for "Will You Come?" create homophonic harmony.

Some of your songs have used *horizontal harmony;* that is, their harmonies have resulted either from the same melody being used by more than one voice singing at the same time but beginning and ending at different times, or from different melodies being performed simultaneously. The use of melodies to produce harmony creates *polyphony*. Examples of polyphonic music are rounds, canons, and fugues. "Will You Come?" produces polyphonic harmony when used as a three-part round with voices entering at four-measure intervals.

When a melody is alone, with no harmony added either homophonically or polyphonically, the music is called *monophony*. Gregorian chant (Tape 2) illustrates monophonic music. "Will You Come?" is monophonic when its melody is used without chordal accompaniment and without the entrance of voices at different times to make it a round.

"Will You Come?" "Hark to the Singing," and "Coffee" are partner songs. They can be performed with each other. This produces a type of polyphony different from the round. Their distinctive melodies combine to produce harmony. The interesting feature of these songs is that they each can also be used as rounds, thus producing their own polyphonic harmony without partnering with the others. Beware: These songs function as partner songs and as rounds because the chord changes of their phrases occur in the same places, and the chords are the same. Songs without compatible chords and chord progressions are not rounds and will not work as rounds.

• Can the three partner songs be used monophonically and homophonically as well as polyphonically?

- Examples of monophonic, homophonic, and polyphonic music are all found in "Hallelujah!" from Handel's *Messiah* (Tape 20). Analyze it aurally to find the different *textures* (horizontal and vertical use of sounds). Locate the textures with the words of the piece that match their occurrences. After you have done this, check your analysis in the Appendix.

Form

Analyze the form of music using your ear alone. Identify phrases that are alike, that are similar, and that are completely unlike each other. Begin by listening to simple songs, then progress to larger works. Find sources in libraries and record shops with scores as well as records or tapes so you can compare your aural analysis with written notation to see if you are accurate.

Music is organized in many forms. You have used a few of them, such as *ABA, AB,* and so on; there are still many others. The forms listed here show some of the contrasting means of organizing music, which are worth more intensive attention in your future attempts at analyzing music aurally.

Fugue: There are many different forms of the fugue. They all use polyphonic harmony. Usually, a given number of parts or voices enter one by one stating the main theme, based alternately on the tonic *(subject)* and dominant *(answer)*. After the initial statement of the subject, the same voice usually continues with another melody called the *countersubject. Episodes* occur between statements of the subject, often using short melodic fragments (motives) derived from the subject or countersubject. The theme(s) may be altered for variety through *diminution* (shortening notes), *augmentation* (lenghening notes), *fragmentation* (using only parts of the themes), *retrograde* (using the notes of a theme in reverse order), *inversion* (using a theme with all its intervals inverted), and so on. Johann Sebastian Bach's *Well-Tempered Clavier* contains many fugues. Each of them is coupled with a *prelude* (companion or introductory piece coming before the fugue.)

Theme and Variations: This form occurs when a main theme is stated and then restated with changes. The changes may amplify, elaborate, or extend the main theme. Good examples of theme and variations are Charles Ives's "Variations on America" (Tape 10) and "Bravour, Variations on a Theme from Mozart" (Tape 17).

Ternary (ABA) Form: This widely used form can be found in simple songs and also in very elaborate works. *Sonata-allegro form* (or *sonata form*) is a large *ABA* form. It consists of an *exposition* (usually stating two main themes), a *devel-*

opment (in which the themes are stated in different ways such as those described under alterations of the fugal themes, as well as modulations, sequences, and so on), a *recapitulation* (in which the themes are stated more closely to the way they were stated in the exposition). Key changes are crucial to the interest generated by this form. A splendid example of sonata-allegro form is Wolfgang Amadeus Mozart's *Symphony No. 40 in G minor,* first movement.

Rondo: Repetition of a main theme between contrasting themes results in a *rondo form.* It can use any of these arrangements: *ABACA, ABACADA, ABA-CABA.* Sonatas by Mozart and Beethoven contain fine examples of rondos. (The use of the word *sonata* in this case refers to a piece containing several *movements* or separate sections. One section usually uses the sonata-allegro or sonata form described above. Another section may use rondo form.)

Timbre

The *tone color, quality,* or *timbre* of voices and instruments used to make music provides some of its greatest interest. Instruments are often classified according to the *families* to which they belong in the *symphony orchestra.*

The four instrumental families of the symphony orchestra are the *strings, brass, woodwinds,* and *percussion.* The most numerous members of the orchestra are the strings; the greatest variety is found in the percussion family.

Strings.   Four members of the string family look very much alike except for their size: the *violin, viola, cello,* and *string bass.* They all are played with a *bow,* except when their strings are plucked *(pizzicato)* for special effects. The movement of the bow hairs across the string sets it vibrating to produce the sound. Pitches are changed by the fingers on the fingerboard. As they shorten the string, the pitch becomes higher. The "f" holes help produce the distinctive sound of these string instruments. A warm string sound is produced when the left hand moves rapidly back and forth while the finger tip remains in contact with the string *(vibrato.)* Violin and viola players can either sit or stand to play. Cello players always sit with the instrument between their legs. The player of the string bass often stands, but has the option of leaning on a high stool.

The member of the string family that is different in appearance is the *harp.* The harpist always sits to play, uses only the fingers, and has pedals to change the pitches from flats to naturals to sharps.

- Listen to "Modere" (Tape 18) to hear the violin and cello. Find at least five other pieces on your tape in which you can identify the sound of the string family. The harp will be most prominent in "Prelude to the Afternoon of a Faun" (Tape 19).

String Family: violin, viola, cello, and double bass.   *(photo courtesy of Jon Blumb)*

The difference between a symphony orchestra and a band is the presence or absence of strings. Compare the sound of the band playing "Semper Fidelis" (Tape 8) and the orchestra playing "Prelude to the Afternoon of a Faun" (Tape 19).

Brass.   All the members of the brass family use a cup-shaped mouthpiece to focus a column of air activated by vibrating lips into the body of the instrument. All brass instruments (except the slide trombone) use valves to help make pitches available by lengthening and shortening the tubing of the instrument. The *trumpet* and *tuba* usually have *piston valves* (some have rotary valves); the *French horn* has *rotary valves;* the *trombone* has a *slide* to lengthen and shorten the pipe when changing pitch. Piston valves work up and down; rotary valves turn in a circular motion.

All brass players use variable lip tension and breath support in addition to changing the length of the tubing for different pitches. Although these instruments are no longer all made of brass, with a few exceptions they are all made of metal. The most notable exception is the fiberglass *Sousaphone* used by marching bands. The Sousaphone was originally developed at the suggestion of John Phillip Sousa as an easier-to-carry substitute for tubas in marching bands. Its bell configuration also broadened the dispersion of sound. The weight of the Sousaphone rests on

Brass Family: tuba, piccolo trumpet, C trumpet, French horn, and alto, tenor, and bass trombones. *(photo courtesy of Jon Blumb)*

the player's shoulder; modern use of fiberglass instead of metal has lightened the weight considerably.

- Listen to "Andante" (Tape 12) for the distinctive sound of the trumpet. *Til Eulenspiegel* (Tape 14) gives a good example of the French horn.

Woodwinds. Instruments with intricate keys and holes belong to the *woodwind* family. Originally their bodies were made of wood; now they are sometimes constructed of other materials. *Flutes* and *piccolos* are generally made of metal, although piccolos may be made of wood or plastic. Very fine flutes may be made of gold or platinum. *Clarinets* are usually made of wood, but plastic is also used. (The use of metal for beginning clarinetists seems to have given way to plastic.) *Saxophones* are traditionally metal instruments.

Alternate materials for making woodwind instruments have been introduced in a quest for improving quality, but other factors have been responsible for changes as well. Some new materials are less expensive or easier to maintain.

Oboes and *bassoons* are not often purchased for children and beginners. This may be a factor in most of them continuing to be made of wood (with very few plastic exceptions). Both of these instruments have their vibrating columns of air activated by a *double reed,* two pieces of reed bound together and carefully shaped, usually by the player. Clarinets and saxophones use *single reeds.* Flutes and piccolos have no reeds. Their column of air is activated by the musician blowing across a round hole held at a right angle to the body. Pitch on these

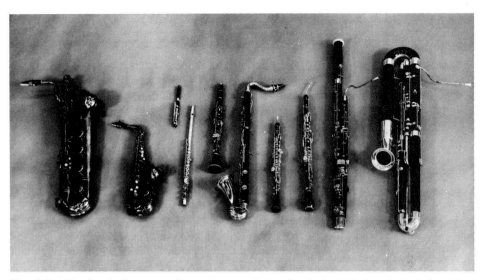

Woodwind Family: baritone saxophone, alto saxophone, piccolo, flute, clarinet, bass clarinet, oboe, English horn, bassoon, and contrabassoon. *(photo courtesy of Jon Blumb)*

instruments is changed by varying the length of the air column, which is controlled by the number of holes covered by the fingers.

- Listen to "Phantasiestücke" for the sound of the clarinet (Tape 11) and "Triste" for the sound of the bassoon (Tape 16). Can you find the sound of the flute in "Prelude to the Afternoon of a Faun" (Tape 19)?

Percussion. The *percussion* family includes the *timpani, gong, cymbals, triangle, celeste, maracas, guiro, tambourine, snare drum, bass drum, marimba, xylophone, glockenspiel, metallophone, whip, wood block, bongo drum, temple blocks,* and *chimes.* It is difficult to list all the members of the percussion family. There are many of them, and for certain literature instruments are added to the orchestra for the special effect desired by the composer. Contemporary composers have added the sound of breaking bottles, brake discs to be hit, and more.

The percussion family includes any instruments that are *struck* (or shaken, tapped, and so on) to produce their sound. Some are pitched; some are nonpitched.

- Listen to the excerpt from *The Young Person's Guide to the Orchestra* for an example of timpani and other percussion sounds (Tape 15).

One of the problems with classifying instruments according to the families of orchestral instruments is that these families are not all-inclusive. The guitar is generally omitted. Ethnic instruments are ignored. The piano is placed in the

Percussion Family: gong, cymbals, orchestral bells (Glockenspiel), xylophone, timpani (kettle drums), snare drum, and bass drum. *(photo courtesy of Jon Blumb)*

percussion or the string family depending upon whether its use of strings, or its hammering action is perceived to be most important.

Erich von Hornbostel and Curt Sachs published another system for classifying instruments in 1914: It deals with the categorization of instruments according to the way their sound is produced. The categories used are the *aerophones, idiophones, membranophones, chordophones, mechanical* and *electrophones:*

AEROPHONES.   These instruments produce sound by the vibration of air. The group includes the woodwinds, brass, bagpipes, whistles, recorders, mouth organs, accordians, and organs.

IDIOPHONES.   The instruments in this classification are made of sonorous material and produce their sound in a variety of ways. They are stamped, shaken, scraped, plucked, hit, rubbed, clashed. Among the instruments in this category are metallophones, xylophones, bells, rattles, jingles, gongs, cymbals, steel drums, slit drums, clappers, Jew's harps, sansa, and celeste.

MEMBRANOPHONES.   The sound of these instruments is made by the vibration of a stretched membrane or skin. It includes any drum with a vibrating head and, of far less importance, the *mirlitons,* whose membrane modifies a sound made in some other way (such as a comb with paper, or a kazoo).

CHORDOPHONES. The vibration of strings produces the sounds of the instruments in this category. It includes lyres, harps, lutes, harpsichords, virginals, pianos, clavichords, dulcimers, guitars, ukuleles, banjos, and orchestral strings.

MECHANICAL AND ELECTROPHONES. Instruments in this group range from music boxes, carillons, hurdy gurdies, and player pianos to electric guitars, organs, and synthesizers.

With the criteria of these categories established, all instruments are included. The effect of using this system is to help musicians (composers, performers, and listeners) realize broader parameters for timbre possibilities to be included in music.

- Locate and list at least two instruments in each of the Hornbostel and Sachs categories. Tell where you located the instruments and who was playing them.

- Reclassify the string, brass, woodwind and percussion families according to the Hornbostel and Sachs categories.

- Listen to Tapes 21 and 22. Determine the appropriate categories for the instruments in those pieces.

MUSIC LITERATURE

This brief section has been separated from the ear-training section to highlight the value of including many different types of music literature in your listening experiences. The broad spectrum of music literature contains abundant contrast, enough so that individuals may find wide variety in music especially appealing to their tastes. When forming those tastes, it is important that the listener be open to new alternatives. Although your present listening experiences may now be highly satisfactory to you, continued receptivity to new musical experiences may help you expand your listening vocabulary to still more fulfilling dimensions.

A characteristic of human beings is that they produce and value music. The development of electronic devices for sound reproduction (tape recorders, radio, television, stereos) has multiplied opportunities for hearing music to an unprecedented degree. In spite of the technological advances, many listeners have neither expanded their horizons nor sought out musical alternatives to keep pace with the opportunities technology has provided. Public media tend to provide an abundance of music within certain restricted categories to the exclusion of other possibilities. Records and tapes, on the other hand, do provide alternatives. Live performances are available to provide stimulating contact with a variety of musical styles. This discussion is intended to suggest alternatives to what may be your conventional listening habits, to challenge you to explore new dimensions of sound, to expand your aesthetic involvement as a listener.

MUSIC OF ALL CULTURES

Cultures throughout the world are represented by their arts. Most cultures have developed a style of music that is unique to them, a distinctive sound that, along with sight, represents cultural differentiation.

• Listen to "Bird Song," American Indian (Tape 21), "Djamu the Dingo" (Tape 22) and "Bungalin Bungalin," Australian Aboriginal (Tape 23). List elements of music you hear in these pieces. Compare them with a piece of music you choose. What common elements do you hear? What elements seem to represent differences?

• Select three pieces of music from three different cultures in collections at the library or from your record collection. Compare the elements of music in these selections. What elements of music would help you identify the pieces and remind you of the culture from which they come?

It is possible that mass media may have a negative impact on cultural differentiation in music. A question worthy of discussion asks if it is necessary and/or desirable to preserve, perform, and value music that uniquely represents distinctive cultures.

MUSIC OF ALL PERIODS

Within the western tradition, music falls into historical periods of development. The periods to be discussed briefly here are the baroque, classical, romantic, and contemporary. All of these periods, as well as periods before the baroque, deserve exhaustive study, which is not possible in this book. You are encouraged to nurture your curiosity about music as it developed throughout history and find resources to enable you to hear more of it. Given dates are approximate.

As public interest in music from before the baroque period grows, authentic, well-recorded examples continue to become available. The only selection of early western music on your tape is the Gregorian chant (Tape 2).

• Find a recording of music that can be traced to a time before the sixteenth century. Describe one of the selections according to its inclusion and treatment of the elements of music.

Baroque, 1575–1750

This period manifested a spirit of theatricalism with decorative elaboration influencing music as well as other arts. Important composers of this period were Bach, Handel, Vivaldi, Scarlatti, Telemann, and Purcell.

- Listen to two selections by Handel on your tape (4 and 20). Use the Music Analysis Sheet to tell as much as possible about what you hear. Adapt the sheet if it does not enable you to reflect adequately on what you hear.

- Analyze "Triste," Telemann, using a *MAS* (Tape 16).

Classical, 1750–1800

The dates for these periods only give an indication of time. There is overlapping of the practices of the periods. In every period, composers use techniques from previous periods. Sometimes contemporary composers deliberately revert to styles used in previous times, becoming *neobaroque, neoclassical,* and so on.

The music of the classical period tended to be objective, reacting against the floridity of the baroque. Refinement, precise organization, symmetry, and contrast were characteristic of this period. Major composers were Haydn and Mozart. Beethoven's early works were in the classical vein, but he gradually changed his writing to become a leader in establishing practices of the romantic period.

- Listen to "Andante" by Haydn (Tape 12). Use the *MAS* to help you analyze its characteristics.

- Select a composition by Mozart. Use the *MAS* to help you describe its characteristics.

Romantic, 1800–1900

The romantic period allowed the individual to become important and music to become emotional and subjective. Because of the individual freedom, distinctive styles became evident. Leaders in this period were Beethoven, Schubert, Berlioz, Mendelssohn, Chopin, Schumann, Wagner, Verdi, Brahms, Tchaikovsky, Richard Strauss, Debussy.

- Listen to Tape 14 and 19. Both of the selections are parts of a complete work. Choose one, then find a recording of the entire composition. Richard Strauss represented *romantic realism;* Debussy was the leading figure of the *impressionist* movement in music. After listening to the complete work and reading the record jacket, try to tell why the term *realist* or *impressionist* was applied to the composer you chose.

- Find a recording of another romantic composer. Analyze the work using the *MAS*.

Contemporary, 1900–Present

More than eighty years after the beginning of this period, it is becoming inaccurate to call this period the "contemporary" period, and difficult to determine what music historians of the future will call it. Composers (as in all periods) continue to use techniques from previous periods, but revolutionaries have turned away from traditional techniques to use exaggerated dissonance, polyrhythms, and nontraditional forms. Jazz has developed in its own right and has also influenced composers who use traditional types of expression. Jazz-influenced popular music has swept across the earth. Leading composers during this time include Vaughan Williams, Schoenberg, Ives, Ravel, Stravinsky, Bartok, Webern, Berg, Prokofiev, Milhaud, Honneger, Orff, Gershwin, Copland, Shostakovitch, Carter, Cage, Britten, Boulez, Stockhausen.

- Your tape includes a number of contemporary works (3, 5, 6, 7, 8, 10, 15, 18). Choose three of them and contrast their treatment of the elements of music. If you heard them without identification, would you know they are from the contemporary period? How would you know?

- Find two works by composers listed above. Analyze them using the *MAS*. Does the written material on the record jacket help you listen to the music? Does it deal with musical or biographical information?

SUMMARY

Since you may spend more time listening to music than engaging in any other activity related to it (singing, playing, moving, creating, reading, writing), your most important priority may be that you continue to develop listening skills. This chapter can only suggest ideas for your future development. It is up to you to move toward the realization of your potential as a listener. A regularly scheduled trip to a record-lending library, or a budgeted amount for record/tape purchase will help you develop breadth in your listening activities.

MUSIC CHECK

You should be able to define, identify, and illustrate musically:

EAR TRAINING	TIMBRE
MELODIC DICTATION	SYMPHONY ORCHESTRA
INNER EAR	STRING
AURAL ANALYSIS	VIBRATO
PERFECT PITCH	PIZZICATO
RELATIVE PITCH	BRASS
TEXTURE	MOUTHPIECE
MONOPHONIC	VALVES
HOMOPHONIC	PISTON
POLYPHONIC	ROTARY
FORM	SLIDE
FUGUE	WOODWIND
SUBJECT	REED
ANSWER	DOUBLE
COUNTERSUBJECT	SINGLE
STRETTO	PERCUSSION
DIMINUTION	SOUND PRODUCING CHARACTERISTICS
AUGMENTATION	AEROPHONES
FRAGMENTATION	IDIOPHONES
RETROGRADE	MEMBRANOPHONES
INVERSION	CHORDOPHONES
PRELUDE	MECHANICAL AND ELECTROPHONES
THEME AND VARIATIONS	MUSIC LITERATURE
ABA	WORLD CULTURES
SONATA-ALLEGRO	HISTORICAL PERIODS
EXPOSITION	BAROQUE
DEVELOPMENT	CLASSICAL
RECAPITULATION	ROMANTIC
RONDO	CONTEMPORARY
SONATA	
MOVEMENTS	

CODA

Do you remember what kind of musician you were when you began using this text? What can you perform now that you couldn't then? What have you heard that was new to you? What have you created that you hadn't tried before? Do you realize that becoming a musician does not happen passively, that your musical skills have resulted from conscientious work on your part? You have heard new things because you took the time to listen. You have created because you were willing to take the risk of being innovative. You know more about music because you studied. You can perform music because you practiced performing music. Music is a splendid reinforcer because it is a subject that provides its own intrinsic rewards. Your future involvement in musical experiences will help you continue to expand your musical horizons and strengthen your musical skills.

MUSIC

African Noel

Andante — C — F — C
pp Sing No-el, sing No-el, No-el No-el.____

accelerando — *p* — F — C
Sing No-el, sing No-el, No-el No-el.

mf Sing we all No-el, sing we all No-el,

Allegro — *f* — *ritard*
Sing we all No-el, sing we all No-el.

mf — F — C
Sing No-el, sing No-el, No-el No-el.____

Andante — F — *pp* C — G7 — C
p Sing No-el, sing No-el, No-el No-el.____

Liberia

Keyboard 14
Autoharp 5
Guitar 5

A Hunting We Will Go

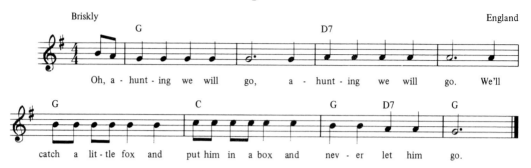

Oh, a - hunt - ing we will go, a - hunt - ing we will go. We'll

catch a lit - tle fox and put him in a box and nev - er let him go.

Keyboard 6

Autoharp 3

Guitar 3

All the Pretty Little Horses

Hush - a - by, don't you cry, Go to sleep - y lit - tle ba - by.

When you wake you shall have, All the pret - ty lit - tle hors - es.

Blacks and bays, dap - ples and grays, Coach and six a - lit - tle hors - es.

Hush - a - by, don't you cry, Go to sleep - y lit - tle ba - by.

Reprinted by permission of the publishers of *On the Trail of Negro Folk Songs* by Dorothy Scarborough, Cambridge, Massachusetts: Harvard University Press, Copyright © 1925 by Harvard University Press; © 1953 by Mary McDaniel Parker.

Alphabet Song

Not too fast

Traditional

A, B, C, D, E, F, G, H, I, J, K, L, M, N, O, P,

Q, R, S, and T, U, V, W, X, and Y and Z;

Now I've said my A, B, C's, Tell me what you think of me.

Baa, Baa Black Sheep

Baa, baa, black sheep, Have you any wool?
Yes, sir, yes, sir, three bags full.
One for my master and one for my dame,
And one for the little boy who lives down the lane.

Twinkle, Twinkle, Little Star

Twinkle, twinkle, little star, How I wonder what you are
Up above the world so high, Like a diamond in the sky.
Twinkle, twinkle, little star, How I wonder what you are.

America

Words by Samuel Francis Smith

Music by Henry Carey

1. My coun - try, 'tis of thee, Sweet land of
2. My na - tive coun - try, thee, Land of the

lib - er - ty, Of thee I sing;
no - ble free, Thy name I love;

Land where my fa - thers died! Land of the Pil - grims' pride,
I love thy rocks and rills, Thy woods and temp - led hills,

From ev - 'ry____ moun - tain - side, Let____ free - dom ring!
My heart____ with____ rap - ture thrills Like____ that a - bove.

3. Let music swell the breeze, And ring from all the trees
   Sweet freedom's song;
   Let mortal tongues awake, Let all that breathe partake,
   Let rocks their silence break, The sound prolong!

4. Our fathers' God, to Thee, Author of liberty,
   To Thee we sing
   Long may our land be bright With freedom's holy light;
   Protect us by The might, Great God, our King.

God Save the Queen

1. God save our Gracious Queen!
   Long live our noble Queen!
   God save the Queen!
   Send her victorious,
   Happy and Glorious
   Long to reign over us.
   God save the Queen!

2. Thy choicest gifts in store
   On Her be pleased to store
   Long may She reign.
   May She defend our laws
   And ever give us cause
   To sing with heart and voice
   God save the Queen!

3. O Lord our God, arise,
   Scatter Her enemies
   And make them fall.
   Confound their politics,
   Frustrate their knavish tricks
   On Thee our hope we fix.
   God save us all.

America, The Beautiful

Words by Katharine Lee Bates

Music by Samuel A. Ward

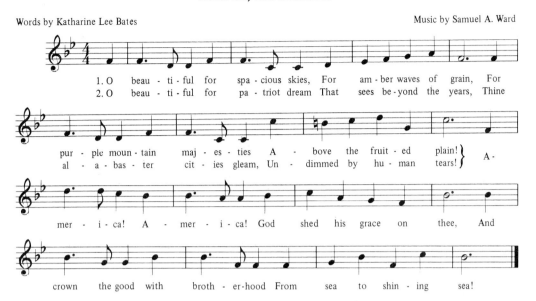

1. O beau - ti - ful for spa - cious skies, For am - ber waves of grain, For
2. O beau - ti - ful for pa - triot dream That sees be - yond the years, Thine

pur - ple moun - tain maj - es - ties A - bove the fruit - ed plain! } A-
al - a - bas - ter cit - ies gleam, Un - dimmed by hu - man tears! }

mer - i - ca! A - mer - i - ca! God shed his grace on thee, And

crown the good with broth - er-hood From sea to shin - ing sea!

Are You Sleeping?

Traditional

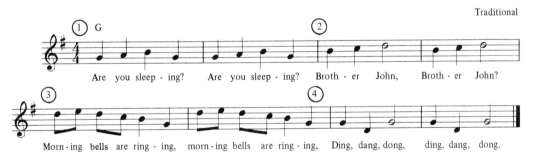

Are you sleep - ing? Are you sleep - ing? Broth - er John, Broth - er John?

Morn - ing bells are ring - ing, morn - ing bells are ring - ing, Ding, dang, dong, ding, dang, dong.

Alternate words: Frere Jacques

Keyboard 4

Recorder 3

Frere Jacques, frere Jacques, dormez vouz? dormez vouz?

Sonnez les matines, sonnez les matines, din, din, don

din, din, don

Or: Where is Thumbkin?

1. Where is thumbkin? Where is thumbkin?
   Here I am, here I am.
   How are you today, sir?
   Very well, I thank you!
   Run away, run away.

2. Where is pointer?
3. Where is tall one?
4. Where is ring one?
5. Where is pinkie?
6. Where's the handful? Here we are.

Artza Alinu

From Patricia Hackett, *The Melody Book,* © 1983, p. 150. Reprinted by permission of Prentice-Hall, Inc., Englewood Cliffs, New Jersey.

You can do the hora with this.

Auld Lang Syne

Andante   Scotland

Should auld ac-quaint-ance be for-got, And nev - er brought to mind?

Should auld ac-quaint-ance be for-got, And days of auld lang syne?

For auld ____ lang ____ syne, my dear, For auld ____ lang ____ syne;

We'll take a cup of kind - ness yet for auld ____ lang ____ syne.

Bella Bimba

From *Songs We Like* © by World Around Songs. Reprinted with permission of the publisher.

The Bird's Song

Keyboard 5

Autoharp 2

Guitar 2

Coffee

Germany

C O F F E E, Don't pass the cof-fee cup to

me! Not for chil-dren is that strong, brown Turk-ish drink For it makes you weak and some-what ill, I

think! Don't be caught wak-ing up, clutch-ing a cof-fee cup!

Used with permission of Hilde Kupfer.

CAFFEE

C A F F E E , trink nicht so viel Caffee! Nicht fur Kinderist der
Türkentrank, schwächt die Nerven macht dich blass und krank. Sei
doch kein Muselman, der ihn nicht lassen kann!

The number over the inserted rest shows the beat necessary to match "Hark to the Singing" when these songs are used as partner songs.

The Cuckoo

1. O I went to Pe-ter's flow-ing spring Where the wa-ter's so good,
2. Af-ter Eas-ter come sun-ny days That will melt all the snow;
3. When I've mar-ried my maid-en fair, What then can I de-sire?

And I heard there the cuck-oo As she called from the wood.
Then I'll mar-ry my maid-en fair, We'll be hap-py, I know.
O a home for her tend-ing And some wood for the fire.

Ho-li-ah, Ho-le-rah-hi-hi-ah, Ho-le-rah cuck-oo! Ho-le-rah-hi-hi-ah, Ho-le-rah cuck-oo!

Ho-le-rah-hi-hi-ah, Ho-le-rah cuck-oo! Ho-le-rah-hi-hi-ah-ho!

From *Songs to Keep* © by World Around Songs. Reprinted with permission of the publisher.

Dance in a Circle

Australia
arr. Barry Palmer

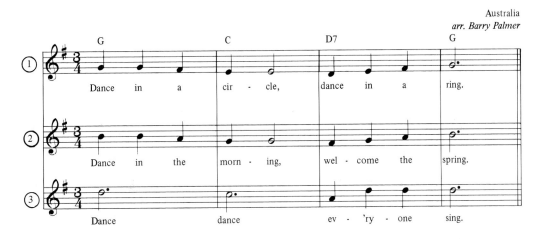

© 1983, Barry Palmer. Used with permission.

Dona Nobis Pacem

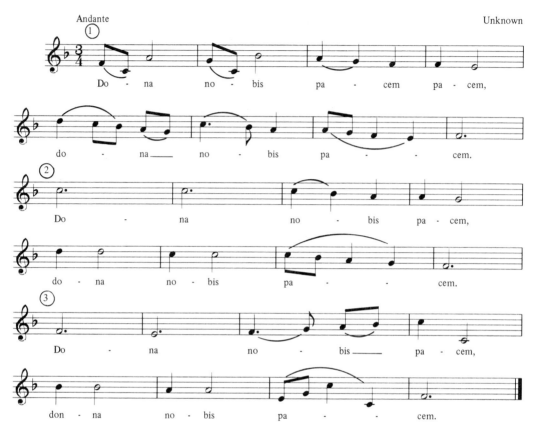

The words to this sixteenth century Latin canon mean "give to us peace." Pronounce them: do-nah no-bees pah-chem.

Eency, Weency Spider

Traditional

Lightly

Een - cy, ween - cy spi - der went up the wa - ter spout;

Down came the rain and washed the spi - der out.

Out came the sun and dried up all the rain, And the

een - cy, ween - cy spi - der went up the spout a - gain.

Show the children how the spider (your hands) climbs the waterspout. Turn your hands into rain that washes the spider out of the waterspout. Then transform them into the sun. Finally, start the spider up the spout again.

El Jarabe

Mexico

Allegro ff

G

There's a dance that is called the ja - ra - be,

D7

It is done with a wide-brimmed som - bre - ro,

G   Fine

Wear - ing chi - na po-bla-na and char - ro, It's a dance from down Mex - i - co way.

A7   D   A7   D

Ev - 'ry - one is so hap - py and care - free, Ev - 'ry - one's at fi - es - ta to - day.—

A7   D   A7   D   D.C. al Fine
D7

There is laugh - ing and talk - ing and sing - ing, Come and join the fi - es - ta, "O - le!"

Reprinted with permission from *The Spectrum of Music with Related Arts*, Book 4, by Mary Val Marsh, Carroll Rinehart, and Edith Savage. © 1983 Macmillan Publishing Company.

China poblana is a woman's dress with a long, full skirt decorated with bright spangles and a white, squarenecked blouse.

Charro is horseman's garb with silver buttons along the outside leg seams.

Erie Canal

2. We'd better get along, old pal, fifteen miles on the Erie Canal,
    You can bet your life I'd never part from Sal, fifteen miles on the Erie Canal
    Get up there, mule, here comes a lock, we'll make Rome by six o'clock,
    One more trip and back we'll go, back we'll go to Buffalo.

The Frogs

Hear the live-ly song of the frogs in yon-der pond,
Crick, crick, crick-i-ty-crick Br-r-r-umph!

Get Along Little Dogies

1.As I was a-walk-ing one morn-ing for plea-sure, I spied a cow-punch-er a-rid-ing a-long. His hat was thrown back and his spurs were a-jin-gling, And as he ap-proached he was sing-ing this song: Whoo-pee ti-yi-yo,— get a long lit-tle do-gies, It's your mis-for-tune and none of my own. Whoo-pee ti-yi-yo,— get a-long lit-tle do-gies, You know that Wy-o-ming will be your new home.

2. It's early in the spring when we round up the dogies,
   And mark them and brand them *and bob off their tails,*
   We round up our horses and load the chuck wagon,
   And then herd the dogies right out on the trail.

3. It's whooping and yelling and driving the dogies,
   Oh, how I wish you would only go on;
   It's whooping and punching, go on, little dogies,
   You know that Wyoming will be your new home.

To simplify the accompaniment, substitute C7 chords for the Gm chords.

Go to Sleep

From *The Music Book,* Book 2, copyright ⓒ 1981 by Holt, Rinehart and Winston, Publishers. Reprinted by permission of the publisher.

Good News

Good news, the char-iot's com-in', Good news, the char-iot's com-in',

Good news, the char-iot's com-in' And I don't want you to leave-a me be-hind.

Hark to the Singing

Oh, hark to the sing_-ing so joy-ful-ly ring-ing.

It says gen-tle spring has come a-gain and shep-herds will play their shawns then.

Tra la la la la la la la la la la la la la la la la.

Es Tönen die Lieder

Es tönen die Lieder, der Frühling kehrt wieder, es spielet,

der Hirte auf seiner Schalmei, tra la la la la la la la la la la la

la la la la la la.

"Hark to the Singing," "Will You Come?" and "Coffee" are all rounds. They are also partner songs; their harmonic construction is compatible so they can be sung together. The songs were shared by Hilde Kupfer (West Germany) when describing her "Klangspur in the Treppenstrasse" (Soundtrack in the Street of Steps) in Kassel, a middle-sized town in Nessen, to music classes at the University of Oregon in 1984. She used them as a nine-voiced quodlibet (simultaneous performance of several melodies). They are used with her permission. The English adaptations are by Lois N. Harrison from English translations provided by Hilde Kupfer.

Hold On

U.S.A.

Verse:

1. When you plow, don't lose your track,— Can't plow straight and keep a-

look - in' back.— Keep your hand on— that plow,— Hold on, hold on, hold on.

Refrain:

Hold on, hold on, Bet-ter keep your hand right on— that plow,—Hold on, hold on, hold on.

From Patricia Hackett, *The Melody Book*, © 1983, p. 90. Reprinted by permission of Prentice-Hall, Inc., Englewood Cliffs, New Jersey.

Originally a social and religious commentary, "Hold On" was easily adapted to the "Freedom Rider's Song" by Blacks attempting to desegregate public transportation in the south. Here are some of those verses:

1. Paul and Silas bound in jail,
   Had no money to go their bail,
   Keep your eyes on the prize,
   Hold on . . .

2. Freedom's name is mighty sweet,
   Soon one day we're gonna meet,
   Keep your eyes on the prize,

3. The only chain that man can stand,
   Is that chain of hand in hand,
   Keep your eyes on the prize,

4. We're gonna board that big Greyhound,
   Carryin' love from town to town,
   Keep your eyes on the prize,

Holla Hi, Holla Ho

German
Words Adapted

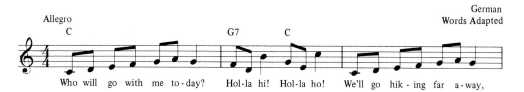

Who will go with me to-day? Hol-la hi! Hol-la ho! We'll go hik-ing far a-way,

Hol - la, Hol - la ho! We will leave in the ear - ly morn, Ho - la hi!

Hol - la ho! Then come back when the day-light's gone, Hol - la, Hol - la ho!

From *Joyful Singing*, © World Around Songs. Reprinted by permission of the publisher.

Home on the Range

Andantino

U.S.A.

1. Oh, give me a home, where the buf - fa - lo roam, Where the deer
and the an - te - lope play,____ Where sel - dom is heard
a dis - cour - ag - ing word And the skies are not cloud - y all day.____

Refrain:

Home, home on the range,____ Where the deer and the an - te-lope play,____

Where sel-dom is heard a dis - cour - ag-ing word, And the skies are not cloud-y all day.____

2. How often at night when the heavens are bright,
   From the light of the glittering stars,
   Have I stood there, amazed, and asked as I gazed,
   If their glory exceeds that of ours.

3. Where the air is so pure and the zephyrs so free,
   And the breezes so balmy and light,
   Oh, I would not exchange my home on the range,
   For the glittering cities so bright.

4. Oh, give me a land where the bright diamond sand
   Flows leisurely down with the stream,
   Where the graceful, white swan glides slowly along,
   Like a maid in a heavenly dream.

Home on the Range

Allegretto   U.S.A.

1. Oh, give me a home where the buf - fa - lo roam, Where the deer and the an - te - lope play; ____ Where sel - dom is heard a dis - cour - ag - ing word, And the skies are not cloud - y all day. ____

Chorus:
Home, home on the range, ____ Where the deer and the an - te - lope play; _____ Where sel - dom is heard a dis - cour - ag - ing word, And the skies are not cloud - y all day. ____

Hot Cross Buns

Moderato   Traditional

Hot	cross	buns.	Hot	cross	buns.	One - a - pen - ny, two - a - pen - ny	Hot	cross	buns.
3	2	1	3	2	1	1 1 1 1 2 2 2 2	3	2	1
mi	re	do	mi	re	do	do do do do re re re re	mi	re	do

Keyboard 1, 2

Recorder 1

Autoharp 1

Guitar 1

Ifca's Castle

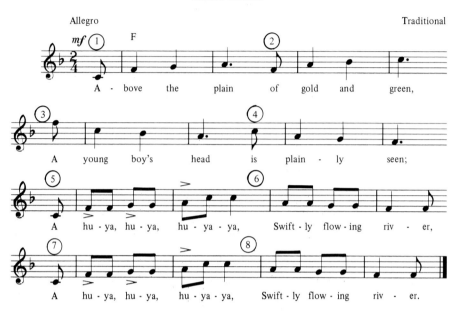

A - bove the plain of gold and green,
A young boy's head is plain - ly seen;
A hu - ya, hu - ya, hu - ya - ya, Swift - ly flow - ing riv - er,
A hu - ya, hu - ya, hu - ya - ya, Swift - ly flow - ing riv - er.

I'm a Little Teapot

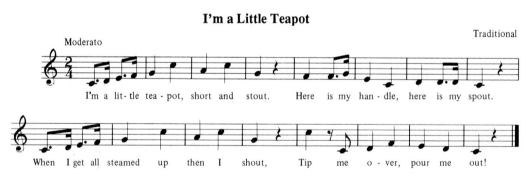

I'm a lit - tle tea - pot, short and stout. Here is my han - dle, here is my spout.
When I get all steamed up then I shout, Tip me o - ver, pour me out!

When singing this song to children, add motions with them. Show the short, stout teapot. Use one arm for the handle, the other for the spout. Tip the teapot on the last phrase by moving your body so the spout looks like it is pouring the tea.

It's Raining

Traditional

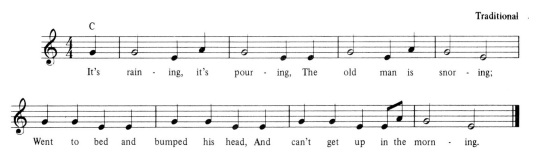

It's rain - ing, it's pour - ing, The old man is snor - ing;

Went to bed and bumped his head, And can't get up in the morn - ing.

Keyboard 7, 8
Recorder 4

Kum Ba Yah
(Come By Here)

Slowly

U.S.A.

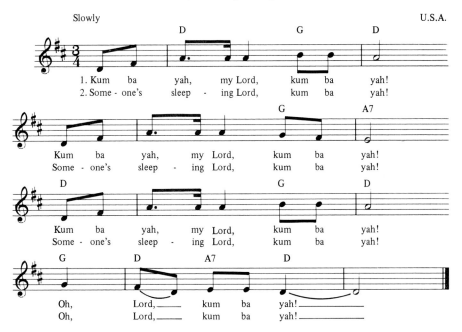

1. Kum ba yah, my Lord, kum ba yah!
2. Some - one's sleep - ing Lord, kum ba yah!

Kum ba yah, my Lord, kum ba yah!
Some - one's sleep - ing Lord, kum ba yah!

Kum ba yah, my Lord, kum ba yah!
Some - one's sleep - ing Lord, kum ba yah!

Oh, Lord,____ kum ba yah!____
Oh, Lord,____ kum ba yah!____

3. Someone's praying, Lord, kum ba yah! (three times)
   Oh, Lord, kum ba yah!

4. Someone's shouting, Lord, kum ba yah! (three times)
   Oh, Lord, kum ba yah!

5. Someone's singing, Lord, kum ba yah! (three times)
   Oh, Lord, kum ba yah!

Lady, Come

England

Lady, come, Can't you see?
1 2 3 3 4 5
do re mi mi fa so

John fell off the white oak tree.
5 4 3 1 3 2 1
so fa mi do mi re do

From Patricia Hackett, *The Melody Book,* © 1983, p. 110. Reprinted by permission of Prentice-Hall, Inc., Englewood Cliffs, New Jersey.

Keyboard 3

Recorder 2

The Little Man Who Wasn't There

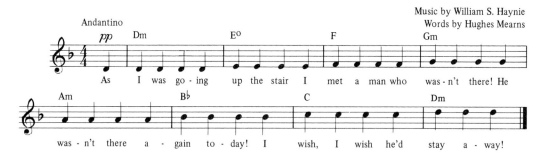

Music by William S. Haynie
Words by Hughes Mearns

As I was go-ing up the stair I met a man who was-n't there! He
was-n't there a-gain to-day! I wish, I wish he'd stay a-way!

From *The Music Book,* K, copyright © 1981 by Holt, Rinehart and Winston, Publishers. Reprinted by permission of the publisher.

Lullaby Round

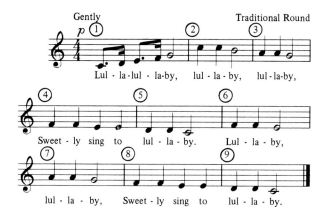

The Muffin Man

England

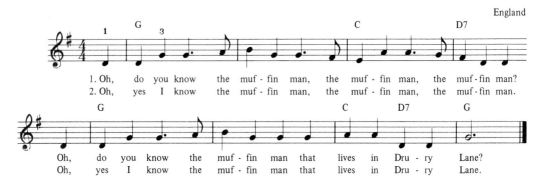

1. Oh, do you know the muf - fin man, the muf - fin man, the muf - fin man?
2. Oh, yes I know the muf - fin man, the muf - fin man, the muf - fin man.

Oh, do you know the muf - fin man that lives in Dru - ry Lane?
Oh, yes I know the muf - fin man that lives in Dru - ry Lane.

Instrumental arrangement by Ken Spanney.

What other occupations can be reflected in this song?
Oh, do you know the carpenter? schoolteacher? doctor? astronaut?
That lives in Tennessee? Awbrey Park? a big white house? Beaverton?

Use last four measures of melody with instrumental introduction.

Non-pitched Percussion

Claves

Play four times each verse, two times for introduction.

Tambourine

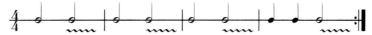

Play twice for each verse, once for introduction.

Triangle

Strike on the word YES each time.

The Muffin Man

Recorders

PITCHED PERCUSSION

Glockenspiel 1, (or Chime Bars)

Introduction

Glockenspiel 2, (or Chime Bars)

Glockenspiel 3, (or Xylophone)

Glockenspiel 4, (or Metallophone)

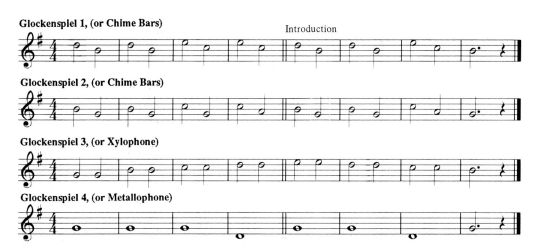

The Old Brass Wagon

Allegramante   U.S.A.

1. Cir-cle to the left, the old brass wag-on, Cir-cle to the left, the old brass wag-on,
2. Cir-cle to the right, the old brass wag-on, Cir-cle to the right, the old brass wag-on,

Cir-cle to the left, the old brass wag-on, You're the one, my dar-ling.
Cir-cle to the right, the old brass wag-on, You're the one, my dar-ling.

Old MacDonald Had a Farm

Allegro   U.S.A.

Old Mac-Don-ald had a farm, E - I - E - I - O!

And on this farm he had some chicks, E - I - E - I - O!
And on this farm he had some ducks, E - I - E - I - O!

With a Chick, chick here, and a chick, chick there   Here a chick, there a chick,
With a Quack, quack here, and a quack, quack, there   Here a quack, there a quack,

Ev-'ry-where a chick, chick.   Old Mac-Don-ald had a farm, E - I - E - I - O!
Ev-'ry-where a quack, quack.

Repetition of line one is optional when adding animals. This is a cumulative song. After the sound of a new animal is sung, all the previous ones are sung in reverse order:

moo, moo

quack, quack

chick, chick

and so on.

Orchestra Song

Andante   Austria

Horn

The horn, the horn a - wakes me at morn, The
horn, the horn a - wakes me at morn.

Keyboard 9

Autoharp 4

Guitar 4

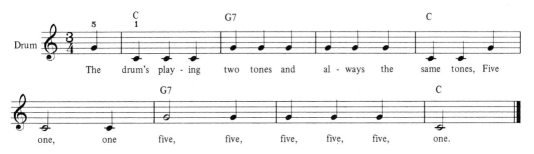

Drum

The drum's play - ing two tones and al - ways the same tones, Five
one, one five, five, five, five, five, one.

Keyboard 10

Recorder 5

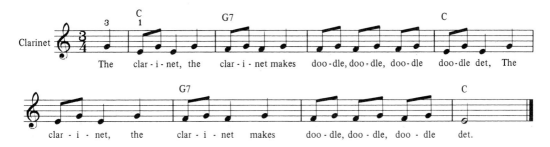

Clarinet

The clar - i - net, the clar - i - net makes doo - dle, doo - dle, doo - dle doo - dle det, The
clar - i - net, the clar - i - net makes doo - dle, doo - dle, doo - dle det.

Keyboard 11

Recorder 6

The trum-pet is sound - ing ti ti ti   ti tu tu ti ti ti ti   ti tu tu ta. The

trum - pet   is   sound - ing ti ti ti   ti tu tu ti ti ti ti   ta - a.

The   vi - o - lin's   ring - ing   like   love - ly___ sing - ing, The

vi - o - lin's   ring - ing   like   love - ly___ song.

Keyboard 12

Recorder 7

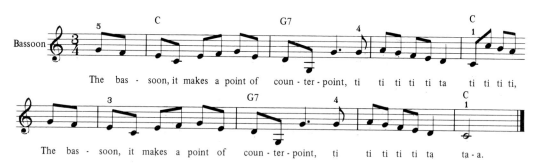

The bas - soon, it makes a point of coun - ter - point, ti   ti ti ti ti ta   ti ti ti ti,

The bas - soon, it makes a point of coun - ter - point, ti   ti ti ti ti ta   ta - a.

Keyboard 13

Recorder 8

Over the River and Through the Woods

Allegro

Traditional

1. O-ver the riv-er and through the wood, To grand - fa - ther's house we
2. O-ver the riv-er and through the wood, And straight through the barn - yard

go;___ The horse knows the way to car-ry the sleigh Through the white and drift - ed
gate,___ We seem ___ to go ex-treem-ly slow It ___ is so hard to

snow.___ O-ver the riv-er and through the wood, Oh, how the wind does blow!___
wait!___ O-ver the riv-er and through the wood, Now grand-moth-er's cap I spy!___

It stings the toes and bites the nose As o-ver the ground we go.___
Hur - rah for the fun! Is the pud-ding done? Hur - rah tor the pump-kin pie!___

Philippine School Song
(Umupo Po)

Philippines

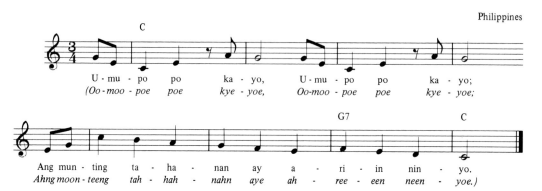

U - mu - po po ka - yo,   U - mu - po po ka - yo;
(Oo - moo - poe poe kye - yoe,   Oo - moo - poe poe kye - yoe;

Ang mun - ting ta - ha - nan ay a - ri - in nin - yo.
Ahng moon - teeng tah - hah - nahn aye ah - ree - een neen - yoe.)

From Patricia Hackett, *The Melody Book,* © 1983, p. 157. Reprinted by permission of Prentice-Hall, Inc., Englewood Cliffs, New Jersey.

Translation:

"Have a seat please, dear sir! (twice)

Feel at home, o dear sir,

as you sit in our chair."

Polly Wolly Doodle

Response Section, Additional Parts (Tape 1)

Rocky Mountain

♩ = 80

U.S.A.

1. Rock - y moun - tain, rock - y moun - tain, rock - y moun - tain high,
2. Rock - y moun - tain, rock - y moun - tain, rock - y moun - tain sky,

When you reach that rock - y moun - tain hang your head and cry.
When you reach that rock - y moun - tain spread your wings and fly.

Refrain:

Do, do, do, do, do re - mem - ber me,

Do, do, do, do, do re - mem - ber me.

From Patricia Hackett, *The Melody Book*, © 1983, p. 176. Reprinted by permission of Prentice-Hall, Inc., Englewood Cliffs, New Jersey.

Roll Over

Allegro   F♯ |1, 2, 3, 4, 5, 6, 7, 8, 9.   U.S.A.

1. There were ten in the bed, and the lit-tle one said, "Roll
2. There were nine in the bed, and the lit-tle one said, "Roll
3.-9.
10. There was

o - ver, roll o - ver," So they all rolled o - ver and
o - ver, roll o - ver," So they all rolled o - ver and

one fell out. lit-tle one said, "Good - night!"

Shalom Chaverim

Moderato   Israel

Shal - om, cha-ve-rim! Sha - lom, cha-ve-rim! Sha - lom, sha - lom!

Le - hit - ra - ot, le - hit - ra - ot, Sha - lom, sha - lom.

Shalom usually is interpreted to mean "peace." It is used as both a greeting and a way of saying farewell.

Shoo, Fly

Moderato
Refrain

U.S.A.

Shoo fly, don't both-er me, Shoo fly, don't both-er me,
Shoo fly, don't both-er me, For I be-long to some-bod-y.

Verse

I feel, I feel, I feel, I feel like a morn-ing star,
I feel, I feel, I feel, I feel, I feel like a morn-ing star. So

Shroom Song

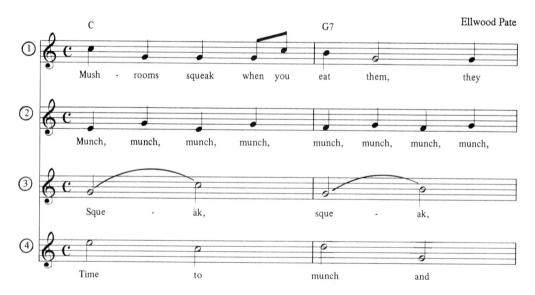

Ellwood Pate

1. Mush-rooms squeak when you eat them, they
2. Munch, munch, munch, munch, munch, munch, munch, munch,
3. Sque - ak, sque - ak,
4. Time to munch and

Written by James Meyer as an assignment for Classroom Instruments in 1984 when he was an undergraduate music education and performance (trombone) major at the School of Music, University of Oregon. Used with permission.

Singing on the Old Camp Ground

We're sing-ing, we're sing-ing to-night, We're sing-ing on the old camp-ground,

We're sing-ing,— sing-ing to-night, we're sing-ing on the old camp-ground.

2. We're clapping . . .
3. We're stamping . . .
4. We're clicking . . .
5. We're walking . . .
6. We're sleeping . . .

Skin and Bones

1. There was an old wom-an all skin and bones, Oo - oo - oo - ooh!
2. One night she thought she'd take a walk, Oo - oo - oo - ooh!

She lived down by the old grave - yard, Oo - oo - oo - ooh! *(To verse 3)*
She walked down by the old grave - yard, Oo - oo - oo - ooh! *(To verse 3)*

Coda
She o - pened the door and BOO!

3. She saw the bones a-layin' around,
   Oo-oo-oo-ooh!
   She went to the closet to get a broom,
   Oo-oo-oo-ooh! *(To coda)*

Collected, with music and additional new words, by Jean Ritchie. © 1952 Jean Ritchie, Geordie Music Publishing Co.

Skip to My Lou

Flies in the but-ter-milk, Shoo fly, shoo, Flies in the but-ter-milk, Shoo fly, shoo,

Flies in the but-ter-milk, Shoo fly, shoo, Skip to my lou, my dar - ling.

Lou, lou, Skip to my lou, Lou, lou, Skip to my lou,

Lou, lu, Skip to my lou, Skip to my lou, my dar - ling.

Summer Is A-Coming In

England

Sum - mer is a - com - ing in; ___ Loud - ly sing, cuck - oo! ___

Grow - eth seed and blow - eth mead, And spring - eth wood a -

new. ___ Sing, cuck - oo! Ewe ___ bleat - eth af - ter lamb; Low'th

af - ter calf the cow; Bul - lock start - eth buck, too, vert - eth;

Mer - ry sing, cuck - oo! Cuck - oo, cuck - oo! ___

Well singst thou, cuck - oo; ___ Oh, cease thou nev - er now.

Swing Low, Sweet Chariot

U.S.A.

Swing low, sweet char - i - ot,___ Com - ing for to car - ry me home!

Swing_ low, sweet char - i - ot,___ Com - ing for to car - ry me home.

I looked o - ver Jor - dan, and what did I see?___ Com - ing for to car - ry me home,

A band_ of an - gels com - ing af - ter me,___ Com - ing for to car - ry me home.

Tell Me Why

2. Because God made the stars to shine,
   Because God made the ivy twine,
   Because God made the sky so blue,
   Because God made you, that's why I love you.

Ten Little Indians

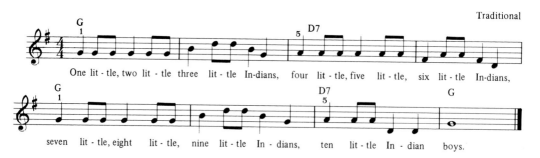

Sing again; start with ten; sing the numbers backwards.

Keyboard 15

Recorder 9

This Train

U.S.A.

Andante

1. This train is bound for glory, this train;
2. This train won't car - ry sleep - ers, this train;

This train is bound for glory, this train;
This train won't car - ry sleep - ers, this train;

This train is bound for glo - ry, I'm not tell - ing you a sto - ry,
This train won't car - ry sleep - ers, It has none but right - eous peo - ple,

1.3. This train is leav - ing, get on board!

The Wild Colonial Boy

Australia
Arranged by Ken Spanney

2. In sixty-one this daring youth commenced his wild career
   With a heart that knew no danger, no foeman did he fear,
   He held up the Beechworth mail-couch and robbed Judge MacEvey,
   Who trembled and gave up his gold to the wild colonial boy.

3. One day as he was riding the mountain side along,
   Listening to the little birds, their pleasant laughing song,
   Three mounted troopers came in view, Kelly, Davis and Fitzroy,
   They swore that they would capture him, the wild colonial boy.

4. "Surrender now Jack Dolan, you see there's three to one,
   Surrender now Jack Dolan, you daring highwayman,"
   He took a pistol from his belt, and shook the little toy,
   "I'll fight but not surrender," said the wild colonial boy.

5. He fired at trooper Kelly, and brought him to the ground,
   And in return from Davis received his mortal wound,
   All shattered through the jaw he lay still firing at Fitzroy,
   And that's the way they captured him, the wild colonial boy.

The Wild Colonial Boy

Arranged by Ken Spanney

Pitched Percussion or Recorders

Will You Come?

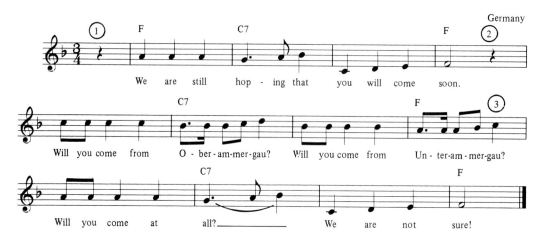

Germany

We are still hop - ing that you will come soon.

Will you come from O - ber - am - mer - gau? Will you come from Un - ter - am - mer - gau?

Will you come at all?_____ We are not sure!

Used with permission of Hilde Kupfer.

Heut' Kommt der Hans

Heut' kommt der Hans zu mir, freut sichdie Lies'; ob er aber uber
Oberammergau oder aber uber Unterammergau oder aber uberhaupt
nicht kommt, ist nicht gewiss.

The number over the rest shows the beat necessary to match "Hark to the Singing" when these songs are used as partner songs.

Yankee Doodle

Allegro U.S.A.

1. Yan - kee Doo - dle went to town, A - rid - ing on a po - ny;
Stuck a feath - er in his hat And called it mac - a - ro - ni.

Chorus

Yan - kee Doo - dle keep it up, Yan - kee Doo - dle dan - dy;
Mind the mu - sic and the step And with the girls be hand - y.

2. Father and I went down to camp
   Along with Captain Gooding;
   And there we saw the men and boys
   As thick as hasty pudding.

3. There was Captain Washington,
   Upon a slapping stallion,
   A-giving orders to his men,
   I guess there was a million.

Yellow Rose of Texas

Moderato   U.S.A.

1. There's a Yel - low Rose in Tex - as I'm go - ing there to see,
2. Oh, I'm go - ing back to find her, my heart is full of woe,

No oth - er fel - low knows her, No - bod - y, on - ly me.
We'll sing the songs to - geth - er We sang so long a - go.

She ___ cried so when I left her, It al - most broke her heart,
I'll ___ pick the ban - jo gai - ly, And sing the songs of yore,

And if we ev - er meet a - gain, we nev - er more shall part.
The Yel - low Rose of Tex - as She'll be mine for - ev - er - more.

Zum Gali Gali

Hechalutz le 'man hab'tulah;
Hab'tulah le 'man hechalutz

Hashalom le 'man ha'amim;
Ha'amim le 'man hashalom.

Repeat the first two measures as an accompanying ostinato for the melody.

APPENDIX

DISCOGRAPHY

The tape accompanying this book contains selected music to help amplify the explanations and musical experiences for you. Because this tape is very short in comparison with the amount of music created through the centuries, it can only be regarded as an *introduction* to a variety of listening experiences. Find additional music to amplify the information presented in this book, particularly when only a portion of a piece is included on your tape. Seek records and tapes in libraries and music stores.

To find musical references on the tape efficiently, use an *audio cassette tape player* with a *counter*. Set the counter to "0", then *write the number* shown on the counter for each *piece* as you listen to the entire tape. The time for each selection is written between the blank for the counter number and the title to help you find the beginning of the pieces. You will hear the number of each selection spoken immediately prior to each selection.

Side One

1. ——— (1:57) "Response Section." Karen J. Wilson, claves; Mary McKean, piano; Coleman Sholl, assorted percussion; Timothy M. Roberson, recorder. (Courtesy of University of the Pacific students, Stockton, CA.)

2. ———— (1:07) "Antiphon: Salve Regina." Schola Antiqua. R. John Blackley, director. (Courtesy of Vanguard Records, a Welk Record Group Company. VSD 71217)

3. ———— (2:40) "Takes Two to Tango," from *The Best of Pearl Bailey.* (Courtesy of Roulette Records, a division of ABZ Music Corp.)

4. ———— (3:42) "Ev'ry Valley Shall Be Exalted," from *The Messiah,* George Frideric Handel. William Kendall, tenor; London Handel Orchestra; Martin Neary, conductor. (Courtesy of Musical Heritage Society.)

5. ———— (2:25) "Sixty-seventh Psalm," Charles Ives. Conservatory of Music, University of the Pacific, A Cappella Choir, William J. Dehning, conductor. (Courtesy of University of the Pacific students and Conductor Dehning.)

6. ———— (7:02) "Danse Sacrale," excerpt from *Le Sacre du Printemps,* Igor Stravinsky. Strasbourg Philharmonic Orchestra; Alain Lombard, conductor. (Courtesy of Musical Heritage Society.)

7. ———— (1:46) "Country Gardens," from *Percy Grainger Plays Grainger.* Player-piano rolls transferred to phonograph discs. (Courtesy of Everest Records.)

8. ———— (2:41) "Semper Fidelis," John Philip Sousa. (Courtesy of EMC Productions)

9. ———— (4:19) "Bring Me Little Water, Silvy," Pete Seeger. (Courtesy of Vanguard Records, a Welk Record Group Company.)

10. ———— (9:15) "Variations on 'America'," Charles Ives. Andrew Davis, organ. (Courtesy of Marquis Records of Canada.)

11. ———— (3:13) "Movement I: Zart und Mit Ausdruck" ("Tenderly with Expression"), from *Phantasiestücke (Fantasy Pieces),* Robert Schumann. William C. Dominik, clarinet, and Wolfgang Fetsch, piano. (Courtesy of the artists, faculty members of the Conservatory of Music, University of the Pacific.)

Side Two

12. ———— (4:23) "Andante," from *Concerto in E-Flat Major,* Joseph Haydn. Maurice Andre, trumpet; Bamberg Symphony Orchestra; Theodor Guschebauer, conductor. (Courtesy of Musical Heritage Society.)

13. ———— (1:53) "Orchestra Song," Austrian. Paul Kimball, horn; Coleman Sholl, timpani; Karen J. Wilson, clarinet; Edwin C. Powell, trumpet; Jody McComb, violin; Jean E. Neven, bassoon. (Courtesy of University of the Pacific students.)

14. ———— (2:46) "Til Eulenspiegel's Merry Pranks," Richard Strauss. Czech Philharmonic Orchestra; Ondrej Lenrad, conductor. (Courtesy of Musical Heritage Society.)

15. ——— (0:38) "The Young Person's Guide to the Orchestra," Benjamin Britten. English Chamber Orchestra; Johannes Somary, conductor. (Courtesy of Vanguard Records, a Welk Record Group Company. VSD 71189)

16. ——— (2:26) "Triste" (*Sonata in F Minor*), George Philip Telemann. Andrew Cordle, bassoon; Christine Daxelhofer, harpsichord. (Courtesy of Orion Records.)

17. ——— (5:05) "Bravour, Variations on a Theme from Mozart, 'Ah! Vous Dirai-Je, Maman'," Adolphe Adam. Margaret Dehning, soprano; Carol van Bronkhorst, flute; Joan Coulter, piano. Produced and recorded by Kuop Productions. Engineered by Doug Huft and Jeff Crawford. (Courtesy of the artists.)

18. ——— (5:22) "Modéré," excerpt from *Trio for Piano, Violin and Cello in A Minor*, Maurice Ravel. Klaus Heitz, cello; Yvon Carracilly, violin; Henri Barda, piano. (Courtesy of Musical Heritage Society.)

19. ——— (4:42) "Prelude to the Afternoon of a Faun" (excerpt), Claude Debussy. Czech Philharmonic Orchestra; Ondrej Lenrad, conductor. (Courtesy of Musical Heritage Society.)

20. ——— (3:33) "Hallelujah Chorus," from *The Messiah*, George Frideric Handel. The Royal Philharmonic Orchestra; London Ambrosian Chorus; Paul Freeman, conductor. (Courtesy of Musical Heritage Society.)

21. ——— (1:45) "Bird Song," from *Indian Music of the Southwest*. Recorded by Linda Boulton. Mojave-Parker, Arizona. Men and women with rattle. (Courtesy of TRF Music, Folkways FW 8850.)

22. ——— (0:43) "Djamu the Dingo," from *Songs of Bamyili*. Artist: David Blanatji, a didgeridoo solo. (Courtesy of Aboriginal Artists Agency.)

23. ——— (2:11) "Bungalin, Bungalin, A Love Song." from *Songs of Bamyili*. Artists: Tjoli Laiwangka, voice; Tom Yorkdjanki, didgeridoo. (Courtesy of Aboriginal Artists Agency.)

TEMPO MARKS

A TEMPO, perform at original speed; often used after a ritard

ACCELERANDO, quickening

ADAGISSIMO, very slow

ADAGIO, slow

ANDANTE, moderately, a walking tempo

ANDANTINO, faster than *andante*

ALLARGANDO, gradually slower

ALLEGRAMENTE, moving faster than andante

ALLEGRETTO, rather fast

ALLEGRO, fast

ASSAI, very (used after another word)

-ETTO, diminutive used at end of a word; makes *larghetto* a little less slow than *largo,* makes *allegretto* a little less fast than *allegro,* and so on

CALANDO, getting slower and softer

CON, with (used before another word, often referring to style rather than tempo), as *con brio,* with vigor; *con moto,* with motion, and so on

GRAVE, heavy, ponderous

-INO, diminutive used at end of a word; makes *andantino* a little less slow than *andante,* and so on

-ISSIMO, suffix meaning "very"; makes lentissimo slower than lento, makes prestissimo faster than presto, and so on

LARGAMENTE, very slow

LARGHETTO, less slow than largo

LARGHISSIMO, very broad

LARGO, broad

LENTO, slow

MENO MOSSO, steady, but slower than preceding tempo

MENO MOTO, same as *meno mosso*

MODERATO, moderate

MOLTO, same as *assai* (used after another word)

PIÙ, more (used before another word)

PIÙ MOSSO, steady, but faster than preceding tempo

PIÙ MOTO, same as più mosso

POCO, a little (used before another word)

PRESTISSIMO, very, very fast

PRESTO, very fast

RALLENTANDO, gradually slower

RITARDANDO, slackening

RITENUTO, holding back

RUBATO, changing in response to music

SMORZANDO, fading away and slowing

STRINGENDO, accelerating swiftly

VIVACE, lively

DYNAMIC MARKS

ALPHABETICAL LISTING

CRESCENDO (CRESC.), becoming gradually louder, also shown by

DECRESCENDO (DECRESC.), becoming gradually softer, also shown by

DIMINUENDO (DIM.), becoming gradually softer

FORTE (f), loud

FORTE-PIANO (fp), loud followed immediately by soft

FORTISSIMO (ff), very loud

-ISSIMO, very (used at the end of a word)

MEZZO, moderately, (used before another word)

MEZZO FORTE (mf), moderately loud

MEZZO PIANO (mp), moderately soft

PIANISSIMO (pp), very soft

PIANO (p), soft

PIÙ, more; **PIÙ FORTE** makes loud into louder

SFORZANDO (sf), sudden accent followed immediately by piano

SFORZATO (sfz), sudden accent followed immediately by piano

GRADATION OF DYNAMICS

← · · · · · softer

ppp　pp　p　mp　mf　f　ff　fff

louder · · · · · →

MUSIC ANALYSIS SHEET

Name of piece

Composer or source

Key   Meter

Characteristics of the melody

Special rhythmic characteristics

Chords needed to harmonize

Form

Dynamics   Tempo

Style of performance (including accompaniment)

Performance media

Other expressive devices

Creative additions

Special problems

Additional comments

MUSIC ANALYSIS SHEET

ELABORATION

When filling out the *MAS,* scrutinize the music as carefully as possible. In addition to filling in the blanks, consider the implications of the analysis. If the music is influenced by the text, tell about it in "additional comments." That is also the space to write about any considerations not previously covered, such as comparisons with other music, or specific characteristics you have noted in other musical examples, historical or sociological settings related to the music, information about the composer or the use of the music.

In discussing the "characteristics of the melody," describe its *shape* (movement up or down, or staying the same), *intervals* (unusual or difficult), *range* (the lowest and highest pitches), *voice leading* (flow of the melody from one note to the other), and so on. When studying the melody, look up new notes on fingering charts in the instrument book if you plan to play it.

Analysis of the "rhythmic characteristics" should result in advance practice of patterns, especially if they are difficult for you. Do patterns repeat? Are they associated with the same pitches when they repeat? Do sequences appear?

How many different chords are needed to harmonize the piece? Is their progression repeated during the piece? If you intend to play the piece, turn to fingering charts for help with new chords. Practice progressions before putting them with the melody if they are new or difficult.

Analysis of the form saves extra work by helping you recognize sections you have already analyzed or can perform, and by challenging you to identify parts differing from previously mastered material that will need attention. Formal analysis can also help you to anticipate differences and so prevent errors.

The tempo and dynamics may or may not be previously assigned in your music. If they are not, you should decide what is appropriate for the piece. Let expressive devices influence your interpretation of the style of the composition. "Style" refers to the combination of the elements of music and the way they are treated to give characteristics to the music that proclaim its individuality. The style should reflect the music's historical period, country of origin, composer, and so on. Just as a jazz vocal solo differs from an operatic aria, so does the way a jazz vocalist performs vary from the way an opera singer performs.

"Performance media" refers to the *timbre* (voices or instruments used to perform the music). Style and expressive devices should be considered when choosing the performance media.

Generally, "other expressive devices" refers to musical devices, but it may also refer to an area especially prepared as a listening arena, a costume worn to enhance the performance of the music, artwork related to the composition, and so on.

As you develop confidence in your music making, you should feel increasingly free to add creatively to the music you perform. At first your creativity may be reflected in expressive devices, such as choosing your own tempo, dynamics, and instruments; later, you may reharmonize melodies or create ostinatos, descants, or countermelodies; then, you may begin to create your own music. The *MAS* will help you organize your decisions when you compose as well as when you analyze other compositions.

If there are special problems with the music, be sure to describe them. The analysis itself may help you deal with the problems more effectively by identifying their nature.

RHYTHM SYLLABLE CHART

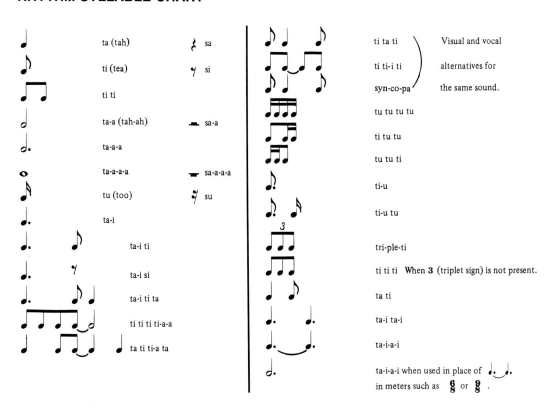

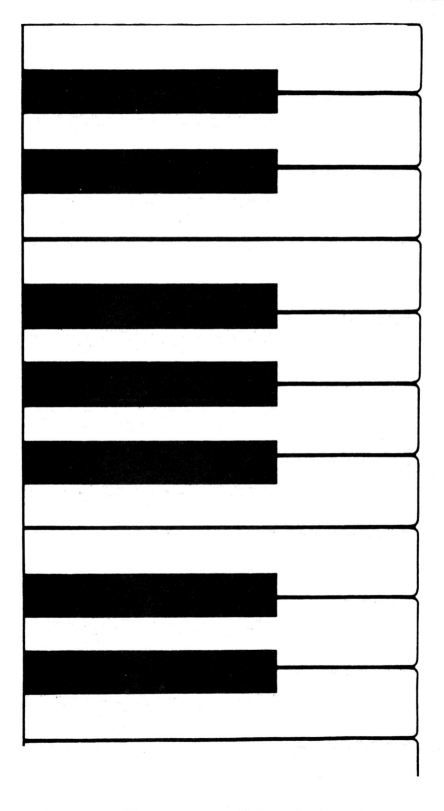

ANSWERS

CHAPTER ONE

p. 8

Old MacDonald Had a Farm

p. 8 The answer depends on what you are looking for in the form of the Pearl Bailey selection. Consider two alternatives:

1. If you are listening for the overall form of the selection on the tape, you may analyze the piece as having an introduction, followed by a vocal rendition of the song, followed by an instrumental section, and finally another similar vocal rendition with a brief coda (ending) after it. The form label matching this description is intro–*AB*–coda.

2. If you wish only to analyze the form of the song as sung once through, you should analyze it as *AB*. This label refers only to the song without considering the parts of the selection played by the instruments.

CHAPTER TWO

p. 14

	Notes	Rests
whole	𝅝	▬
half	𝅗𝅥	▬
quarter	♩	𝄽
eighth	♪	𝄾
sixteenth	𝅘𝅥𝅯	𝄿

p. 16

Dat - sun   Volks - wag-en   Ford

Colt   Su - ba - ru   Bu - ick

Chev-ro-let   Vol - vo   Hon - da

Olds-mo-bile   Chrys - ler   Au - di

Pon-ti-ac   Ca - dil - lac   Lin-coln-Mer-cu-ry

p. 22

F E E   G A G E   C A B B A G E   D E E D   A

D E A D   F E E D   A D A G E   B E D   B E E F

p. 22

B A G B   A G   G   G   G A   A   A   B A G

p. 23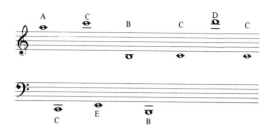

p. 24

p. 24

CHAPTER THREE

p. 27

p. 27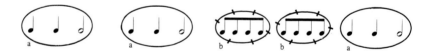

p. 29 There are four measures in "Hot Cross Buns."

p. 29 When using the time signature $\frac{4}{4}$ for "Hot Cross Buns," the half-note gets two beats; eighth-notes get half a beat.

p. 29

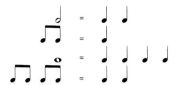

p. 29   These examples all use the $\frac{4}{4}$ meter signature. The top number tells you there are *4* beats in a measure; the bottom number tells you the *quarter* note gets one beat.

p. 29

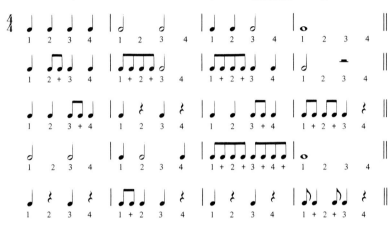

p. 36

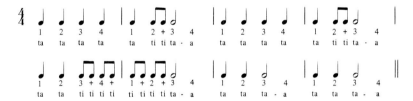

p. 36

p. 39   This one ($\frac{3}{4}$) shows that there are _3_ beats in a measure, and the _quarter_ note gets one count.

p. 39

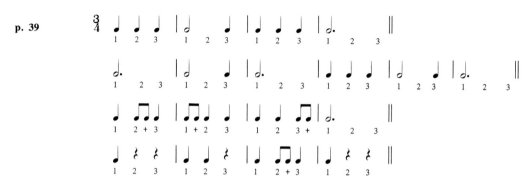

p. 40

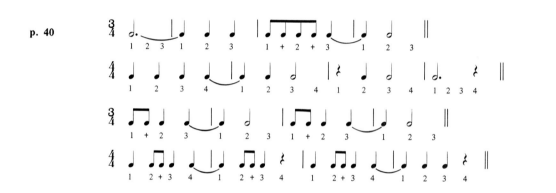

p. 40   The meter signature ¢ stands for $\frac{2}{2}$. That means there are _2_ beats in the measure, and the _half-note_ gets one beat. If the half-note gets one beat, what will the dotted half-note get? _1½_

p. 41   With a meter signature of $\frac{2}{2}$,

$\textstyle\frac{}{}$ 𝅗𝅥 = 1

𝅗𝅥. = 1 1/2

♩ = 1/2

♪ = 1/4

𝅘𝅥𝅯 = 1/8

𝅝 = 2

p. 41

p. 42

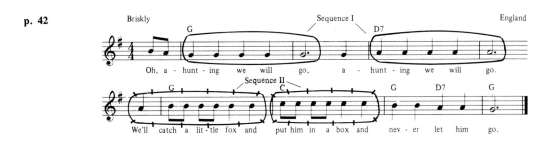

p. 44
1. Are all the sections in the same key? *Yes*
2. What key are they in? *Key of C*
3. What meter signature is used? $\frac{3}{4}$
4. Analyze the form of each section. Notate the form with letters under each section. *All AA' except the horn (AA).*

p. 45
5. How many different chords are needed to accompany this piece? *2*
6. Compare the placement of chord changes in all the sections. *Change in the same measures for all sections.*
7. With what pitch does each section begin? *All begin on G.*
8. Which of the sections begin with an anacrusis? *All do.*

p. 47

p. 48

Rossini, theme from
"William Tell Overture"

Scarlatti, Sonata in G

p. 50

p. 50

p. 51 • Put the number of the matching rhythm pattern after the composer's name: Gounod <u>4</u>, Schubert <u>3</u>, Schumann <u>5</u>, Tchaikovsky <u>2</u>.

p. 51 • Draw *one* note to equal these tied notes.

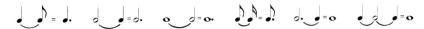

p. 51 • Draw *two* notes to equal these dotted notes.

p. 52

p. 52

1.

a. ta si ti ta si ti ti ti ti ti ta sa ta si ti ta si ti ti ti ti ti ta sa

b. ta-i ti ta-i ti ti ti ti ti ta sa ta-i ti ta-i ti ti ti ti ti ta sa

2.

a. ta sa ti ti ti ti ta si ti ta si ti ta si ti ti ti ti ti ta-a sa-a

b. ta sa ti ti ti ti ta-i ti ta-i ti ta-i ti ti ti ti ti ta-a sa-a

3.

a. ta-a sa ta si ti ti ti ta-a sa ta si ti ti ti ta-a sa

b. ta-a sa ta-i ti ti ti ta-a sa ta-i ti ti ti ta-a sa

4.

a. ta si ti ti ti ta si ti ti ti ta si ti ti ti ti ti ti ti ti ta sa sa

b. ta-i ti ti ti ta-i ti ti ti ta-i ti ti ti ti ti ti ti ti ta sa sa

p. 54

African Noel

The four examples of syncopation are circled.

p. 55

Key of G: I = G, IV = C, V_7 = D_7.

p. 56

The least definite cadence in the "Alphabet Song" is at the end of the second (*B*) phrase. Its last melodic pitch is D, instead of the final sounding key-tone C that ends the first and third (*A*) phrases; the last chord of the phrase is a G chord instead of the C chord that finalizes the *A* phrases.

p. 58

Each phrase of the melody for "Ten Little Indians" is two measures long. The last cadence seems more final than the others because (1) the last note is held longer; (2) the pitches before the last one lead into it very strongly as they leap from the lower D to the higher G; (3) the harmony of the last two measures uses two chords (one in each measure) that help give a feeling of final resolution on the last measure.

p. 58   "Auld Lang Syne" is in the key of G. Its form is *ABCB*. Notice that the second measure appears in the *A* and *B* phrases. It also appears in the *C* phrase with only the last note altered. The first measure of the *B* phrase is the same as the first and third measures of the *C* phrase. Three different chords are used: G, D7, and C. The meter signature indicates four beats in a measure with the quarter-note getting one beat.

"Dance in a Circle" is in the key of G. It is a round whose three phrases differ from each other. Phrase two is sequential to phrase one. Phrase three is completely different. The recorder and percussion parts that accompany it are ostinatos that repeat indefinitely and are compatible with all the phrases. Three different chords are used: G, C, and D7. The meter signature indicates three beats in a measure with the quarter-note getting one beat.

"The Muffin Man" is in the key of G. Its form is *AA'*. Although the percussion parts for this piece are ostinatos, the recorder parts are not. They have an introduction and differ in each phrase. It uses three chords: G, C, and D7. The meter signature indicates four beats in a measure with the quarter-note getting one beat.

"Polly Wolly Doodle" is in the key of G. Its form is *ABCB'*. The beginning of the *B* phrases are sequential to the beginning of the *A* phrase. Two different chords are used: G and D7. The meter signature indicates four beats in a measure with the quarter-note getting one beat.

The "Shroom Song" is in the key of C. Its form is *AA'* for each of its four independent parts. The parts combine polyphonically. It uses two chords: C and G7. The meter signature indicates four beats in a measure with the quarter-note getting one beat.

p. 59   The excerpts are from:
1. "The Birds' Song"
2. "African Noel"
3. "Go to Sleep"
4. "Jesu, Joy of Man's Desiring" (Bach)
5. First theme, fourth movement, *Ninth Symphony* (Beethoven)
6. "Jingle Bells"

CHAPTER FOUR

p. 64   In $\frac{4}{4}$ meter, the ♩ note gets the beat and may be subdivided into 2 ♪
In $\frac{2}{2}$ meter, the 𝅗𝅥 note gets the beat and may be subdivided into 2 ♩.
In $\frac{6}{8}$ meter, the ♪ note gets the beat and may be subdivided into 2 ♫.
In $\frac{3}{16}$ meter, the ♬ note gets the beat and may be subdivided into 2 ♪

p. 65   This means that the eighth-note gets one beat. When this happens, the quarter-note gets _2_ beats, the dotted quarter-note gets _3_ beats, the dotted half-note gets _6_ beats, the half-note gets _4_ beats. How many beats are in each measure? _6_

p. 66   The form of "The Wild Colonial Boy" is *ABCA*.

p. 67

Note	Value in $\frac{6}{8}$ time
	half - beat
	one beat
	two beats
	four beats
	three beats
	one and a half beats

p. 67

Vivace

p. 68

First Theme

Second Theme

Third Theme

Fourth Theme

p. 69   Bach: 3 beats in each measure.

        Handel: 4 beats in each measure.

p. 69

Notes	Value in $\frac{6}{8}$ counting two beats in a measure
♩.	one beat
♩ ♪	one beat
♩	two thirds of a beat
♪	one third of a beat
♪	one sixth of a beat
♩. ♫	one beat
♫♪	one beat
♩.‿♪	one and two-thirds beats

p. 70

$\frac{6}{8}$ counted in six

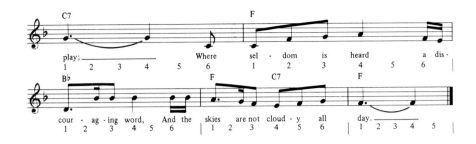

p. 70 §8 counted in 2

p. 72

Kind of note	Number of beats when ♪ gets the beat.
♪	half-beat
♩	one beat
♩	two beats
♩.	three beats
♩. ♩	five beats

p. 73

Kind of note(s)	Number of beats when $\frac{6}{8}$ is counted with two beats in a measure.
♪	one third of a beat
♪ ♪ ♪	one beat
♩ ♪	one beat
♩.	one beat
♩. ♪	one and a third beat

p. 73   "Over the River and Through the Wood" is in the key of _D._
What is its form? _ABAC_

p. 75   In $\frac{2}{2}$:

What kind of note gets one beat? _half-note (♩)_
What kind of note gets half a beat? _quarter-note (♩)_
What kind of note gets three quarters of a beat? _dotted quarter-note (♩.)_

p. 75

p. 75 Sometimes ¢ appears in the meter signature instead of $\frac{2}{2}$. The meaning is the same. How many beats are in a measure of this piece? _2_ What kind of note gets one beat? ♩ What kind of note gets half a beat? ♪ What kind of note gets three quarters of a beat? ♪. What kind of note gets one-and-a-half beats? ♩. What kind of note gets one quarter of a beat? ♪ What kind of note gets three eighths of a beat? ♪.

p. 76

p. 77

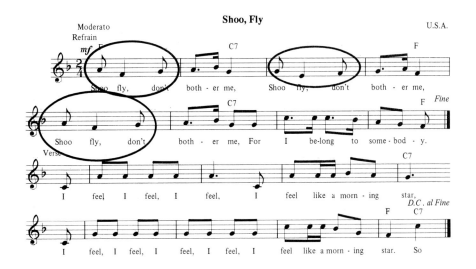

p. 77   <u>*D.C.*</u> means "Go back to the beginning," <u>*al fine*</u> means "continue to the end" (*fine*). "Somebody" is the ending word.

p. 77    is held for 2½ beats

p. 77   The tie is a curved line used with notes of the same pitch. It indicates that the sound carries through the length of as many notes as are tied together with no break in between.

The slur is a curved line used with notes of different pitches. It indicates that there is no break in sound in moving from one pitch to the next. Recorder players should tongue only for the initial pitch. Singers carry the vowel of the first word or syllable into the following pitch.

CHAPTER FIVE

p. 86

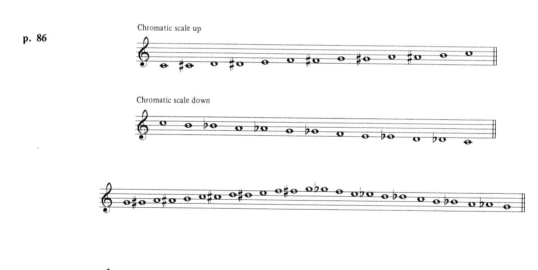

p. 87

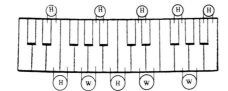

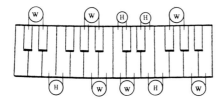

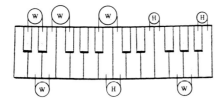

p. 88

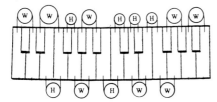

p. 88   <u>6</u> different notes are in a whole-tone scale.

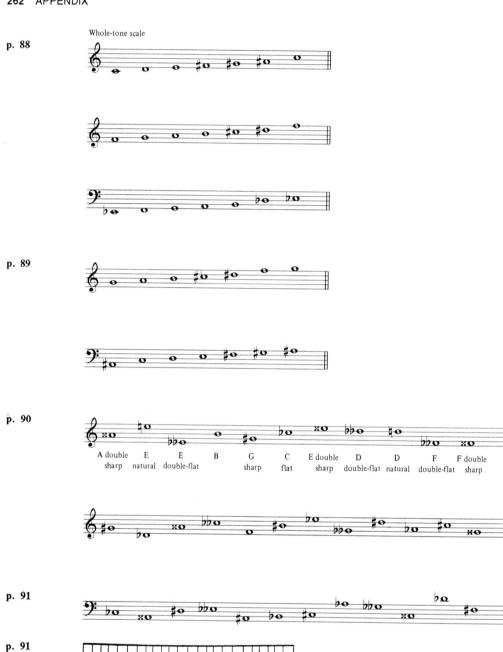

CHAPTER SIX

p. 94

G major scale

D major scale

p. 95

Numbers, syllables, letter names

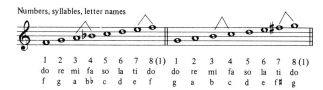

1	2	3	4	5	6	7	8 (1)	1	2	3	4	5	6	7	8 (1)
do	re	mi	fa	so	la	ti	do	do	re	mi	fa	so	la	ti	do
f	g	a	bb	c	d	e	f	g	a	b	c	d	e	f♯	g

p. 96

B-flat major scale, numbers, syllables, letter names

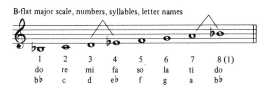

1	2	3	4	5	6	7	8 (1)
do	re	mi	fa	so	la	ti	do
bb	c	d	eb	f	g	a	bb

p. 97

E-flat major scale

A-flat major scale

D-flat major scale

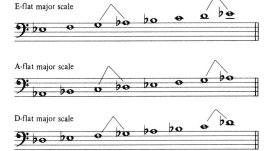

p. 97

A major scale

E major scale

B major scale

p. 98

Analysis of "Lullaby Round"

incomplete ascending C major scale

descending C major scale

Gently

① ② ③

p Lul - la-lul - la-by, lul - la - by, lul - la - by,

④ ⑤ ⑥

Sweet - ly sing to lul - la - by. Lul - la - by,

incomplete descending C major scale

⑦ ⑧ ⑨

lul - la - by, Sweet - ly sing to lul - la - by.

p. 98   There are four beats in each measure; the quarter note gets one beat.
A dot adds half the original value of the note.
Six measures have this rhythm: ♩♩♩
Two measures have this rhythm: ♩♩♩♩
Only one measure has the dotted rhythm.

p. 99   Measures 3 and 7 are the same; so are 4, 6, and 8 and 5 and 9. Six measures have ♩♩♩; two
have ♩♩♩♩.
The form can be described as
introduction (1–2), phrase *A* (3–5), bridge (6), phrase *A* (7–9)
or
introduction (1), phrase *A* repeated (2–5 and 6–9) with the first measure of
both *A* phrases (2 and 6) being the only parts of the phrase that differ.

p. 100   Analysis of "Philippine School Song"

U - mu - po   po   ka - yo,   Oo - mu - po   po   ka - yo;
(Oo - moo - poe   poe   kye - yoe,   Oo - moo - poe   poe   kye - yoe;

Ang mun - ting   ta - ha - nan   ay   a - ri - in   nin - yo.
Ahng moon - teeng   tah - hah - nahn   aye   ah - ree - een   neen - yoe.)

p. 100   Note naming

Eb   Eb   Ab   Bb   Ab   Ab   Bb   Bb

C#   D#   F#   G#   C#   F#   D#   G#

p. 101   Key naming

Eb   Ab

p. 101   Bb   Eb   Ab   Db   F

p. 102   D   A   E   B

p. 102   **Keys of Pieces**
"Skip to My Lou," F major
"Holla Hi, Holla Ho," C major
"Rocky Mountain," E-flat major
"Kum Ba Yah," D major
"Old MacDonald," G major
"Roll Over," F-sharp major

p. 104

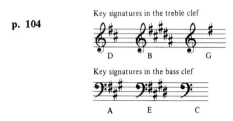

p. 105

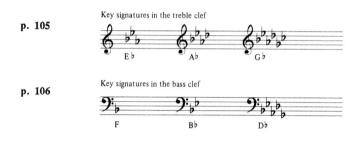

p. 106

p. 107

p. 108 "Roll Over" is in the key of F-sharp major. It is also in F-sharp pentatonic.

CHAPTER SEVEN

p. 111

p. 112

5th 4th 5th 4th 3rd 6th octave prime 6th 3rd 2nd 7th

3rd 5th 2nd 6th 4th 7th prime octave 5th 3rd

Key of D

5th 4th 3rd 6th 7th 2nd

Key of B♭

3rd 6th 4th 5th octave prime

p. 113

maj. 2nd, min. 2nd maj. 3rd, min. 3rd

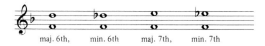

maj. 6th, min. 6th maj. 7th, min. 7th

maj. 2nd, min. 2nd maj. 3rd, min. 3rd

maj. 6th, min. 6th maj. 7th, min. 7th

p. 114

maj. 2nd,   min. 7th   maj. 3rd,   min. 6th

maj. 6th,   min. 3rd   maj. 7th,   min. 2nd

maj. 2nd,   min. 7th   maj. 3rd,   min. 6th

maj. 6th,   min. 3rd   maj. 7th,   min. 2nd

Key of B♭   Key of D   Key of E♭   Key of A   Key of A♭

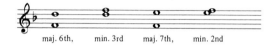

maj. 2nd   min. 7th   maj. 3rd   min. 6th   min. 2nd[

p. 115

perfect: prime octave 4th 5th   5th 4th octave prime

perfect: prime octave   4th   5th   5th   4th   octave   prime

dim. 5th   dim. 3rd   dim. 4th   dim. 7th   dim. octave   dim. 7th   dim. 4th   dim. 3rd

p. 116

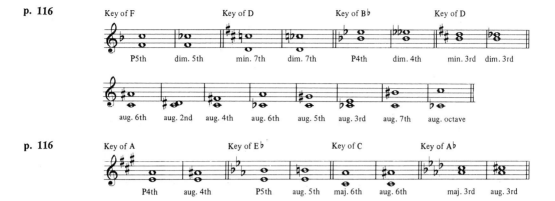

p. 116

The intervals above have been augmented by raising their top note. This could also have been augmented by lowering their bottom note:

p. 117

p. 117

p. 118

p. 119

10th   13th   9th   10th

P5th   maj. 3rd   min. 3rd   min. 2nd   P4th   maj. 2nd   aug. 4th

P octave   min. 6th   maj. 6th   maj. 7th   min. 7th

maj. 7th min. 7th maj. 6th   maj. 7th maj. 6th min. 7th   min. 7th maj. 7th maj. 6th

p. 120

CHAPTER EIGHT

p. 125

p. 127

p. 127

p. 127

p. 129

p. 129

p. 130

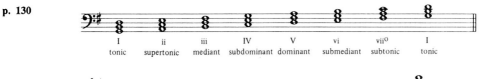

p. 130

p. 131

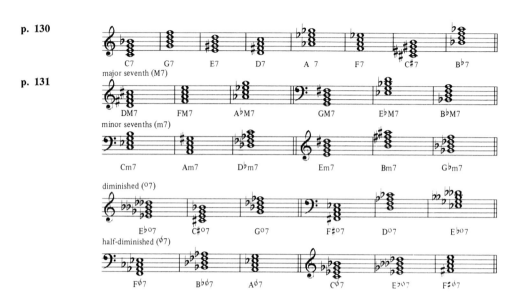

major seventh (M7)

minor sevenths (m7)

diminished (°7)

half-diminished (ø7)

p. 132

p. 132

Holla Hi, Holla Ho

German
Words Adapted

Allegro

Who will go with me to-day? Hol-la hi! Hol-la ho! We'll go hik-ing far a-way,

Hol-la, Hol-la ho! We will leave in the ear-ly morn, Ho-la hi!

Hol-la ho! Then come back when the day-light's gone, Hol-la, Hol-la ho!

p. 132

Kum Ba Yah
(Come By Here)

Slowly and evenly

U.S.A.

Skip to My Lou

p. 133

CHAPTER NINE

p. 136

p. 137 The half-steps of the E natural minor scale occur between *2 and 3* and between *5 and 6*.

p. 137

p. 138 Half-steps in the natural minor scale occur between *2 and 3* and between *5 and 6*.

p. 138 The melody for "The Little Man Who Wasn't There" is based on a D natural minor scale.

p. 138

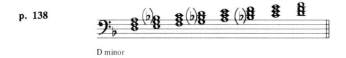

p. 138

p. 139

G Major

p. 140 In major keys, chords numbered *I, IV, V* are major.
In major keys, chords numbered *ii, iii, vi* are minor.
In major keys, the chord numbered *vii* is diminished.

p. 140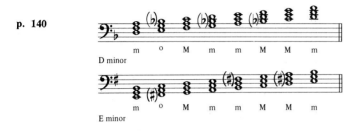

D minor

E minor

p. 140 In natural minor keys, chords numbered *III, VI, VII* are major.
In natural minor keys, chords numbered *i, iv, v* are minor.
In natural minor keys, the chord numbered *ii* is diminished.

p. 140 A minor's relative major is C.

p. 140 It is possible to play only the D minor chord throughout the piece, but that gets monotonous. Try your own ideas: this is one you may like.

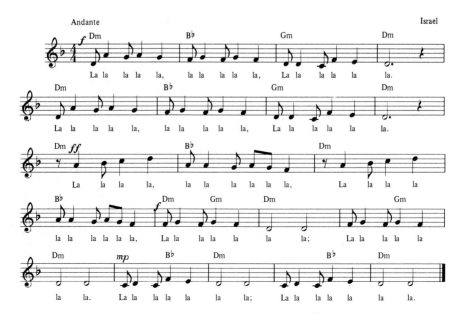

p. 141 These chords are used to accompany "Zum Gali Gali": i (m), iv (m).

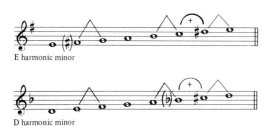

E harmonic minor

D harmonic minor

p. 142 Half steps in the natural minor scale occur between 2 and 3, 5 and 6.
Half steps in the harmonic minor scale occur between 2 and 3, 5 and 6, 7 and 8.
An augmented second is found between 6 and 7 in the harmonic minor scale.

p. 142

E harmonic minor

p. 142

D harmonic minor

p. 142 In harmonic minor keys, chords numbered *V, VI* are major.
In harmonic minor keys, chords numbered *i, iv* are minor.
In harmonic minor keys, chords numbered *ii, vii* are diminished (ii°, vii°).
In harmonic minor keys, the chord numbered *III* is augmented (III+).

p. 142

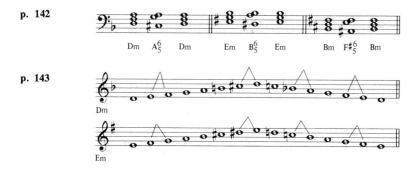

p. 143

Dm

Em

p. 143

p. 143

p. 144 What is the relative minor for these major keys?
A *F♯min*   B-flat *G min*   D *B min*   E *C♯min*
What is the relative major for these minor keys?
Fm *A♭*   A♯m *C♯*   C♯m *E*   Gm *B♭*

p. 144

p. 145

p. 146 The key signature could be either G major (tonic chord: GBD) or e minor (tonic chord: EGB).

p. 147

p. 147

p. 147

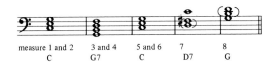

CHAPTER TEN

p. 150

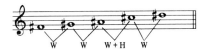

p. 151 In a pentatonic scale,

whole steps occur between *1 and 2, 2 and 3, and 4 and 5.*
a minor third occurs between *3 and 4.*
half-steps occur between *(none).*

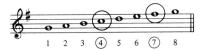

F pentatonic

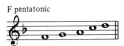

Eb pentatonic

C pentatonic

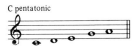

A pentatonic

p. 153   "Old MacDonald" is in the key of G pentatonic. Its meter signature tells that there are four beats in each measure and a quarter-note gets the beat. Its form is AA'BA.

p. 153   The new key for "Old MacDonald" is G-flat pentatonic.

p. 153   "Rocky Mountain" is in E-flat pentatonic. It can be harmonized as if it is in a major key by using the I and V_7 chords.

p. 154   "Rocky Mountain" transposed up a half-step is in E pentatonic.

p. 154   "Swing Low, Sweet Chariot" is in G pentatonic.
Its melody contains no C's or F-sharps.

p. 154   "Singing on the Old Camp Ground" is in F pentatonic.

p. 154   "Ifca's Castle" is in the key of F major.

p. 154   "The Old Brass Wagon" is in G-flat pentatonic.

p. 155   "Skin and Bones" is in G pentatonic.

CHAPTER TWELVE

Since you may wish to consult the score of "Hallelujah," measure numbers are used below along with the words to help identify the texture and the places where it changes.

Measure 4	homophonic entrance of voices (in four parts), "Hallelujah"
Measure 12	monophonic, all voices and orchestra on same melody, "For the Lord God," etc.
Measure 14	homophonic, "Hallelujah"
Measure 17	monophonic, "For the Lord God"
Measure 19	homophonic, "Hallelujah"
Measure 22	polyphonic, "For the Lord God"
Measure 33	homophonic, "The Kinsdom of," etc.
Measure 41	polyphonic, "And He shall reign," etc.
Measure 51	polyphonic, contrast of women's voices in unison with men's voices in harmony, "King of Kings"
Measure 58	moving away from polyphonic to homophonic with sopranos sustaining long tones over alto, tenor, and bass homophonic singing of "Hallelujah"
Measure 69	polyphonic, "And He shall reign"
Measure 74	moving back to homophonic with tenor sustaining long tones while soprano, alto, and bass sing homophonically, "King or Kings"
Measure 78	homophonic with alto suggesting polyphony for one measure, "And He shall reign," then straight homophonic to the end.

AUTOHARP

AUTOHARP 1:
"HOT CROSS BUNS"

These pictures show alternate ways to hold the autoharp. Cradling it in your arms gives you greater mobility. Placing it on a table is easier.

- Put the fingers of your left hand on the buttons for the chord-bars. Cross your right hand over the left to strum the strings from the bottom (fat, long strings) to the top (thin, short strings.) References to "bottom" or "top" will mean pitch, not location, since the location changes, depending upon the method adopted for holding the instrument. "Bottom" refers to low sounds; "top" refers to high sounds.

- Look at the instrument to see what happens when you push a bar down. The bars under the chord buttons stop vibration of strings not in the chords. Chord-bars are not arranged in the same places on all autoharps. Become familiar with the bar arrangement of your instrument as quickly as possible. Autoharps are made with different numbers of chords.

This position allows the musician to move around the room. (Joan Anderson, Lincoln Unified School District)

Notice the player's posture and right hand crossing over left hand.

- Press the G major chord-bar with your left index finger; strum the strings with your right index finger. If it sounds wrong, perhaps

  1. You are not pressing the button firmly enough. Be sure the felts on the lower side of the bars contact the strings firmly to prevent the unnecessary ones from sounding. Is the sound better when you press harder with the left hand?

2. The instrument is not in tune. If this is the case, ask for help. A beginning musician should not be challenged with this task too soon. Learn from an experienced musician how to tune the autoharp. Be sure to obtain an *autoharp tuner* (an implement similar to the one used by a piano tuner) whose opening matches your tuning pins.

    a. One way to tune the autoharp is to tune the notes named on the body of the instrument in the order named, using the pitches of a keyboard instrument as a reference for their desired sound. This procedure is difficult because it necessitates movement between the keyboard and the autoharp, as one plays and checks the sound between the two instruments for each pitch.

    b. A more desirable alternative is to begin with the lowest note on your autoharp. Tune it to match its equivalent on an in-tune keyboard instrument. Then tune all the notes with the same name on the autoharp, referring to the first-tuned low note for the pitch reference. If the low note was an F, after all the F's are in tune, follow the same procedure with the A's (the next note in the F chord), and then the C's (also in the F chord). While tuning the notes of the F chord, press the F chord button frequently to help you hear if the chord is in tune, and to find the proper note to tune. (Next-door-neighboring notes that you might mistakenly pluck will not sound with the chord button pressed.) Move to the C chord next. Then tune the remainder of the autoharp pitches by moving from chord to chord. It is too soon for you to worry if you do not understand the above directions about tuning chords. This is one reason you need help with tuning now. Chords will be gradually introduced in this text.

• Use the fingernail of your right index finger to strum, moving quickly from bottom (low pitch) to top (high pitch). Hold the G chord-bar down as you count 1–2–3–4 and strum on count 1 only. Move your hand back to the bottom strings quickly enough to be ready for the next strum on 1. Allow no break between count 4 and count 1.

• As soon as you have established a regular chord strum, pluck the B string to give the pitch for the beginning melody note, then sing "Hot Cross Buns" with the G chord accompaniment. When this seems easy, strum on counts 1 and 3 to accompany your singing of the melody.

• Is your autoharp constructed so you can strum on the right side of the chord-bars? If it is, strum on the right, listening carefully to the timbre as you do so. Does it sound different from the strum on the left of the chord-bars?

AUTOHARP 2:
"THE BIRD'S SONG"

- Strum the autoharp from lowest pitches to highest pressing the G major chord-bar.

- Find the D7 chord-bar. Press it with a finger other than the one pressing the G bar. Because the arrangement of autoharp chords varies from instrument to instrument, take a moment to study the placement of the chords, then put your fingers comfortably over the chord-bars you will use.

- Practice alternating the G and D7 chords.

- Pluck B to give your starting pitch. Sing "The Bird's Song," changing chords as indicated by the symbols above the melody.

- Play each chord on the steady beats, moving to a different chord when indicated by the letter over the melody. When strumming in this fashion, you will play two G chords, two D7 chords, six G chords, two D7 chords, and so on.

- Vary your strum:
  1. On beats 1 and 3, use your index finger to play all the strings from bottom to top. On beats 2 and 4, use your thumb to play all the strings from top to bottom.
  2. Use your index finger to play all the beats from bottom to top.

AUTOHARP 3:
"A-HUNTING WE WILL GO"

- Play the G and D7 chords alternately, being sure to press the bars down firmly and use a different finger for each bar.

    What is the name of the new chord in "A-Hunting We Will Go"?

- Put another finger on the C chord, then memorize the association of finger with chord. Which of your fingers will play the G chord, which the D7, and which the new C chord?

- Strum the three chords in the same progression they follow in the piece.

- Strum twice in each measure. Remember to continue the chord last named until a new chord is indicated.

- Sing the melody as you play the chordal accompaniment. Be sure to start singing on the correct pitch and to keep the rhythm steady and accurate.

- Vary the style of the accompaniment:

  1. Strum, using all the strings for beat 1, the upper half of the strings for beat three.

  2. Use alternating up and down strums on all four beats.

  3. Strum the same as number 2, but use all the strings for beat 1, and only the upper strings for beats 2, 3, and 4.

     As you become familiar with the autoharp, experiment with different styles of playing. Chord symbols will be shown only where the chords change. Between the chord symbols, use your ear to help you determine how often the chord should be strummed. Frequently, strumming only where the chord symbols are written produces an accompaniment with too little support for the melody.

AUTOHARP 4:
"HORN" ("ORCHESTRA SONG")

It is possible to use the G chord instead of G7, but using the G7 chord adds more tension. The G7 demands resolution to the C chord and results in more of a sense of reaching the proper destination when the C chord is heard. Assign one finger to C, another finger to G7. Practice so that you can switch comfortably from C to G7 without moving the assigned finger away from its chord-bar. If you are not comfortable, try different finger combinations until you are.

- Accompany your singing of the "Horn" with the C and G7 chords. Then accompany your singing of the "Horn" with the C and G chords. Which combination gives you a stronger sense of harmonic movement?

- Try these different strums as you accompany the melody.

  1. Strum the appropriate chord from bottom to top at the beginning of the measure only.

  2. Strum low strings on beat 1, high strings on beats 2 and 3.

  3. Strum low strings on beat 1, middle strings on beat 2 and high strings on beat 3.

  4. Strum quickly across all strings from bottom to top on both beats 1 and 3. Rest on beat 2.

  5. Create new strums as you accompany this and other parts of the "Orchestra Song" after you learn their melodies.

AUTOHARP 5:
"AFRICAN NOEL"

- Find the F chord on your autoharp. Put one finger on it, another finger on the C chord. Be sure you can alternate chords without moving your fingers away from their chord-bars.

- Try these strums to accompany the melody of "African Noel":

  1. Strum on beat 1 only, using all the strings from the bottom to the top.

  2. Strum on both beats using all the strings from the bottom to the top.

  3. Strum this pattern in each measure:

  up   down   up

  4. Strum this pattern in each measure:

  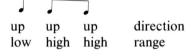

  | up | up | up | direction |
  | low | high | high | range |

  5. Create a different strum.

AUTOHARP 6:
"THE WILD COLONIAL BOY"

- Put a different finger on the D, G, and A7 chord-bars. Practice the chord progression alone, then add the melody to it.

AUTOHARP 7:
"ZUM GALI GALI" AND
"ALL THE PRETTY LITTLE HORSES"

If your autoharp does not have the chords needed for the music you wish to play, *transpose* it to a closely related key. For example, move from E minor to D minor. The problem is that autoharps with fifteen or fewer chord-bars may not have enough minor chords to play in the keys you need even if you try to transpose. Autoharps with twenty-one chord-bars enable you to play the i, iv, and V7 chords in four minor keys. It is possible to purchase extra bars for chords not presently on your autoharp.

By this time you probably realize that the autoharp has definite limitations. The advantage of the instrument is its accessibility. It is easy for a beginning musician to use once it is in tune. When you become frustrated with the autoharp's lack of chords or its limited style, it is time for you to learn to play another harmonic instrument that will give you a greater variety of musical options.

GUITAR

GUITAR 1:
"HOT CROSS BUNS"

There are several ways to hold the guitar. Choose the position most comfortable for you.

Crossed legs without a stand for the left foot.

Notice the stand for the left foot. (Terry Mills, University of the Pacific, guitar faculty)

Use the fingers of your left hand to stop the strings and produce the chord notes. Use the right hand to strum. Before beginning to play, be sure your instrument is in tune. If you have access to a piano, tune the guitar strings to these notes on the keyboard.

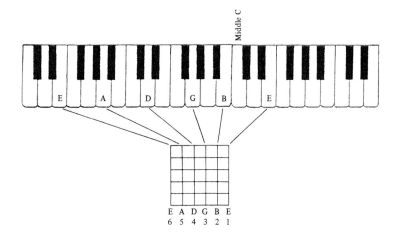

Low	High
Thick strings	Thin strings
Bottom	Top
Below	Above

Reference to "low" or "high" is related to pitch, not the position of the instrument. No matter how the guitar is held, the low, thick strings are described as being at the bottom, and below other strings. The high, thin strings are described as being on top, above the lower strings. This becomes confusing when holding the guitar in playing position, since what looks like the highest string emits the lowest pitch. *Refer to the pitch, not the position of the string.*

If you do not have access to a keyboard, tune the instrument to itself.

- Play an E on a fixed-pitch instrument or a pitchpipe so the guitar can be tuned to play with other instruments. After you have tuned the low E, press a finger firmly on the low E string just below the fifth fret. (When describing fingered notes, also refer to pitch, not position. "Below" the fifth fret means toward the tuning pegs, even when the guitarist seems to be holding the fingerboard in such a way that the finger placement seems to be "above." Remember, *the longer the string, the lower the sound.* The finger placed "below" the fifth fret makes the string longer, with a lower sound than a string with a finger placed "above" (toward the body of the guitar) the fifth fret.

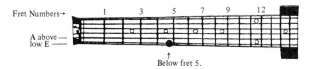

Below fret 5.

- Compare the sound of this fingered *(stopped)* string with the open A string just above. The two strings should sound exactly the same. If the sounds are not the same, adjust the tuning of the open A until it matches the fingered E.

- Next, finger the A string just below the fifth fret.

The sound of that stopped string should be the same as the sound of the open D above. If the two strings do not agree, change the open D until it matches the fingered A sound.

- Continue to tune the rest of the strings. All will be fingered below the fifth fret to match the open string above except the G, which must be fingered below the 4th fret to match the open B.

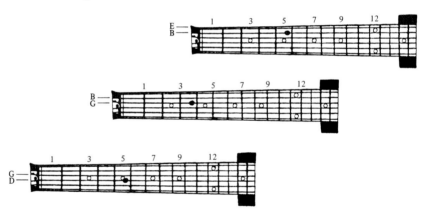

At first, strum only the *four highest strings* on the guitar. This will enable you to begin with *simplified fingering* for your first chord. Place the fourth finger of your left hand just below the third fret on the high E string. Although other fingers may seem stronger and so better able to hold the string down, use the fourth finger so it is in place for the time you play the complete chord and need that finger. Consistently place the finger as close to the fret as possible without touching it. If the string is placed halfway between two frets or close to the one below, the string may buzz because it is not being stopped firmly by the fret above.

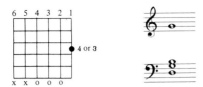

In the diagram above, which is a conventional guitar-fingering diagram, *x means the string is not to be played* and *o means the string is to be played open,* without a finger stopping it. *The numbers above the diagram identify the strings from 1 (high E) to 6 (low E).*

- Brush your right thumb (or a *pick*) across the top four strings (D–G–B and fingered E.) Play the G chord on count 1 as you say 1–2–3–4.

These pictures show the sequence for using a thumb brush strum.

Thumb brush preparation: thumb on bass string, fingers prepared to brush.

Thumb completes stroke.

Completion of finger stroke; thumb and fingers clear of strings.

- As soon as this seems easy, pluck the B string to give you the starting pitch for "Hot Cross Buns." Sing the song as you strum on count 1. Practice this until it is easy for you to strum and sing.

- Strum on counts 1 and 3 to accompany your singing. When this is easy for you, practice the complete fingering for the G chord, strumming on all the strings.

If you have access to a *baritone ukulele* instead of a guitar, use the fingering and tuning instructions for the top four strings of the guitar. The baritone ukulele

1. is smaller than the guitar.
2. does not have the bottom two strings of the guitar.
3. is lighter in weight.
4. is generally less expensive.

Size comparison of baritone ukulele and guitar.
(Hope Harrison, Klamath Falls Union High School)

GUITAR 2:
"THE BIRD'S SONG"

- Strum the G chord using the top four strings.

    This is the fingering for the D7 chord using the top four strings:

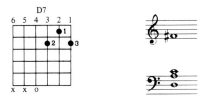

    Be sure to place the fingers as close to the fret above as possible.

- Practice moving from the G chord to the D7 chord.

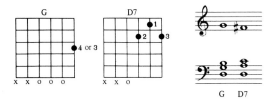

- When you can change from G to D7 fluently, sing the melody and play the chords to accompany it, changing them as indicated in the music for "The Bird's Song."

- Be sure to repeat the same chords rhythmically until a new chord letter tells you to change to the next chord.

- When this seems easy, try changing from the complete G chord, using six strings, to the D chord, using four strings.

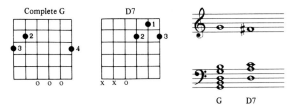

    As a preliminary exercise, move each finger alone:
    second finger from the A string, second fret, to G string, second fret.

third finger from low E string, third fret, to high E string, second fret.

Check your left hand position.

Left hand position: fingers on tips, fingers close to frets (in direction of sound note).

Left hand thumb position: center on width of the neck.

GUITAR 3:
"A-HUNTING WE WILL GO"

- Play the G and D7 chords in the order in which they appear in the notation for "A-Hunting We Will Go." When you come to the new chord (C), stop and practice placing your fingers as shown in this chart.

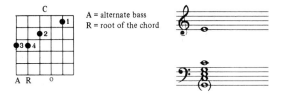

- Practice moving your fingers from the G chord to the C chord and back again.

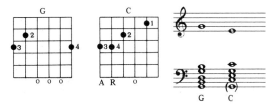

- If it is helpful to you, practice moving one finger at a time from its position in the G chord to its position in the C chord.

- Practice moving your fingers from the G chord to the C chord to the G chord to the D7 chord to the G chord. Strum eight steady beats on each chord before changing to the next one.

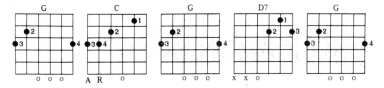

- Play the chords in the order they follow for "A-Hunting We Will Go."

- Strum twice in each measure as you play the chord progression for the piece again. Remember to continue the chord last named until a new chord is indicated.

- Sing the melody as you play the chordal accompaniment. Be sure to keep the rhythm steady and accurate even if it means you must sing the song very slowly at first.

- Try to quicken your tempo until you are singing and playing as fast as is indicated by the tempo marking.

GUITAR 4:
"HORN" ("ORCHESTRA SONG")

This is the fingering for the G7 chord.

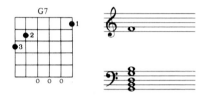

How does it differ from the G chord?

You can use the G chord in the "Horn" if you wish, but it will not give the feeling of harmonic tension that the G7 gives. It is also easier to move from G7 to C than it is to move from G to C.

The C chord will establish its tonality more firmly if the lowest string is not played. This allows the root of the chord (the fingered C on the A string) to sound as the lowest note of the chord. Use the fingered G on the low E string as an alternate bass.

- Practice moving from the C chord to the G7 chord many times before you use that progression to accompany the melody of the "Horn" in correct rhythm.

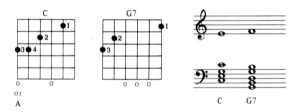

- Compare the sound of the C–G7–C progression with the sound of the C–G–C progression.

- Practice these strums to accompany the "Horn" and the other parts of the "Orchestra Song":

    1. Strum once in each measure.
    2. Pluck the roots (lowest notes) of the chords (fifth string for the C chord, sixth string for the G7 chord) with your thumb on beat 1. (The single notes plucked are C and G, the roots of the C and G7 chords.) Strum the rest of the strings on beats 2 and 3.
    3. Pluck the roots of the chords with your thumb on beat 1. Strum two eighth-notes (up, down) on beat 2 and one quarter-note (up) on beat 3.

pick   strum- - - - - - -
P   ↑ ↓ ↑

4. Create an original strum.

GUITAR 5:
"AFRICAN NOEL"

The new chord for "African Noel" is F.

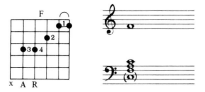

- Practice moving from C to F before using these chords as the accompaniment for "African Noel."

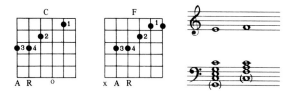

- Play these strums as you sing the melody:

    1. Strum on beat 1 only.

    2. Pluck the root of the chord on beat 1, strum the rest of the chord on beat 2. The root is:
        string 5 for the C chord
        string 4 for the F chord
        string 6 for the G7 chord

    3. Pluck the root of the chord on beat 1. Strum two upward eighth-notes on beat 2 using the rest of the notes in the chord.

    4. Create another strum.

GUITAR 6:
"THE WILD COLONIAL BOY"

Learn these new chords to accompany the melody for "The Wild Colonial Boy."

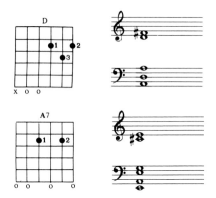

- Play the D, G, and A7 chords in the order they are used for "The Wild Colonial Boy." Play eight beats for each chord at first, then four, then two.

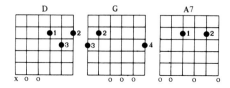

GUITAR 7:
GUITAR CHORD CHART

The left column of chords shows fingerings for *major chords*. The third column from the left shows *dominant seventh chords*. The other columns show fingerings to add as the chords are demanded by music you will learn in the future.

X means: Don't play the string.

R shows the string sounding the root of the chord.

A shows the fifth of the chord, often used in alternation with the root.

⌒ *shows the finger laid flat across the strings (barre).*

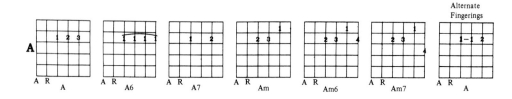

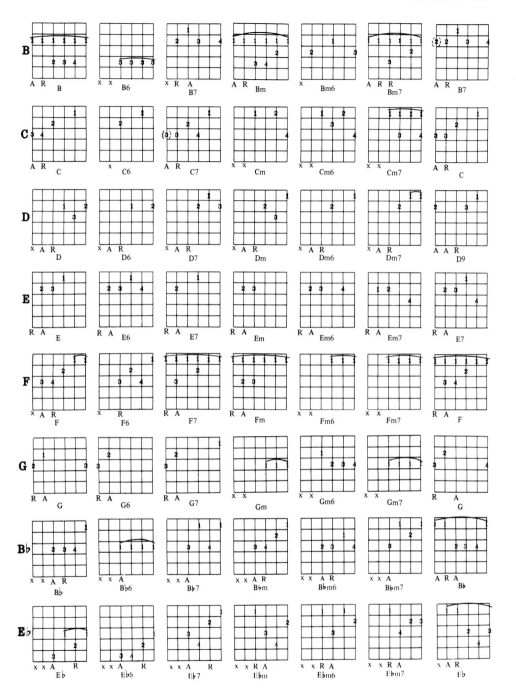

KEYBOARD

KEYBOARD 1:
"HOT CROSS BUNS"

Because many different kinds of keyboard instruments may be available to you (such as piano, electric organ, electric piano, synthesizer, pipe organ), this section will be called "Keyboard" to indicate the inclusion of these varied instruments and their similar capabilities.

The large printed keyboard included in this text is not intended to substitute for a real instrument, but it may help you when you are not near a sounding keyboard.

Victor Steinhardt, University of Oregon, School of Music, piano faculty.

This picture shows how you should sit when playing a keyboard instrument. The speed of the hands comes only after much practice!!

Sit in front of the middle of the keyboard. If the instrument has a name over the keyboard, it will almost always help show the location of the middle. Put your music for "Hot Cross Buns" on the rack in front of you.

Keep your fingers curved as if you are holding a tennis ball.

Notice the black keys in sets of twos and threes alternating for the whole length of the keyboard. Locate the set of three blacks to the right of the center of the keyboard. To play "Hot Cross Buns," you will use the white keys just to the right of the set of three black keys: G, A, B.

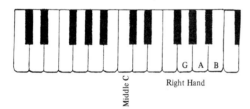

- Put your right thumb on G, your second finger on A, and your third finger on B. Combine what you have learned about the pitches and the rhythm to play "Hot Cross Buns."

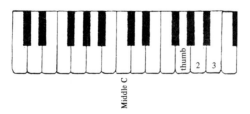

KEYBOARD 2:
"HOT CROSS BUNS"

- Find the set of three black notes to the left of the center of the keyboard.

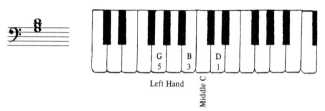

G will be in the same relative location as it was when you used it for the melody, but now you will use the left hand to play it an octave (eight notes) lower. Put your little finger (5) on G, your middle finger (3) on B, and your thumb (1) on D. Notice the finger numbers for the left and right hands are 1 for the thumbs, 5 for the little fingers, etc.

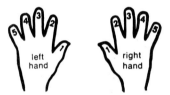

- Use 5–3–1 of your left hand to play G, B, D together without allowing your other two fingers to play the keys under them. You are now playing a G chord.

- Practice playing the G chord on count 1 as you say 1–2–3–4 several times.

- As soon as you can do this easily, instead of counting, sing "Hot Cross Buns" accompanying yourself by continuing to play the G chord on the first count. Play a B to give yourself the starting melody pitch.

- As soon as you can, accompany your singing by playing the chord on beats 1 and 3.

- Next, use the keyboard to put the melody for "Hot Cross Buns" (right hand) and the G chord harmony (left hand) together.

KEYBOARD 3:
"LADY COME"

You will need all the fingers of your right hand to play the melody for "Lady, Come." Put your fingers on the keyboard as this picture shows. Keep your hand in position so each note has its own finger.

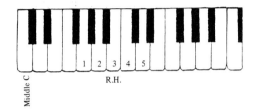 

When you can play the melody with accurate rhythm, return to Chapter 3.

KEYBOARD 4:
"ARE YOU SLEEPING?"

- Begin to play "Are You Sleeping?" with your right hand in the same position you used for "Lady, Come." Put your thumb on G; have one white key under each of your other fingers. When you get to the beginning of measure 5, get ready to change the position of your hand. Put your fourth finger (instead of your fifth finger) on D. Use your fingers over the notes indicated in the picture below, stretching the thumb over to the G at the end of the measure.

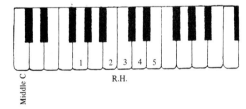 

- Practice changing from measure 4 to 5 until the change from the fifth to the fourth finger on the high D is smooth. Rather than changing position again for the other new note, low D (just above middle C), use the thumb of your left hand on that note, being ready to insert it rhythmically in the last two measures.

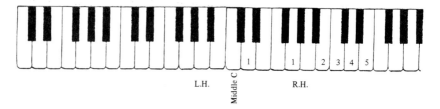

- Practice the last two measures several times before playing the piece from the beginning.

- Practice the melody of "Are You Sleeping?" with correct rhythm until you can play it well. When you are ready, return to Chapter 3 for a discussion of the harmony of this piece.

KEYBOARD 5: "THE BIRD'S SONG"

This piece uses a chord progression that includes the G and D7 chords. Because it is easier (and the voice leading is better) to move from G to D7 by staying on common tones and moving from the notes of the G chord to the closest notes of the D7, the latter will not be used in root position (name of the chord as its bottom note). The relationship of the notes to each other in the rearrangement of the D7 chord, results in the D7 being called a D^6_5 chord.

$$\text{G} \qquad \text{D}^6_5 \qquad \text{G}$$

- Use your left hand to play several G chords as you did for "Hot Cross Buns."

- To change from the G chord to the D^6_5, move your fifth finger from the G to the F-sharp (black note just below the G.) Practice playing G to F-sharp with your fifth finger.

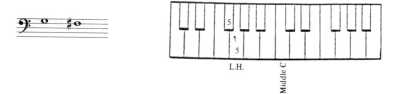

- Instead of using your third (middle) finger in the D⁷ chord, play C with your second finger. Practice playing B to C several times using your third and second fingers.

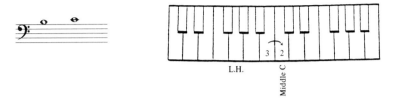

- When changing from G to D⁷, your thumb should stay the same. It will play D in both chords.

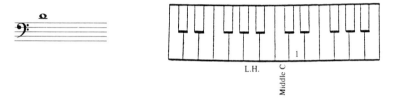

- Practice changing from G to D⁷ using the separate finger movements described above all at the same time.

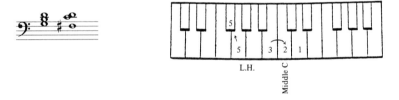

- When you can change from G to D⁷ fluently, play them as accompanying chords while you sing the melody for "The Bird's Song." Change the chords as indicated in the music.

- When you can sing the melody and change the chords with accurate rhythm, play the melody with the right hand and the chords with the left hand at the same time. Instead of trying to play the low D where it occurs in the melody with the right hand, use the left-hand thumb.

KEYBOARD 6:
"A-HUNTING WE WILL GO"

- Review the G and D$_7^6$ chords by playing them several times.

What is the name of the new chord in "A-Hunting We Will Go"? What is the chord played just before the new chord?

For the same reasons that you have used the D7 chord in the $_3^6$ position, you will use the C chord in the $_4^6$ position. The figures $_4^6$ indicate the relationship of the upper notes to the lowest one as notated here:

In the change from the G chord to the C chord, the fifth finger of the left hand will remain on G. This is called a *common tone* because it appears in both chords.

Instead of moving the third finger from the B (of the G chord), use the second finger to play C in the new chord.

- Practice changing from B, third finger, to C, second finger.

 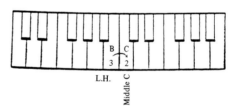

- Practice changing from B to C while the fifth finger plays the G.

 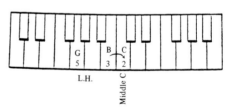

- Move the thumb (first finger) from D to E.

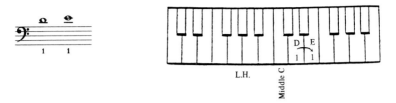

- Combine the movements you have practiced above to change from the G chord to the C$^6_4$ chord.

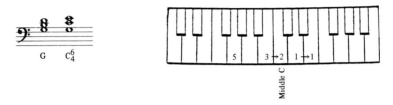

- Play the three chords (G, D7, and C) in the progression they follow in "A-Hunting We Will Go."

- As soon as you can play the chord changes smoothly, sing the melody in rhythm and change the chords without interrupting the rhythm. Be sure to start singing on the correct pitch.

- Play the melody and harmony together with accurate rhythm.

**KEYBOARD 7:
"IT'S RAINING"**

The most efficient way to play a keyboard instrument is to place your hand over most of the notes in the pattern to be played. If you leave your right hand with the thumb on G, where it has been for previous pieces, it will be difficult to hop down for the low E. Instead, put your third finger on G. This enables you to play the E with your thumb and still have the fourth finger free to play A.

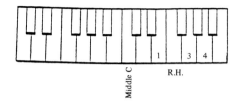

Middle C   R.H.

KEYBOARD 8:
"IT'S RAINING"

Although you will use the C chord to accompany this melody, it will be used in root position,

C

with the C on the bottom, rather than the $\frac{6}{4}$ position you have used before.

$C\frac{6}{4}$

Note that the C chord in root position and the C chord in $\frac{6}{4}$ position contain the same notes; they are arranged differently. Since "It's Raining" is in the key of C, that key is more firmly established when its key chord is used in root position.

The same fingers of the left hand will be used to play the C chord in root position that were used to play the G chord, 5–3–1. Put finger 5 on the C, 3 on E, and 1 on G. Play C, E, G together without allowing fingers 2 and 4 to depress the notes under them.

C

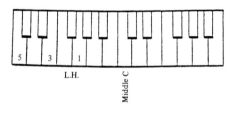

L.H.   Middle C

KEYBOARD 9:
"HORN" ("ORCHESTRA SONG")

The finger movement from the C chord to the G§ chord is the same as the movement you used when moving from the G chord to the D§ chord. Unlike the D§ chord, which has one black key, the G§ chord has all white keys.

 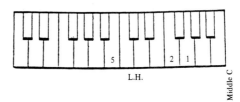

L.H.

- Change from the C chord to the G6 chord. If you experience difficulty in moving all the fingers at once, practice them separately: finger 5 from C to B, then finger 3 on E to finger 2 on F. Finger 1 stays on G. When your fingers can execute these separate moves fluently, execute them together.

 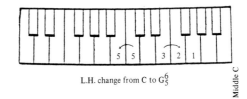

L.H. change from C to G§

KEYBOARD 10:
"DRUM" ("ORCHESTRA SONG")

- Place your hand with your right thumb on middle C and finger 5 on G.

 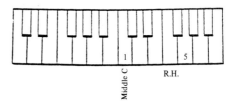

R.H.

KEYBOARD 11:
"CLARINET" ("ORCHESTRA SONG")

- Shift your right hand back to the position you used for "It's Raining" with your thumb on E. Play F with finger 2.

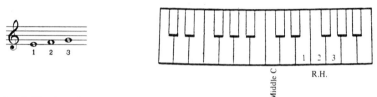

- Play the "Clarinet" using another set of fingers:

    The weakest finger in keyboard playing often is finger 4. To strengthen that finger, play the "Clarinet" with finger 5 on the G, finger 3 on the E and finger 4 on the F.

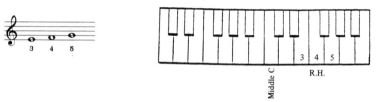

KEYBOARD 12:
"VIOLIN" ("ORCHESTRA SONG")

- Shift your hand position again to play the "Violin." This time put finger 1 of the right hand on G and finger 4 on C.

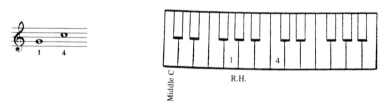

- At the beginning of measure 3, stretch your hand so finger 5 can play high F, 3 can play D, and 2 can play B. Keep your thumb on G.

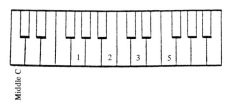

- At the beginning of measure 4, hop quickly to play C with finger 3. The hop is necessary because finger 3 is also used for the last note of measure 3. Conscientiously use the fingerings suggested so you don't use the keyboard like a "hunt and peck" typist.

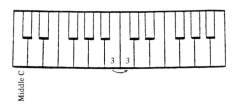

KEYBOARD 13:
"BASSOON" ("ORCHESTRA SONG")

- Begin to play the "Bassoon" with finger 5 on G. At the beginning of measure 2, stretch from finger 2 on D to finger 1 on low G without moving your hand. Practice keeping your hand in a stable position.

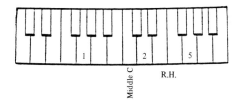

- To free a finger for the A at the beginning of measure 3, hop from finger 5 on the G just after low G, to finger 4 on the last G in that measure.

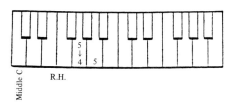

- Hop again from finger 1 on the last note in measure 3 to finger 1 on the first note in measure 4, then stretch so finger 5 can play C an octave higher.

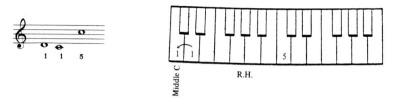

- At the beginning of measure 5, use a *cross-over* fingering for the first time. Play the F at the end of measure 4 with finger 1, then cross finger 3 over and have finger 1 ready immediately to play middle C.

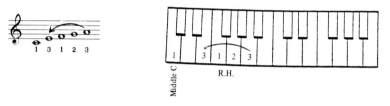

The other fingerings in this piece repeat what you have already tried. Be sure to read the fingering marked over the melody.

KEYBOARD 14:
"AFRICAN NOEL"

The movement from the C chord to the F$^6_4$ chord in "African Noel" is the same you used to move from G to C$^6_4$ in "A-Hunting We Will Go." Move from E, finger 3, to F, finger 2. Play G with finger 1, then shift finger 1 to A. Leave finger 5 on C.

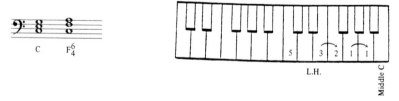

- Practice moving your fingers from the C to the F chord until it becomes easy. Then play the chord progression as it appears in "African Noel."

When you are ready, sing the melody with the chordal accompaniment.

KEYBOARD 15:
"TEN LITTLE INDIANS"

Since this piece is in the key of G, be sure to make F a sharp (♯) every time it appears in the melody. F-sharp is the black key to the right of the F.

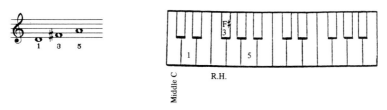

KEYBOARD 16:
"THE WILD COLONIAL BOY"

C-sharp is the black key to the left in the set of two blacks on the keyboard. The C-sharps used in this piece are middle C-sharp and the C-sharp an octave above middle C-sharp.

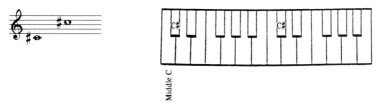

The numbers above the notation for "The Wild Colonial Boy" are for your fingering. Use both hands to play the melody. Place your hands on the keyboard like this to use the suggested fingering for both hands:

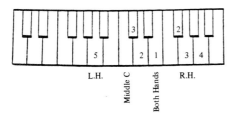

Shift your right hand at the beginning of the phrase starting with "Of poor."

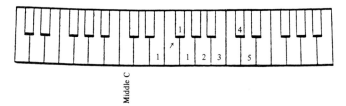

Shift back to the first right-hand position for the last phrase.

KEYBOARD 17:
"THE WILD COLONIAL BOY"

The new chords for "The Wild Colonial Boy" are D and A♮.

- Play the D chord using this left-hand fingering.

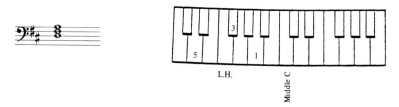

Use this fingering for the A♮ chord.

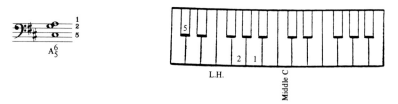

Rather than playing the G chord in its root position as you have done before, use a different position to make its place in the chord progression easier to play.

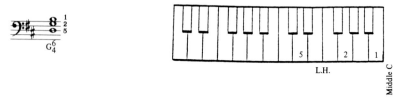

• Play the chord progression for "The Wild Colonial Boy" without singing the melody until you can move your fingers easily from one chord to the next.

KEYBOARD 18:
"ZUM GALI GALI"

The finger action in moving from chord I to chord IV$^6_4$ is similar in major and minor keys. The difference is in how much to move each finger.

The little finger of the left hand (5) stays the same when moving from the E minor chord to the inverted A minor. The third finger of the left hand plays G in the E minor chord; the second finger plays A in the A minor chord (a whole step away). The thumb (1) plays B in the E minor chord, then moves to C in the A minor chord (a half-step away).

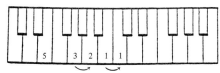

L.H. E minor chord to inverted A minor chord.

Compare the movement from I to IV in minor keys with that same movement in major keys.

KEYBOARD 19:
"ALL THE PRETTY LITTLE HORSES"

The chord progression in "All the Pretty Little Horses" from E minor to A minor is the same as described in *Keyboard 18*. The progression from E minor to B$^6_5$ is similar to the I to V$^6_5$ progressions you have played in major keys. The difference is the distance from the third to the second finger. In a minor key, it is a whole step.

Finger 5 moves down a half-step. Finger 3 gives way to finger 2 a whole step higher. Finger 1 stays on the same note.

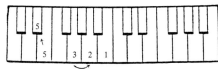

L.H. E m chord to inverted B7.

When you get to the G chord at the beginning of the third line, move your hand up to play it in root position; then move back to the E minor chord in root position.

RECORDER

RECORDER 1:
"HOT CROSS BUNS"

- Hold your soprano recorder as these pictures show. Use your left hand to cover the top holes; your right hand to cover the bottom holes.

Note position of mouthpiece.

Recorder: left hand covers top holes.
(Tim Roberson, San Andreas School)

- Before blowing into the instrument, say "ti-ti-ti-ti." When you do this, you are using your tongue to interrupt the flow of air. To produce your first recorder sound:

    1. Close no holes with your fingers.

    2. Put the mouthpiece between your lips.

3. Without touching the mouthpiece with your tongue, initiate the sound using the same action you did when you said "ti-ti-ti-ti."

4. Blow gently.

Initiation and interruption of air flow using the tongue is called *tonguing*. For now, tongue the beginning of each note you play.

To play "Hot Cross Buns," you must learn the fingering for three notes: B–A–G. These three notes require your thumb to cover the hole in the back of your recorder. To play B, use the thumb and index finger of your left hand.

To play A, add the second finger of your left hand to the B fingering.

To play G, add the third finger of your left hand to the A fingering.

- Practice playing B–A–G until your tongue and fingers coordinate. Practice these exercises.

- When you have mastered the exercises, and can remember the fingering for each note, play the melody for "Hot Cross Buns."

- Take care of your recorder:

  The *plastic* recorder (recommended for beginners) is easy to care for. Frequently give it a mild soap and water bath followed by a clear water rinse. Always wash it between uses by different players.

  Never wash *wooden* recorders. They must be dried carefully after each use with a special swab or delicate, absorbent cloth attached to a cleaning rod.

RECORDER 2: "LADY COME"

- Review the fingering for the three notes you used in "Hot Cross Buns." Find those notes in "Lady, Come."

  Here are fingerings for two new notes you will need in this piece:

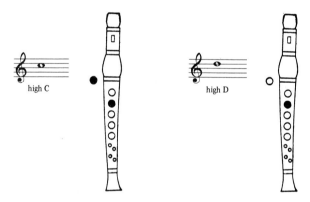

high C   high D

- Practice playing the new notes in these exercises.

- Locate the new notes in "Lady, Come."

- Practice the melody for "Lady, Come" using the correct rhythm.

RECORDER 3:
"ARE YOU SLEEPING?"

These fingerings are for the two new notes you will need to play "Are You Sleeping?"

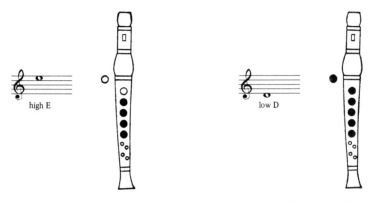

- Play them in these exercises.

- Practice playing from high D to E.

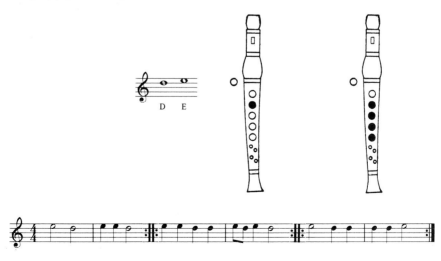

- Practice playing from G to low D.

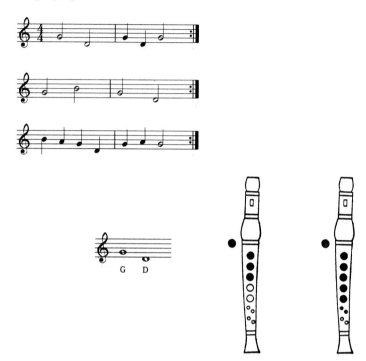

- Play "Are You Sleeping" with accurate rhythm. Play it slowly at first if you have trouble remembering the new notes. Even when you play it slowly, try to keep the relative rhythmic values of the notes.

RECORDER 4:
"IT'S RAINING"

The only new note in "It's Raining" is low E.

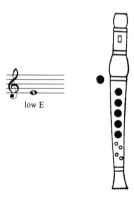

• Play it in these exercises before playing it rhythmically as part of the melody.

RECORDER 5:
"DRUM" ("ORCHESTRA SONG")

The new note in the "Drum" is probably the most difficult note you will play on the recorder because it requires you to close *all* the holes of the instrument. Use your finger cushions to completely stop the air from escaping. *Blow gently.* Problems with playing low C generally result from:

   1. Over-blowing (using too much air).

   2. Partial closure of holes.

This is the lowest note on the soprano recorder.

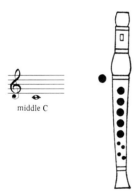

middle C

• Practice these exercises.

RECORDER 6:
"CLARINET" ("ORCHESTRA SONG")

The new note for the "Clarinet" is another difficult one because it does not follow a predictable fingering pattern if you are playing a Baroque (English) soprano recorder.

If you are not sure if your recorder is Baroque or German, look at the holes on the front of the instrument. Count down from the top. If hole number five is larger than hole four, use the Baroque fingering. If hole four is larger, or if the holes seem to be the same size, use the German fingering. Use your ear to determine if the fingering produces a pitch that is in tune.

If you are playing a German soprano recorder, this is the fingering for F.

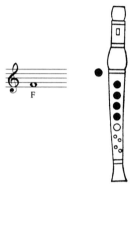

If you are playing a Baroque soprano recorder, the F fingering for the German recorder will produce a note that is out of tune. To get the best intonation, add an extra finger to flatten the pitch. Use your right ring finger to cover the two small holes circled below.

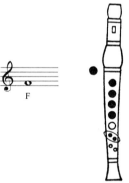

Some Baroque recorders require the addition of two fingers to produce the best intonation. Use your right ring finger to cover the two small holes as shown above, and your right little finger to cover the set of two small holes below them. Use your ear to select the correct fingerings to help you play the notes in tune.

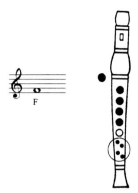

Before playing the "Clarinet," practice playing these exercises until you can produce the F readily.

RECORDER 7:
"VIOLIN" ("ORCHESTRA SONG")

The only new note in the "Violin" is high F. Play it with the same fingering you used for low F except for a half hole with the thumb to make it sound an octave higher.

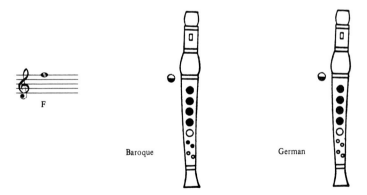

Baroque   German

- Before playing the "Violin" part using the correct rhythm, practice these exercises.

Slurs are created on the recorder by using the tongue less frequently. In previous pieces you have been asked to begin each note using your tongue as if you were saying "ti". When you see a slur in your music from now on, tongue the first note of the slur, such as the B over "ring," then move your fingers for the following note, but do not tongue that note.

When playing the four notes over "love-," tongue the high F, then change your fingers for the D, B, and G, but do not tongue them. Keep a steady stream of air going to play the notes, but do not interrupt the airstream with the tongue. If you slur correctly, you should produce a legato effect.

- Practice these exercises:

RECORDER 8:
"BASSOON" ("ORCHESTRA SONG")

You cannot play the new note for the "Bassoon" part on the recorder. The very low G is below the range of this instrument. When you encounter music written with some notes below the range your recorder can play, try to devise substitutions. In this case, substitute the second line G for the G below the staff. Play the piece as written except for the two places where you will change the G's.

- Practice these exercises to help you with the "Bassoon":

RECORDER 9:
"TEN LITTLE INDIANS"

This is the fingering for F-sharp.

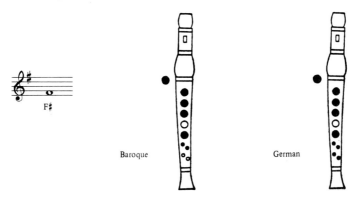

- Before you play the whole piece with correct rhythm, practice these exercises:

RECORDER 10:
"HOME ON THE RANGE"

Remember the fingering necessary to play F in tune on the Baroque recorder. In the key of F it is sometimes more efficient and just as much in tune to use this fingering for B-flat:

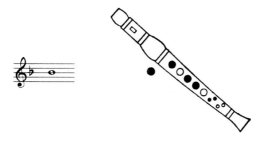

It is especially useful when going from low D to B-flat, or when moving back and forth between B-flat and F. (Another fingering for B-flat is found on the fingering chart, *Recorder 12*.)

If you have trouble with low C, check to make sure that all your fingers are covering the holes. Be careful not to over-blow. Decrease the expulsion of your breath to see if you are better able to set the note you want.

As you continue to play the recorder, be curious about alternate fingerings. The fingering chart (*Recorder 12*) does not give all possible fingerings. You may find alternate and cross-fingerings to suit certain musical purposes by experimenting with the sounds you can produce on the instrument. Listen carefully to see if the sounds are in tune. Don't be afraid to find alternatives.

The soprano recorder you have played is one of many different members of the recorder family. Longer instruments produce lower sounds.

Recorder family from top down: garklein flötlein, sopranino, soprano, alto, tenor. Missing from picture: bass, grossbass, subbass.

RECORDER 11:
"THE WILD COLONIAL BOY"

This fingering is for low C-sharp. Be sure to blow gently and cover all the holes except the one illustrated.

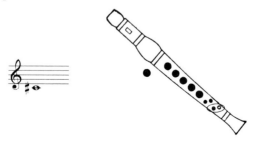

- Practice playing from D to C-sharp until you can produce C-sharp easily.

This is the C-sharp fingering one octave higher than the one you just played.

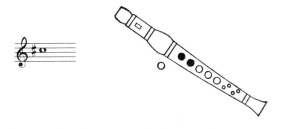

- Practice playing from D to C-sharp until you can produce C-sharp easily.

Find two notes in "The Wild Colonial Boy" that are below the playing range of the soprano recorder. Circle these notes. In both cases, when playing this piece, either leave out the low A, substituting an eighth-rest, or play a C-sharp in its place. The latter alternative will change the melodic line and is probably the least desirable of the two.

RECORDER 12:
BAROQUE RECORDER FINGERING CHART

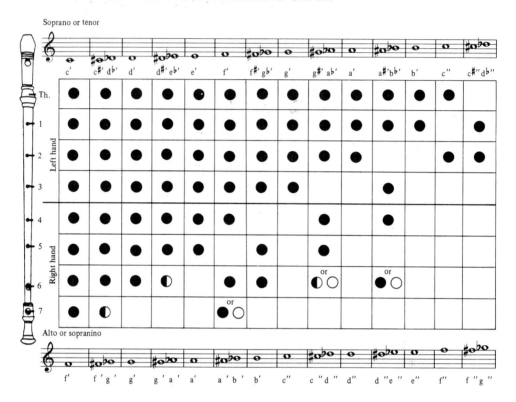

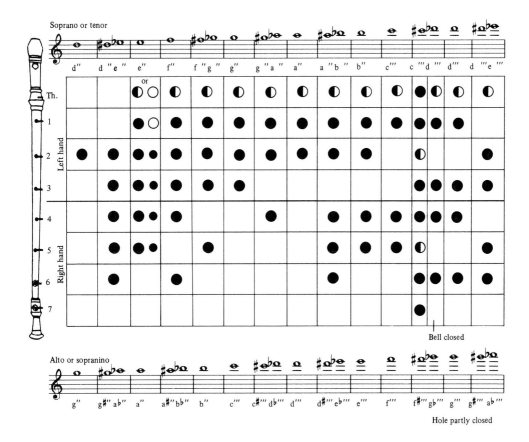

VOICE

Are you surprised to find a voice section in the instrument section of this book? If so, your surprise may be caused by your exposure to references differentiating the voice from other "instruments." According to the 1970 edition of the *Harvard Dictionary of Music* (Willi Apel, Harvard University Press, p. 413), instrumental music is "music performed on instruments, as opposed to music performed by voices." In contrast, the 1954 edition of *Grove's Dictionary of Music and Musicians* (ed. by Eric Blom, St. Martin's Press, Inc., Vol. IX, p. 43) says that "singing is primarily that branch of the art of music of which the human voice is the instrument." Grove's (1954, Vol. IV, p. 487) further defines instruments as the "tools by means of which we manipulate the raw materials of music." The 1980 Grove's quotes Hornbostel as saying "for purposes of research everything must count as a musical instrument with which sound can be produced intentionally," but the article is then completed with no reference to the voice as being one of those producers (*The New Grove Dictionary of Music and Musicians,* ed. by Stanley Sadie, Macmillan, 1980, Vol. IX, p. 237). In that same edition of Grove's, Owen Jander calls the voice "the most subtle and flexible of musical instruments" (Vol. XVII, p. 338).

This section is included in the instrument section because the voice is perceived by the author as a musical instrument. It is not matched with discussions in the text as are the other instruments because specific fingerings are not needed by the singer. This section is in narrative form and is intended to be used by teachers and students as is desirable for their particular emphases. The musical experience of the student is well served if opportunities for participation using the voice are incorporated regularly.

Singing can and should be a wonderful, natural form of human expression. It is a very personal one. A student playing a recorder can thrust the instrument aside with a casual comment about it squeaking; it is not part of the student. The voice, on the other hand, is difficult to disassociate from the singer; it cannot be casually disowned. Voices help represent who we are as people. In order to improve your singing voice, use it. In order to gain confidence, sing with and for other people.

To improve your voice, learn proper breathing techniques, correct vowel placement, use of consonants, appropriate tone quality, sensitive use of expressive elements, precise intonation, and general musical accuracy.

To gain confidence, sing as much as possible. Practice techniques suggested below as you listen carefully to your voice. Seek opportunities to sing *with* other people. As you improve, sing *for* other people. You may wish to begin with a very appreciative audience such as a small child. Not only will a youngster appreciate you, but you can also help the child sense that singing is something to be enjoyed by everyone. Don't worry about whether or not your friends appreciate your voice. Encourage them to sing too. Keep trying!

BREATHING

Breath is the fuel that makes the voice function. It moves from the lungs to the larynx where it passes between flexible vocal cords, causing them to vibrate and produce the sound. Singing from the throat with mistreatment of the vocal cords is likely to result in laryngitis or serious damage.

- Lie down on the floor, flat on your back. Relax for a few minutes and daydream about something other than the breathing process. After a few minutes, notice how the hard floor changes your body alignment. Take several deep breaths. Put your hands on the lower part of your chest. Notice how your chest cavity expands as you inhale. Also note that your shoulders do not move up and down. If you were asked to take a deep breath standing up, the chances are that you would suck your lower chest in and raise your shoulders. Neither of these movements helps you breathe. When inhaling, the idea is to fill your lungs, *not* compress them. It is likely that you will breathe more naturally when lying on the floor.

- Continue to breathe deeply while observing the action of your lungs on your lower chest. If they are expanding properly, you can feel the rib cage expanding also. After the next deep breath, use your hands to help expel the air from your lungs; force the air out rapidly, being aware of the action of your muscles in getting rid of it. The most important muscle is the diaphragm, a large muscle under the chest cavity. Can you expel the air rapidly, using your muscles with no help from your hands?

Be careful! Don't carry anything to extremes when dealing with your voice. If you are tense or uncomfortable when singing, see a voice teacher for an individual diagnosis as to what the problem(s) may be.

Learn to breathe so the tone you produce is well supported. Become conscious of the mechanism that deals with the intake and expulsion of air. Still lying on the floor, take a deep breath, then sing "coo" and hold the vowel as long as you can. As you sing it, be aware of the breath supporting your tone; it is the foundation upon which your successful singing experiences are built. If you seem to be running short of breath, gently push with your hands on either side of your lower chest cavity to help your muscles support the tone. For variety, sing "who," "too," and "moo."

When you feel that you understand the breathing process and can use your breath to support the words you sing in a relaxed way, then try the same exercises while standing. Be sure the shoulders remain still, the lower chest expands with the intake of air, and the lungs contract as they expel the air. Carry the body alignment you had while lying on the floor into the carriage you assume while standing. Good posture is essential for singing well. Be careful that stereotypes of posture do not influence your singing posture. You cannot breathe properly if you continuously concentrate on holding your abdomen in. Good singing posture is responsive to the demands of the breathing mechanism; the lungs must expand and contract.

If you sing when seated, use the best posture possible: back straight, seat on the front half of the chair, feet flat on the floor.

VOWELS

Singing differs from speaking because the sung vowels are elongated on variable pitches. Sing a few words with attention to the vowels. Sing the word "go." Notice that "o" is the sound you sustain. Sing the word "see." Sing the "s" sound alone, then the "ee" sound alone. Try to change the pitch of these letters as you sing them. Compare the sound of the sustained "s" sound with the "ee" sound as you try to change the pitch. Although you can change the pitch of the "s," it does not contribute to the musical sound in the same way as the "ee."

To determine the correct placement of vowels when singing, try a variety of pronunciations. Depending on the interpretation of the text, the pitch of the word, the musical approach to it, and the individual voice, each of those vowels will have many varied sounds. Sustain the vowel "e." While you hold it, experiment with variations on the "e" sound:

1. Change the shape of your mouth.
2. Put the "e" up in your nose.
3. Drop your jaw.

Notice how many shadings of "e" you were able to produce. Experiment with other vowels. See how much variation you can get with each of them while still striving to maintain their particular identity. In general, singing a vowel in the back of the throat is the least desirable placement. The most desirable placement of the vowel

1. Maintains the identity of the vowel.
2. Enables the singer to produce it with no tension.
3. Helps the singer to produce good tone quality.

• Choose a favorite song. Sing it slowly, concentrating on the sounds of the vowels for each word.

• Sing the same song again. This time, sing the entire song using the sound of only one vowel (no consonants). Repeat the song using a different vowel each time you sing it. As you do this, concentrate on maintaining the same vowel sound throughout. Can you do it? Do different pitches of the melody influence your capability for maintaining any of the vowel sounds?

Singing a song through with a vowel that is especially comfortable for your voice is a good way to warm up for a singing session.

CONSONANTS

Although the vowels carry the singing sound, the consonants are necessary for *articulation*. Choose a comfortable pitch and on that pitch sing "e-o-a-o" listening carefully to the vowel sound. Now add the consonants so you are singing "sweet potato." Articulate the consonants sharply, moving immediately through them to reach the sustained vowel. Choose other words to articulate on one sustained pitch.

Use the sustained vowel sound, and the swiftly articulated consonant on varied pitches such as:

Hel - lo

Good morn - ing

Choose a comfortable range for this activity. Concentrate on pleasing tone quality, proper breathing, succinct articulation. Improvise on pitch-word combinations that sound good to you.

As you work with consonants, you will become aware that some of them (such as T, K, F, P) cannot be articulated on pitch. Others (such as D, G, L, M, N) can be pitched. Under some circumstances (as when M or N is used for humming), the pitched consonants are effectively used to sustain the sound. More often, they serve only to terminate the vowel sound. Even though the pitched consonants may be short, when used to terminate the sustained vowel, they should be sung at the same pitch as the preceding vowel.

- Choose another familiar song. Sing it slowly, concentrating on clean articulation of the consonants and quick movement to the sustained vowel(s) of each word.

TONE QUALITY

Each voice has its own unique timbre or tone quality, with the possibility of producing many variations on the basic sound. Correct breath support will enable the singer to produce a clear tone. Vowel placement helps the singer produce the type of quality most desirable and appropriate for the music being performed. Singers turn to voice teachers to help them produce the best quality possible for their particular instrument. Singers are influenced, too, by recordings epitomizing the quality most appropriate for the literature to be performed.

EXPRESSIVE ELEMENTS

Sensitive use of the expressive elements is crucial for vocal interpretation of music. In addition to timbre (see *tone quality* above), variety in tempo and dynamics helps the singer express shades of meaning either associated with the text or intrinsic to the music.

INTONATION

Singing in tune, or using good *intonation,* means that the singer is precise in producing correct pitches. Inexperienced singers may be unable, at first, to match pitches; they may be unable to sing a recognizable melody. Most people who are willing to try, and are able to get help from a sympathetic teacher, can improve their ability to sing correct pitches.

Learning to sing with good intonation may be a series of successive approximations in which the singer gradually gains skill with in-tune singing. A singer who sings *under* the pitch is said to sing "flat." One who sings *higher* than the pitch is said to sing "sharp." A necessary part of learning to sing in tune is the development of the singer's ear, that is, the singer's ability to discriminate between right and wrong or flat and sharp pitches through paying attention to the sound and then adjusting the voice appropriately.

MUSICAL ACCURACY

General musical accuracy will include some of the items discussed above (such as singing in tune, using expressive elements accurately, and so on), but it includes still more components of music. The musical singer must be able to integrate all musical elements to produce accurate and expressive music. The singer's rhythm must demonstrate pulse, understanding of meter, correct patterns. Melodic concepts of phrasing must also utilize appropriate dynamics and tempo. The singer must be aware of the harmonic structure of the selection and fit the vocal line accurately into its place as part of the total harmony. Understanding of form works with the other elements to demonstrate appropriate variety while maintaining the integrity of the entire composition.

RANGES

Do you know the classification of your voice? The common way of identifying voices after they have changed from children's to adult voices, is to put them in categories of high or low male or female voices. The highest voice is the *soprano,* the next lowest the *alto,* then the *tenor,* and finally the *bass.* The ranges of these voices overlap considerably. Identification of voices should be done by quality as well as range, but this factor is often obscured by other considerations that may seem more pertinent at the time the voice classification is made:

1. The choir needs people in the "x" section.
2. The singer can read a harmony part.

3. Friends want to sit in the same section of the choir.

4. The range seems to be where the singer feels most comfortable.

If you are interested in finding the proper classification of your voice, contact a skilled voice teacher or choir director for an analysis of your vocal instrument and its potential.

These ranges are approximate. Ranges associated with voices vary with training, experience, and desire to expand the extremes of the range. The tenor part is usually written in the treble clef, but it is actually sung an octave lower than written. Tenor parts should show an "8" under the clef sign to indicate that they are to be sung an octave lower. In common practice, tenor scores frequently do not include the "8." It is assumed that musicians understand the octave transposition.

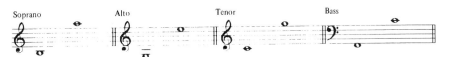

Many adults say that they cannot sing high notes. That is generally an inaccurate statement, made because the voice has been used infrequently, or perhaps used improperly. The will to expand the singing range, coupled with proper breath support and much practice, is conducive to extension of the vocal range.

Rock singers often demonstrate a wide vocal range. Some of the male singers have developed their falsetto voices so they can sing from a bass through a soprano range. The falsetto is used to sing pitches not normally within the male singer's natural range. To use the falsetto, the singer vibrates only part of the vocal chords, adding higher pitches to perform wide-ranging melodic material.

SOLO AND UNISON SINGING

As you develop your singing voice, sing solos. This will help you focus on your sound, its quality, and, most important, your intonation (ability to sing in tune). Sometimes you will want to sing your solo literature with other people. Group singing of melodies is called *unison* singing. Although you may enjoy unison singing, convince yourself that you can sing the songs alone also. Even if you are an inexperienced singer, it is not too early to think about the mood, the style, and the unique characteristics of the music to which you can apply your individual expressive interpretation. Use pieces from this text if you do not have solos in mind.

In every case, if you need help with the melody, teach it to yourself by playing it on your melody instrument. There may be a few difficult intervals you need to play to help your voice sing accurately. Strive to read vocally as well as instrumentally. If the key is too high or too low, transpose it to a comfortable singing range when necessary. Try different keys to challenge yourself to expand your range. When you find a key for a particular song that is good for your voice, note the starting pitch and give it to yourself on an instrument or pitchpipe each time before you begin to sing.

SINGING IN HARMONY

An added attraction of group singing is the potential for members of the group to sing in harmony as well as in unison. Your musicianship is strengthened when you develop the ability to hold a harmony part on your own. Do not try to sing harmony until you can sing melodies accurately.

Some of the easiest harmonies are created vocally through singing *rounds*. Sing the rounds listed below first as unison songs, then in harmony, with different singers beginning the melody when the singers who started first reach the circled numbers shown above the melody. Four numbers above the melody mean that there can be up to four different singers or groups of singers joining the harmony when the first singers reach those four different places.

If you have not yet studied all the songs listed below, delay singing them until they are introduced in the text so their particular musical problems are explained before you try them as rounds.

"Are You Sleeping"   "Lady, Come"

"The Bird's Song"   "Lullaby Round"

"The Frogs"   "Shalom Chaverim"

"Ifca's Castle"   "Summer Is A-coming in"

• Sing a round that is not explained in the text, "Dona Nobis Pacem."

The *ostinato* provides another way to add harmony to a melody in a comparatively easy fashion. The first two measures of "Zum Gali, Gali" form an attractive ostinato. Sing the melody while other musicians sing or play the ostinato. It should be repeated as many times as necessary to end with the melody.

The "Orchestra Song" treats voices like instruments, giving them each their own distinctive part to sing. Sing one of the orchestra parts by yourself while friends try other orchestral parts.

Once certain individual songs are learned, they can be combined to create harmony as *partner songs*. At first, to increase your confidence, sing "Hark to the Singing," "Will You Come?" and "Coffee" together with their words. As you gain confidence, substitute syllables for the words. If all the singers use a uniform syllable, such as "tu," a simulated orchestral effect can be achieved that is more attractive than the jumble of many unrelated words. Songs can only be used as partner songs if their chord changes occur in the same places, if they are in the same key, and if there is compatibility between the melodies.

The "Shroom Song" gives you an opportunity to sing in four part harmony.

Tell Me Why

Chromatics (tones that do not belong in the key) add a different flavor to harmony. Half-steps are not easy to sing, so be careful. A harmony part above the melody is sometimes called a *descant*. If you have trouble singing the descant, play it on the recorder or piano to get the sound in your ear.

The rule for accidentals (signs used to show chromatic alterations) is that they are good only for the measure in which they appear: The bar-line cancels them. In actual practice, music printers usually put the sharp, flat, or natural in the next measure even though the key signature indicates the correct note. An example of this occurs in measures 3 and 4, line 2, of "Tell Me Why." The B-natural in the third measure should automatically return to B-flat in the fourth measure, but the music printer has inserted the flat sign as a reminder. The reminder may be put in parentheses (♭).

VOCAL MUSIC READING

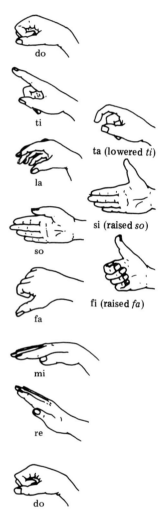

Reading music with your voice may be more difficult than reading with an instrument. If you wish to improve your vocal reading, try *solfege* (*so-fa* syllables). Excellent sightreaders have learned to read using the syllables alone, or coupling them with hand signs. The *Kodaly method* of vocal reading, based on a combination of syllables and signs, is used in many parts of the world. Musicians who have used this combination successfully derive value from the physical coupling of the hand sign with the syllable label of the sound they both represent.

- Apply the syllables and the hand signs to pieces you have already sung so the combination will represent sight and accurate sound. Then, apply the syllables to new material. If you are singing in a major key, *do* will be the name of the key. If you are singing in a minor key, *la* will be the name of the key. Although fixed *do* is used in parts of the world (where *do* is C and never changes), you will use the moveable *do*. The placement of *do* changes, or moves, to the tonic of whatever major key is used; *la* moves to the tonic of whatever minor key is used.

- Memorize the hand signs and their corresponding syllables.

- Write the syllables under the notes in these pieces:

  "The Frogs"   "Home on the Range"

  "Hold On"   "Ifca's Castle"

- Choose two other pieces and write the syllables under their notes.

- Sing the pieces whose syllables you have written; use the corresponding hand signs as you sing the syllables.

VOCAL IMPROVISATION

Much fine singing is done extemporaneously. Groups that encourage creative singing form around campfires, in churches, in jazz ensembles, sometimes in classrooms. Once you have the sounds of harmony in your ear, apply them to harmonizations of your own creation that you think will add to the music.

Creative singing is done by soloists also. Vocal jazz singers display great virtuosity in singing solos of their own design related to the chord progressions being played by the combos with which they sing. Before and during Bach's time (1685–1750) soloists were expected to *embellish* (ornament) the melodies they sang.

- Listen to Margaret Dehning embellishing a tune you know (Tape 17).

- Sing the tune Margaret Dehning sang. After you sing it the way it is written, sing it again with changes of your own making. Sing it a third time with different changes.

- Describe the variations you made on the melody. Share them with a class member to help both of you enlarge your creative vocabularies.

Singing is an attractive human activity. Persist in developing your vocal skill to maintain it as part of your enjoyable association with music-making. One advantage of singing is that the instrument is always nearby.

MUSIC CHECK

You should be able to define, identify, and illustrate musically:

PROPER BREATHING

ELONGATION OF VOWELS

ARTICULATION THROUGH CONSONANTS

APPROPRIATE TONE QUALITY

EXPRESSIVE ELEMENTS APPLIED TO SINGING

ACCURATE INTONATION

VOCAL RANGES

    SOPRANO

    ALTO

    TENOR

    BASS

FALSETTO

SOLO SINGING

SINGING IN UNISON

SINGING IN HARMONY

    ROUNDS

    OSTINATOS

    DESCANT

CHROMATICS

ACCIDENTALS

    EFFECT OF BAR-LINE

    REMINDER

SO-FA SYLLABLES

HAND SIGNS

VOCAL IMPROVISATION

TERMINOLOGY REVIEW

ACCELERANDO   accel.
Gradually getting faster.

ACCENT   >
The stress placed on notes.

ACCIDENTALS   ♯ ♭ ♮ × ♭♭
Sharps, flats, naturals, double-sharps, double-flats placed before notes rather than in the key signature.

AEROPHONES
Instruments that produce sound by the vibration of air.

ANACRUSIS
A partial measure with which a piece begins. The strong beat is not on the beginning note(s).

ARIA
A song or elaborate air often associated with opera or oratorio.

AUGMENTED
Made larger. A musical theme will take more time because its notes will be made longer. An augmented interval or chord will be larger than normal.

AURAL ANALYSIS
Determination of the nature of music through listening.

BAR
A *measure* of music.

BAR-LINE
Divides music notes into convenient counting groups (*measures* or *bars*).

BAROQUE
Historical period, 1575–1750.

BASS CLEF
Also called *F-clef*. Appears at beginning of staff to show location of note F on fourth line.

BEAT
The underlying, evenly spaced pulse providing a framework for rhythm.

BINARY FORM
Piece of music with two sections (*AB*).

BLUE NOTES
Flatted notes normally associated with jazz.

CADENCE
The conclusion of a musical idea, most often associated with complete or incomplete harmonic resolutions.

CHORD
Three or more notes that are generally sounded together, but that can also function with notes sounding successively (a *broken* chord).

CHORD PROGRESSION
Series of chords.

CHORDOPHONES
Instruments that make sound with vibrating strings.

CHROMATIC

Notes that are a half-step away from each other; note(s) outside the major or minor organization of the composition.

CLASSICAL

Historical period, 1750–1800.

CLEF

Sign that locates notes on the staff. Normally appears at the beginning of the staff.

CODA

An ending section to a piece of music.

COMPOUND METER

Meter in which the beat is divided into three rather than two.

COMPOSITION

Act of creating and writing music; or the piece of music itself.

CONCERTO

Musical work for orchestra with soloist(s).

CONSONANCE

Combination of pitches that does not demand resolution.

CONTEMPORARY

Historical period, 1900–present.

CRESCENDO   cresc. or

Gradually getting louder.

DA CAPO

Go back to the beginning of the piece and play or sing again.

D. C. AL FINE

Go back to the beginning and play or sing through to *Fine*.

DIMINISHED

Made smaller. A musical theme will take less time because its notes will be made shorter. A diminished interval or chord will be smaller than normal.

DIMINUENDO   dim. or

Gradually getting softer.

DISSONANCE

Combination of pitches that demands resolution.

DOT

After a note, indicates note is to be held half as long again.

DOUBLE-BAR LINE

End of piece, or end of section.

DOUBLE-DOTTED

Two dots to the right of a note head. The first dot elongates the note by half, the second dot elongates it by a quarter. The double-dotted note is three quarters longer than its original value.

DOUBLE FLAT   ♭♭

The note that follows the double flat is one whole step lower in pitch than it is without the double flat.

DOUBLE SHARP   ×

The note that follows the double sharp is one whole step higher in pitch than it is without the double sharp.

DYNAMICS

Gradations of louds and softs.

ELECTROPHONES

Instruments that make sound with some form of electrical assistance.

ENHARMONIC

The pitch is the same, but the appearance of the notes, scales, chords, or intervals are different.

FERMATA

Pause or hold; alter count at point indicated so note or rest beneath the fermata is held longer than usual (at the discretion of the conductor or performer).

FINE

The end.

FLAT

Play or sing indicated note one half-step (semitone) lower than usual pitch.

FORM

Plan or structure showing order and balance of composition.

FORTE *f*

Loud.

FORTISSIMO *ff*

Very loud.

FUGUE

A highly developed polyphonic composition.

HALF STEP

The smallest interval commonly used in Western music; the distance between any two adjacent notes on a keyboard. Synonym for *semitone*.

HARMONY

The simultaneous sounding of at least two different pitches.

HOMOPHONIC

Texture caused by chordal support of a melody.

IDIOPHONES

Instruments made of sonorous material that produce sound through some type of striking action.

IMPROVISATION

Spontaneous creation of musical material often related to given composition or chord progression.

INNER EAR

Musical imagination that enables musical recreation without overt sound.

INTERVAL

The difference in pitch between two notes.

INTRODUCTION

A short section acting as a beginning of a composition to show the key, tempo, meter, and dynamics before the main melody is introduced.

INVERSION

Transfer of the lowest note of an interval or chord to the next highest octave.

KEY SIGNATURE

Found at the beginning of each line of notation, indicates the sharps or flats to be used throughout the composition.

LEDGER LINE(S)

Line(s) added above or below the staff to extend the written note range.

LEGATO
> Smoothly join notes.

MAJOR SCALE
> A successive array of notes. In one octave, whole steps (whole tones) occur between all consecutive pitches except steps 3 and 4 and steps 7 and 8, which are separated by half steps (semitones).

MEASURE
> Units of musical time found between a bar line and the one that follows it; sometimes called a bar.

MELODY
> A succession of musical pitches arranged in a rhythmic pattern.

MEMBRANOPHONES
> Instruments whose sound is made by a vibrating skin or membrane.

METER SIGNATURE
> Numbers placed at the beginning of a composition's notation. The top number tells the number of beats (counts) per measure; the bottom number tells the kind of note that gets one beat (count). Also called *time signature*.

M.M.
> *Malzel's metronome,* gives steady beat that can be adjusted to show tempo indications.

MINOR SCALE
> Scale with whole steps between all consecutive notes except for the following: half-steps between 2 and 3, and 5 and 6 (*natural*); or 2 and 3, 5 and 6, and 7 and 8, and an augmented second between 6 and 7 (*harmonic*); or 2 and 3, and 7 and 8, going up, and 6 and 5, and 3 and 2, going down (*melodic*).

MONOPHONIC
> Melody with no harmony.

MOVEABLE *DO*
> A system of sight-singing for which *do* is always the key note of the composition.

MOVEMENT
> Section of a large musical composition.

NATURAL SIGN ♮
> Takes away the effect of a flat or sharp sign.

OCTAVE
> The interval between a note and its nearest namesake, eight letter names away.

OCTAVE SIGN *8 va.* -
> Sign above indicates passage is to sound one octave higher; below, one octave lower. The number *16* indicates two octaves higher or lower.

OSTINATO
> An obstinately repeated pattern.

PATSCHEN
> Thigh slap.

PENTATONIC
> Uses five pitches.

PERFECT PITCH
> Ability to identify and produce pitches accurately with no outside help.

PHRASE

A portion of a melody sensed as a musical entity. Can be compared to a sentence, phrase, or clause as used in language.

PIANISSIMO   *pp*

Very soft.

PIANO   *p*

Soft.

PICK-UP

Same as anacrusis.

PITCH

How high or low the sound is; a measure of the frequency of vibration.

PITCH SYLLABLES

Do, Re, Mi, Fa, So, La, Ti.

PIZZICATO   *pizz.*

Pluck instead of bow.

POLYPHONIC

Texture formed by simultaneously sounding melodies.

RALLENTANDO   *rall.*

Gradually getting slower.

RECITATIVE

Vocal style used especially in opera and oratorio to advance understanding of the story or to provide narrative.

RELATIVE MAJOR AND MINOR

Use of the same key signature for a major key and a minor key, their keynotes being separated by a minor third: For example, G major and E minor both have one sharp.

RELATIVE PITCH

Given a starting pitch, determine subsequent pitches by relationship to that starting pitch.

REPEAT SIGN

Repeat music between this sign and beginning of composition, or where there is a repeat sign with two dots on the opposite side.

ROMANTIC

Historical period, 1800–1900.

RONDO

A musical form in which the main theme alternates with secondary themes: *ABACA, ABACABA,* or the like.

ROUND

A song whose phrases are compatible so that voices can enter singing the same tune at different predetermined places and produce harmonious polyphonic texture.

RHYTHM

The time-pattern made by notes of varying length.

RHYTHM SYLLABLES

"Ta," "ti," "tu," and so on.

ROOT POSITION

The chord is arranged by thirds with the name of the chord as the lowest note.

SCALE

A consecutive arrangement of notes in a predetermined pattern.

SEMITONE

See *half step*.

SEQUENCE

Repetition of a melodic pattern in which the melodic shape and rhythm remain the same, but the pitch changes.

SEVENTH CHORD

In addition to the three notes on the root, third, and fifth, a fourth note is added to the chord. The added note is a seventh up from the root.

SHARP ♯

Play or sing indicated note one half step (semitone) higher than usual pitch.

SLUR

Used with two or more notes of different pitches. Play all notes under or over the slur legato.

STACCATO

Dot used under or over a note. Indicates the pitch should be short, detached. Not to be confused with dot to the right of the note.

STAFF

Five parallel lines on which pitches are notated.

STRESS MARK >

See *accent*.

STYLE

Combination of elements of music and the way they are treated to give characteristics to the music that proclaim its individuality.

SYNCOPATION

Dislocation of expected pattern of strong and weak beats.

TEMPO

Speed at which music is performed.

TERNARY FORM

Composition constructed in three sections (*ABA*); the second section contrasts with the first and third, which are the same or very similar.

TETRACHORD

Four notes of a scale.

TEXTURE

Relationship of horizontal and vertical musical lines described by the terms monophonic, homophonic and polyphonic.

THROUGH-COMPOSED

Song with new music for each stanza as opposed to strophic in which the same music is used for each stanza.

TIE

Curved line joining two or more notes on the same pitch. Hold note for duration of both notes with only one attack at the beginning of the first note.

TIMBRE

Tone color or quality of sound.

TIME SIGNATURE

See *meter signature*.

 Three beats (counts) to a measure; a quarter note gets one beat (count).

Six beats (counts) to a measure; an eighth note gets one beat (count).

Two beats (counts) to a measure; a half note gets one beat (count).

TREBLE CLEF

Appears at the beginning of a staff to show the note G on the second line from the bottom. Also called *G-clef*.

TRIAD

Chord containing three notes.

TRIPLET

Three notes in the time normally taken by two notes.

UPBEAT

Same as *anacrusis*.

VIBRATO

Small pitch changes caused by shaking motion of the hand on string instruments or small variation of pitch produced vocally.

WHOLE STEP

An interval made up of two *half steps*. Also called a *whole tone* (made up of two *semitones*).

WHOLE TONE

See *whole step*.

MUSIC INDEX

GENERAL INDEX

*These terms appear consistently throughout the book. Page numbers are included only for their initial appearances.

*These terms appear consistently throughout the book. Page numbers are included only for their initial appearances.

*These terms appear consistently throughout the book. Page numbers are included only for their initial appearances.

*These terms appear consistently throughout the book. Page numbers are included only for their initial appearances.